Don't Tell Me Goodbye

Becca Blue

Don't Tell Me Goodbye

The Guardians Of Your Heart Series

Don't Tell Me Goodbye
(The Guardians of Your Heart Series)
Written by Rebecca Carrigan (author pen name: Becca Blue)

To contact the author please email:
sakurabluestudios@gmail.com

Cover Design & Typesetting by:
Rebecca Carrigan under her company Sakura Blue Studios

Facebook.com/beccablueauthor
Facebook.com/sakurabluestudio
Tiktok: @authorbeccablue
www.sakurabluestudios.ca

Printed in the United States of America For Worldwide Distribution

ISBN 978-1-0697013-1-2

"Be careful how you think, your thoughts could shape your reality" - Fate

1
A New Girl

"Be careful how you think, your thoughts could shape your reality." It was true. My life was a lot different now, better now that he was gone. I had managed to move on in the short time since he left or at least trick my mind into believing I had. Successfully cutting everyone and everything out of my life that had caused me any emotional or physical distress, past or present. Hiding away and burying myself in my acting career, I had no time for anyone or anything—not even to think. If I did start to think about my old life or him, I immediately snapped myself out of it and began a new task or hobby to keep busy. I had even moved out of our—well, my old place and into a small run-down apartment just big enough for me. The idea was to erase everything from my old life, including him. I wanted everything new and fresh. Different. Because I knew if I thought for just one split second about him, it would destroy me. So this was all I could do to try and live a normal life. This was me controlling my thoughts, holding tight to the life I had left, the life that hadn't been what I planned. I had seen, experienced, and lived through more than the average person and I didn't care to relive any of it. I was a whole new girl now. I was... one piece of a life.

It was springtime in Vancouver again and the cherry blossoms were in full bloom. I always avoided Burrard Station, making sure the slow climb from the SkyTrain stop below up to ground level wouldn't haunt me with memories. The blossoms surrounded the station, filling the sky with a pink umbrella—blanketing the universe with a scent of hope and love.

The Cherry Blossom tree, also known as the Sakura tree, is known for its short but brilliant blooming season which ends with an inevitable fall of the blossoms to the ground. For the Japanese, it's reminiscent of human life, where the rise and fall are the main elements in limited time. They say the tree tends to evoke a positive response in anyone who tries to associate themselves with any aspect of it. Clearly this was a folklore tale, otherwise he would've—no, I have to stop. That was too far.

I continued my walk to the film set, trying my best again to clear my mind. I had landed a regular part on the new TV drama series, "Boundary High." It was the same one Charlotte had told me about a while ago. She had hooked me up with an audition after she finished the promo shoot for season two. I immediately landed the role of "Becca."

Becca was a mischievous character, a drama starter really. The kind of girl who wouldn't take crap from anyone, a trait I was happy to emulate in my own life thanks to the role.

Charlotte texted me every day asking me how I was, until I cut her off. I had to, there was no other way. She couldn't get it through her head that I had moved on. When she finally stopped texting, Alex showed up. He usually visited every few days or so, careful not to overstep my boundaries. For the most part, Alex gets me, but this time he begged me to speak to Charlotte. She had told him she couldn't give up on our friendship and would do whatever it took to make things right. Eventually, I agreed. But with ground rules. Well actually, one ground rule: we could only talk about what was currently going on in our lives from this day forward and that was it.

Charlotte and Alex had become very close. In fact, they were living together. Stupid choice in my opinion to get involved with a supernatural being but whatever, it wasn't my life, and as long as they didn't bring that crap into my world we would remain friends. Recently, Alex had the idea we should all join a running group. But this wasn't just any ordinary running group. There were workout challenges with obstacles along the way to make our muscles stronger. I'm not sure why he was so persistent on doing this. I mean, both Charlotte and I hate anything to do with exercise. But on the other hand, I sometimes enjoyed it. It was a welcome distraction and I was pretty sure his exercise idea had something to do with all the changes happening in my life right now. Alex always challenged me—no matter what we were doing. He never annoyed me either for some reason. No matter what we did. Charlotte on the other hand, struggled every day with our interactions. I had to give her kudos though, she never gave up or complained—not once. No matter how many times I shut her down. I could tell she hated every moment of this new life I was living, but she just kept showing up.

My new view and approach to life was working well for me so far. I didn't care how many friends I had. I was perfectly fine on my own. I preferred to be on my own and I was getting stronger every day. Unbelievably, my family was also respecting me now. Every couple weeks, we'd have a nice phone conversation, share our updates and then head to bed. It was the most we ever spoke about my acting career in my entire life. Another person who was completely happy with my change was my agent, Audrey. Since I'd been landing every audition, she felt the need to harass me about why I insisted on living in such a small, shitty apartment when I made such good money now. The other great thing in my life right now was my nightmares. They had completely vanished. There was no haunting and I was sleeping a full eight hours. Most nights. Everything was pretty great considering what I had gone through. Well, everything except for that annoying hole inside of me, not to mention the mood swings that would sneak up at any moment. They were random, violent and almost bi-polar, but no one had the guts to ask me about them. I assumed it was a left over reaction from purgatory. It was hard to believe I had been there. Mostly, it seemed like a far-off nightmare.

Thinking about it too long scared me. Their nails—the blood—and her. No one would ever understand what I felt, what I keep feeling. It was and still is, indescribable.

 As I reached set, the damp Vancouver streets had completely dried. All the stories about the city were true, it rained a lot, but there were also just as many bright days as there was dull. I reached for my bag to grab my pass to check in when my phone went off. I felt around until I finally grabbed the vibrating cell.

"Hello?" I said, without checking who it was.

"Hey Soph, on the way to set I'm guessing?"

"Hey Alex, yea I am. But it's only a half day of work today, so if you want to do a run tonight, we can."

"Actually, I can't. I sprained my ankle last night, but maybe dinner and a movie with me and Charlotte later if you want?" He waited patiently for my answer.

"Alright, that's fine. I'll run when I get home from set, then grab a shower before I head over." I said, showing my pass at the gate.

"Sounds good, see you around six then?"

"See ya then." I quickly hung up the phone and headed into hair and makeup. That was one thing I loved about Alex, I could be quick and blunt and he never took it personally. I never had to explain my mood or anything else and slowly, he was teaching Charlotte to be the same.

I slipped off my cardigan and dropped my bag to the ground.

"Good morning Sophie," my hairdresser said, greeting me with my usual caramel macchiato from my favorite coffee shop.

"Morning Claire," I replied, settling into the chair.

"Ready for your girl fight today?" She teased.

"Always," I smiled, pulling my hair back into a tight ponytail. I looked forward to filming every day—always.

$$2$$

Wicca

The flames burned brightly, filling the room with light. His eyes slowly rolled back into his head as the energy picked up—charging his body from head to toe. He had tried numerous times to communicate with Gabriel, but nothing worked. Every spell, every mirror or any other witchcraft route had failed tragically, but he refused to give up. He spent every second he could searching the dark realm of purgatory through his new scrying mirror and every attempt was done with urgency in case anything was to arise here in their home. It was the safest way he could think of without physically going there himself.

A series of images began to flash through his mind. He had done this enough times to pick up exactly where he left off in the search. The only problem was, purgatory was endless. A realm with no borders, no time, and no cause for anything. Recently when he entered, he began lose his memory, just for a split second and with every exit from that world he would be shaken up uncontrollably for almost two days. Making no sense of his words or actions. His body was becoming weaker too. He could feel it, the more he tampered in purgatory, the more bruises and scrapes would grace his skin. Unfortunately, he only had to be there mentally for the spirits to hurt him physically and it got worse each time.

A sudden knock at a door made his eyes twitch.
"Alex?"
He heard footsteps around him.
"Come on, Alex… come back to me." The voice spoke again.
Alex's face grew tense as he gripped the mirror tightly,
"Guide me swiftly, guide me true, guide me back to the world
I once knew…"
He repeated the words over and over, slowly becoming louder
and more aggressive with each round.
"Alex." The voice repeated, worried.
Sweat dripped from his forehead as he ripped through the
same sentence another time. Suddenly, the touch of a hand
made his eyes fly open. He blinked a few times then dropped
the mirror to the ground. Charlotte quickly wrapped her arms
around him and held him tight.
"You're okay, take a breath." She whispered.
He pushed her back quickly.
"Don't touch me…" he trembled.
"It's okay, it's me. Charlotte." She spoke, moving slowly back
towards him. "You're fine, you're home. Okay?"
She waited for his reply, then carefully reached out to touch
his cheek with her hand. Eventually, his eyes calmed and
flickered a few more times before releasing his breath and
lowering his head.
"Charlotte," he sighed in relief. "How long was I out this
time?"
"Not too long, but it seems to be effecting you quicker these
days. I mean, by the time you get in, some thing's on you
and…" She paused, noticing some blood dripping down his
left arm. She pushed the sleeve up carefully.
Alex flinched from the pain. There were scratches everywhere
across his shoulder.
"Oh Alex," she sighed. "You better get cleaned up. Sophie will
be here soon. I'll get you a new shirt."
He nodded and gripped her arm as she helped him up.
"Are you going to be able to carry on a conversation tonight?"
She then asked.

Alex rubbed his forehead, a little light-headed as he attempted to step away towards the doorway.

"You really should have waited until after she came to do this. You know how you get," Charlotte sighed.

"I'll be fine. I don't feel that bad. Promise." He half smiled. "Help me to the bathroom, then get dinner started. I'll be out in ten minutes."

She looked at him, still worried.

"I'll do a relaxation spell. It'll help my nerves. I'll be fine. I promise." He smiled again.

"Alright, but only because this is an emergency. I don't like you using any more magic than you have to. I need you to stay you, Alex. Please." She said, stepping towards him again.

He wrapped his arms around her in pain, resting his weight on her shoulders.

"I know Char, I'll be fine." He then kissed her on the forehead. "Now come on, she'll be here soon."

Charlotte walked him to the bathroom, then hurried off to start dinner.

Alex leaned against the door frame for a moment to catch his breath. His hands trembled as he gripped the wall. Painfully, he stepped into the bathroom and closed the door behind him.

About fifteen minutes later there was a knock at the door.

"Hey Soph, how are you?"

"Good, a bit tired. Lots of running on set today," I said, entering the apartment. My eyes searched for Alex who was nowhere in sight. Normally he was first to answer the door.

"So, your character had lots of excitement today, huh? That sounds fun." Charlotte replied, guiding me into the living room.

I stopped in the middle of the room. Something was wrong. It was oddly cold in here, the air was thick too. It was quiet—too quiet.

"Soph?" Charlotte spoke, nervously.

"Shh..." I replied.

"What is it? What's wrong?" She asked again.

A chill ran up my spine. A presence I had felt before lingered in their home. I twitched a bit as a tingling sensation prickled the tips of my fingers. I felt my hand shoot up and begin to scratch at my right ear. What was I doing? I hadn't done this in quite some time. My fingers slid down my face to lace into the long strands of my hair, they immediately got tangled. That's when I stopped.

"Sophie? Are you having one of your episodes again?" Charlotte asked, preparing herself. "It's okay, I'm here. Why don't you come sit down and relax with me?"

I felt her hand touch my elbow, attempting to guide me to the couch. A burning sensation shot through me and I ripped my arm from her.

"Don't touch me!" My shriek filled the apartment.

Before I knew it I had lunged at her.

"Stop!" Charlotte screamed, fighting back.

But I didn't see Charlotte. I only saw them. I swung at her a few more times before a set of arms wrapped around me tight. Charlotte scrambled back quickly on the ground.

"You're okay! You're safe. You're not there. You're here with Charlotte and I. No one is getting past me."

His voice instantly reached me.

Alex's grip was strong, but safe. I jerked in his arms a few more times until my vision cleared and Charlotte came into focus. She trembled on the floor below me.

"I'm fine," I said, taking a deep breath.

I wasn't sure what had set me off so quickly in their apartment, but it was strong. I hadn't reacted like this in quite some time and I hadn't attacked Charlotte since—I was upset with myself—and annoyed. Alex's grip loosened. He then stepped around me to help Charlotte up from the ground.

"Are you alright?"

She nodded, then looked to me. "Are you?"

I stared at her for a moment with mixed emotions. I then straightened my shirt and pulled myself together as best I could.

"I said I was fine." I repeated, brushing my hair back into

place. I didn't mean for that to come out so rude.

They continued to stare at me.

"Look, I'm just gonna go." I then said. "I'm actually pretty tired from set."

"Sophie," Alex protested, hurrying to place himself between me and the front door.

I stared at him, trying desperately not to show my emotions. He gently touched the side of my face, looking deep into my eyes, then straight into my soul. I could feel him, digging around in me. But sadly, he would find nothing in my empty eyes. If anything, he'd feel how anxious I was to get out of there.

"I'm fine, Alex." I repeated calmly, then lowered his hand from my face. I tried my best to remain still in front of him, but the adrenaline was still rushing through me.

"I have to go." I said, stepping past him towards the door again. As my hand touched the doorknob, I glanced back at Charlotte.

"Sorry." I said, then left.

   I walked aggressively down the street, upset with my recent outburst.

"Nice one Sophie," I mumbled to myself. "Your friends invite you over for dinner and you thank them by attacking them thirty-seconds after walking in the door."

I kicked the air as I continued to harp on myself.

"Pull yourself together. I mean seriously, enough of this crap. Just be normal." I was getting more upset by the minute.

I had worked so hard to forget everything, to shut my mind off and this happens. I was sick of this. How long was this going to linger inside me?

"Just shut it off!" I shouted. "Otherwise it's a complete waste of time being here."

I stopped, running my cold fingers through my long hair. I stood silently in the middle of the sidewalk. I took a deep breath in, hoping to release some stress. Then eventually continued my way home.

My fingers twirled through my hair as my mind continued to race with random thoughts.

This hair was getting to be too much. I thought. *It's too tangled. Too long.*

I thought many times about cutting it all off. Holding a long strand of hair between my fingers, by accident, I thought of him. How he used to run his fingers through my hair and touch my cheek ever so gently on the way by. My eyes began to water from the hate I felt inside for him. I hated him so much for what he did. His name, his touch, his dark eyes, even the wispy hair that fell across his face when he would lay next to me. My chest began to ache.

I swallowed hard as the pain continued to grow, making me stop dead in my tracks. The park was dark and silent now. It was the same park I had been attacked in years ago. The one he had saved me in. But tonight, he wouldn't come for me, even if I needed him. But I didn't worry about strangers or danger anymore. Nowadays, nothing bothered me. If something were to happen, I would let it, because I didn't care anymore. My legs trembled as I slowly bent down, resting my knees against the cold pavement. I thought for a moment about lying there in the bitter damp air until my heart stopped. Would he come for me then if he knew I was about to take my last few breaths? I then remembered Gabriel's warning from long ago. Should I have listened to him? Would it have been better if I'd never fell for my guardian angel? If he hadn't got his second chance? If we hadn't kissed or spent that night together? My head dropped and I began to cry.

"Please, make this stop." I sobbed. "I can't stand it. I miss him so much." I admitted out loud. "I do. I miss you…"

It was hard to breathe. I could barely get the words out as I continued to cry.

"Nathan!" I screamed aloud, my voice echoing in the quiet park. The name I tried hardest not to speak, now poured tragically from my lips, breaking my heart into what felt like a million pieces. That sad excuse of a pure heart Gabriel once

spoke of. I knew it would never fully heal.
"It's getting harder to hide this from everyone. I don't know
how much longer I can do this." I whispered. "Gabriel, you
said you'd watch over me..." I grabbed my chest in pain.
How had everyone left me? Was I worth nothing to them
now? My entire life, I had felt as if I was worth nothing—to
everybody. Everyone had let me down, everyone had broken
my heart in some way or another. I was useless—to everyone.
Even to the angels. I watched as a few more of my tears fell to
the pavement below. I wiped my eyes and slowly attempted to
pull myself back up to my feet. He had too much power over
me still... *No. I can't keep doing this. It has to stop.*

  Alex dropped his fork at the dinner table and suddenly
clenched his chest in pain.
"Alex," Charlotte quickly grabbed his other hand.
"I can feel her..."
A while back after Nathan left, Alex had cast a spell on
Sophie enabling him to feel her emotions when they were at
their peak. This way, he could keep an eye on her without
physically being there.
"She's hurting—bad." He said, holding his chest.
Charlotte's lips trembled watching his expression change.
His eyes closed as he followed Sophie in his mind.
He watched her fight to walk straight and hold herself
together. He watched her gasp for air.
"I've never felt so much sadness from a person in my entire
life. She's trying too hard to hold it all inside. It's going to
destroy her if she carries on like this."
"What can we do?" Charlotte asked, squeezing his hand.
"I'm going to calm her, just for tonight. Then at least we know
she'll make it home safe."
"Alex," Charlotte said, worried.
"It's needed. I promise. I'll just relax her mind. It's a natural
act for spirit guides, it won't take much."
He thought about Sophie deeply, sitting very still at the table

as he touched his left hand to his heart. He concentrated on her mind, her body, and what used to make her happy. Using the positive energy from his body and soul, he collected it in the center of his heart. He then pushed it out into the universe, towards her. He began to visualize twelve petals. As each one peeled back, he soon saw her in-dwelling altar of her heart chakra, the most sacred point of her consciousness.

 Sophie stopped on the sidewalk for a moment as a warm feeling began to grow inside her chest. Alex watched as the pink heart flame began to illuminate. Her hand rose to her heart and slowly, her breathing became much easier.

"I invite the angel of love to dwell in your heart," Alex spoke. The flame suddenly changed into a golden-pink, six pointed star as the energy grew inside of her. It flowed throughout her body, then outward—surrounding her, before eventually ascending into the sky and protecting her for the night.

"Be happy Sophie. Even if it's just for tonight."

Alex then opened his eyes.

Charlotte smiled, touching her chest. The calm and peacefulness Alex's body was radiating was wonderful. The energy that hovered around them now was light and smelled of lavender.

"That was amazing. I didn't know you could do that."

He smiled, then reached over and touched her cheek.

"It's one of my favorite parts of being a spirit guide."

"Is she okay?" Charlotte asked, still worried.

"She'll be fine, she's almost home. She'll probably go right to sleep. I'll call her tomorrow." Alex then stood up from the table. "I'm pretty tired as well. I'm going to head to bed if you don't mind." He then leaned down to kiss her on the head.

"I'll be in soon," Charlotte spoke. "I'm just going to clean up." She then watched as he slowly made his way down the hallway towards their bedroom. She didn't like the way he was looking lately. The work he was doing was taking a toll on him.

3

Purgatory

The cold air cut across his face. Something he hadn't felt in a long time. Nathan pulled his legs in tight against his chest trying to keep warm as Serena cuddled in close. Her scent, the smell that used to come from her hair as the wind blew through it was gone now. She was pale and she didn't shiver from the wind like he did. Her hands wrapped around his arm tight. She looked as if she was sleeping but she wasn't. She didn't sleep anymore. She physically couldn't. She was dead.

They had just found Serena a few days ago and along with her—Anna, who immediately took off at the sight of them. Unfortunately, Gabriel went after her and he hadn't seen the Archangel since.

When Nathan called for Anna, ready to enter purgatory, she didn't appear as she said she would. Her voice only responded in the back of his mind, telling him what to do next. She told him to go deep into the woods by the harbor and call for her again. He arrived not long after that with Gabriel by his side. He called to her again, but this time she didn't answer. They waited patiently, unsure of what to do. Soon enough, the bead in Nathan's hand became warm to the touch. Gabriel's energy reacted to it and suddenly a small portal opened in front of them. They stepped through and before they could look back, it closed behind them—permanently.

Now that Nathan was on his own and just a human, he could only trust Serena to protect him from what lingered in the darkness. He wasn't even sure if it had been a few days ago that Gabriel left. It felt more like weeks now, maybe more. Alex was right, there was no sense of time in this horrible place. He and Gabriel had spent what felt like months fighting against supernatural beings in search of Serena, and now that they were together, Nathan found it hard to speak with her. For days they walked in silence, but Serena didn't care. He was so upset with her for all that she had done to Sophie, but on the other hand, still had feelings for her. He couldn't get his emotions straight and he just couldn't find the right words to start a proper conversation. Most days, they spent their time fighting off spirits and trying to keep a low profile. But for Nathan, now that he had Serena, he needed to find Gabriel to finish what they had come to do. Sadly, the longer he spent in there, the harder it was becoming to see a way out. This was much more difficult than he thought it was going to be.

Everything Alex had told him, everything Raphael had expressed about this horrible place was true. It was exhausting mentally and physically, not to mention the disturbing sounds and terrifying screams that would be indefinitely embedded in his mind from this day forth. What he saw, even the haunting landscape was much worse than any horror movie he had ever seen. Everything was contorted, disgusting and more importantly—dead. He couldn't bear the thought of Sophie facing this place on her own. He now understood completely what she was dealing with inside. He desperately wanted to fix that for her, to make her feel safe again.

"Nathan?" Serena interrupted, lifting her head from his shoulder.

He continued to stare straight ahead.

"Nathan, please look at me."

When he didn't answer a second time, she moved herself in front of him, placing her hands down on his knees.

"This is silly Nathan, please just talk to me. We've been waiting so long for this—for us to be together again. Won't you just speak to me?"

He stared into her eyes.

"I can feel your emotions racing…" She said.

"There's a lot going through my mind right now." He finally answered.

"Like what?"

He looked away from her again.

"Isn't it nice being together again? It's almost like a second chance for us, isn't it?"

His eyes returned to hers, "Not much of a second chance being in here though is it?" He replied. "Serena, I had my second chance, but now I'm here with you instead of living my life out there where I should be."

She frowned, a little upset with him.

"You know what I mean, Nate." She then pulled her hands from his knees.

He continued to shiver in front of her.

"Do you know what I wish?" He then said. "I wish we could have sat down like normal people and talked about all of this. The way we used to talk long ago. When we were honest with each other and shared everything." He paused. "How did it get to this, Serena? When did you turn into such a—"

"A what?" She said, pulling back from him more.

"This isn't you, this isn't the Serena I loved." He said.

"So let's talk then Nathan, this is as good of a time than ever. Right?" She huffed.

"No, it's not. I mean, I've done nothing but run for my life since I got here. There hasn't been a second for us to get things straight. I need answers. I need you to be honest with me, but I'm afraid to let my guard down for one second in case something pops out and tries to kill me." He said, nervously looking around. He then zipped his jacket up a little more, the cold was really getting to him.

"Nathan, I'm here. Nothing is going to kill you." She said, touching his hand again.

"Anna could." He responded, "Or Fate, or even—you." He said, truthfully.

She froze, unimpressed with his words.

"You think I would hurt you?" She said sadly.

"Maybe. I mean, you haven't really been in the right state of
mind since you've died and I feel like..." he paused trying to
be careful with his words.
"What? What are you trying to say, Nathan?"
"I feel like I don't really know you anymore," He looked at
her sadly. "I miss the old Serena. I miss the sweet girl who
wouldn't hurt a fly. I mean, the things you did to Sophie... It's
hard for me to believe that you would do such things. Gabriel
told me that Anna had a lot of influence on you, that she fed
your mind with crap because of her own issues, but even so. I
can't see the real Serena attacking someone or acting the way
you did." He sighed, a little disgusted as he ran his fingers
though his hair. It was full of dirt and grime.
"Anna doesn't control—"
"She does, Serena!" Nathan snapped.
"No!"
"Serena, think about it. The things you did to Sophie... Do you
know how much you hurt her? How much it hurt me? The real
Serena would never act that way. It has to be her. I refuse to
think that you chose to act like that."
"Nathan, she took my place. She doesn't care about you. She
just needs you to—"
"No, you know what?" He interrupted, "I change my mind, I
actually don't want to hear it."
She looked at him worried.
"Maybe you have changed too much," He paused.
She didn't answer.
"Since I found out about you, I've fought blindly for you—
foolishly even because you're my friend. Because you deserve
not be controlled like a puppet, and even after all that you
did to Sophie, and my friends, I never thought once about
not trying to help you. No matter what people said to me.
But right now, I just realized something." He paused. "I was
always thinking of your feelings and what was best for you—
what you deserved, but you... in all your actions didn't once
think about what was best for me." He choked at the thought.
"Did you ever stop to think that maybe I was happy with my

new life?" He waited for her to say something, but she didn't.
"It's clear to me now, I've been fighting for the person you used to be—a memory. It's just not you in there anymore and I hate that, but it's the truth."
"Nathan," She spoke, clearly hurt by his words.
"You need to pass on Serena. It's the only way you can be at peace. The only way you can be free. Don't you see that?"
Her eyes began to water as she stared back at him.
"Don't you love me, Nathan?" She asked, quietly.
"I love who you used to be," He replied.
"Then isn't that enough? I know I've messed up, but everything I did, I did because I couldn't bear to be without you. I've never felt this way about anyone—ever—in my entire life. It was so new to me and before I got to truly experience what we had, you were gone. Taken from me before we even got a chance!"
Nathan's eyes softened, "I know…"
"No, you don't. You said you loved me and that you would never let anything happen to me. Then you left and I was alone and scared, and…the pain. It was unbearable."
Her hands began to shake as the anger grew inside.
"If things were the other way around and I was taken from you, then fell in love with someone else… How would you feel about it?"
Nathan reached out and touched her hand, feeling a little guilty for snapping on her.
"Don't you remember how much we loved each other, Nathan?" She spoke again. "Don't you remember the feelings we had when we first met? Sitting in the back of the classroom, borrowing your pen when I already had one?"
He smiled at her.
"Remember when you made me breakfast? And we walked to school together talking about our lives, our hopes and dreams? Do you remember me telling you about the Cherry Blossoms and how I wanted to walk through them someday?"
He nodded.
"But instead, you walked through them with her."

"I know, and I'm so sorry. But I only did that because I was
thinking of you. I remember everything about us, Serena. I do,
but things are different now. It just didn't happen for us. I hate
to say it, but clearly we weren't meant to be together."
A tear fell from her face as she shook her head in denial.
"But what I do know, is that we were meant to meet." He then
said. "Because since I met you, I changed my outlook on life
and when I became a guardian, I pushed that onto others as
well. You brought out so much good in me. Things I didn't
know I had." He carefully wiped a tear from her cheek.
"I love you, I do… but my heart belongs to Sophie now and
always will."
"No," She begged, looking up at him. "You're just confused.
If we had some more time together you would change your
mind. You would remember the feeling we had long ago. I
know it."
"Serena.… I—"
Just then Nathan was ripped from her arms and thrown across
the ground. He rolled across the dirt, cutting his arms against
jagged rocks until his body came to a stop.
"Nathan!" She yelled, taking off after him.
A ghostly spirit latched onto Serena by the arm, his growl
ringing in her face. Nathan covered his ears as the horrifying
sounds rippled around them. Serena's hands laced around the
neck of the spirit, tightening by the second. She had learned
many techniques being in here alongside Anna. One being how
much power she had inside if she could just learn to harness
it—like how she had learned to creep into Sophie's mind
at night. There were so many things spirits could do when
powered by a bit of negativity. She just needed to concentrate.
Nathan looked around for something to fight with, there were
only sticks and other useless pieces of nature around them.
He finally spotted a large branch, scooped it up and charged
at them. Thoughts of Sophie ran though his mind as he went
forward fearlessly. Just as he reached them, Serena threw out
a powerful dark orb of light that shot the spirit far from them.
Nathan stopped, out of breath. "Where is it?" He yelled.

Taunting voices began to whisper through the wind from all sides.

"Here…" a deep voice hissed in his ear.

Immediately, he swung around to nothing. A chill ran down his spine as he gripped the branch tighter. Suddenly, something snagged Nathan around the neck, forcing him to drop the branch. He desperately fought to release the tension that wasn't physically there. Something was strangling him, but he couldn't see it. Each of the spirits in this world were different. These ones were the worst. You could barely see them. Sometimes not at all. It was more like a gust of dark smoke that blew by you. Sometimes, if they stayed still long enough you could piece together the shape of a person. But mainly, the smoky air flowed quickly around you—too quick to see and it usually hit you with a forceful blast that could knock the wind right out of you—or in this case—cut it off completely. It was hard to fight what you couldn't see.

"Ser…ena…" Nathan attempted to call out.

Serena appeared before him and gripped onto his neck with both hands. He could feel it. The spirit, Serena and his life slipping away. Why wasn't she stopping it? It seemed like she was adding to it. Her eyes grew black as her arms flexed with force. Nathan dropped to his knees. He wanted to fight, but the two of them were too strong. His mind began to race, where was Gabriel? Then he thought of Sophie. Who would take care of her if he died? A burning sensation began to grow within. A flame in the gut of his stomach sparked like it did back in his bedroom long ago. He remembered this sensation. But this time, he concentrated on it. This energy was powerful, unlike anything he had felt before as a human—or an angel. A light began to illuminate around his body.

Serena looked at him nervously. "Nathan, what are you doing?!"

A soft red glow began to illuminate around them. He could feel the spirit's grasp loosen. It began to scream in his ear. Nathan continued to concentrate on the power within because whatever this was, it was working.

"Come on!" He cried, closing his eyes and impatiently clenching his fists with strength. Just then, the red energy exploded from his body, throwing Serena and the spirit far from him. His eyes shot open. Adrenaline was pumping through his veins now. He quickly rose to his feet and took off. Serena immediately chased after him with the spirit close behind. Nathan kept his head down, running as hard as he could. Every part of him ached. He was cut all over, his bones were weak and he hadn't eaten in days, but he was still alive! Serena was closing in, following the red energy that trailed behind him. He could feel her. He could also feel the other dark energies surrounding him now. They liked a chase, they always did. Any type of frantic movement excited them. They were out to feed on your fears, your doubt and there was nothing you could do once they dug into you.

Smokey shadows appeared beside him as he continued to run. They were on both sides now. Their voices taunted him and his mysterious energy was fading fast.

"Keep going, Nate!"

The familiar voice startled him, making him stumble for only a second.

"I'm trying to get to you, but I need your help!"

Nathan's eyes widened. Was it a trick? Did he really hear it? He knew that voice, but how was it reaching him? It was impossible.

"Don't give up!!" The voice echoed again.

"It's him, it has to be..." Nathan gasped, out of breath.

The sound of Alex's voice ached his heart, it was too good to be true, but it made perfect sense. Alex had broken in before to save Sophie, so why not now? He was looking for them. If anyone could save them, it would be Alex. Just like he had hoped. But something bothered him about his friend's voice. It sounded different. It sounded deeper and accompanied by someone—or something else. Perhaps it was a trick? Whatever it was, it left a wonderful, yet horrible feeling inside.

"Alex?!" Nathan shouted as the spirits screeched around him.

"Help me, please!"

● ● ●

Charlotte woke from her sleep with a heavy feeling in her heart. The atmosphere had changed in the room and the air was thick. She turned to Alex. He was not in bed beside her. Frantically, she searched the room with her eyes, then quickly pulled the covers away.
"Alex?!" She called out, searching the apartment for him.
"Run! Nathan! Run!" She heard him say.
As she turned the corner into the living room, she found him sitting in the middle of the floor, eyes wide open—staring straight ahead.
"Alex, what's happening?!" She asked, nervously.
He didn't respond.

● ● ●

"Alex, are you there?" Nathan hollered again.
"I'm right beside you," He responded.
Nathan looked around, but saw nothing. The spirits were getting closer, and easier to see. They were feeding off his fear. Suddenly, a quick slice ripped across Nathan's skin. They were in reach of him now. Nathan watched as their ghostly figures morphed into bony bodies that were now stringed in dark bloody veins and rotted flesh.

● ● ●

"Alex! Talk to me, please!" Charlotte yelled, again. "Can you see him? Can you see Nathan?" She quickly gripped his arm. The positive energy and hope from Charlotte's voice lit him up immediately. A yellow glow illuminated around them and suddenly, she saw a flash of Nathan running in her mind. She dropped to her knees at the sight. Her other hand gripped her chest in pain. She could not only see Nathan, she could feel him too. She could feel his fear.

"Alex..." she cried. "Save him!"

●●●

Nathan continued to stumble over his feet and just as he was about to fall to the ground, he felt himself suddenly jerked up and pulled onward.

"I'm right here," Alex repeated, appearing beside him this time—forcing him to keep running. The sight of Alex weakened Nathan with happiness and not only that, he could now feel Charlotte's presence too.

"Run Nate! You have to keep running!" Alex urged.

Nathan stumbled a few more times, but the spirit guide didn't let go.

"Don't give up, Nathan!" Charlotte's voice chimed in. "Come home to us!"

The sound of her voice suddenly ignited the red energy around him again just as a figure appeared in front of him about ten feet away.

"Stop!" The deep voice shouted.

It rippled throughout the dead trees and thundered like an earthquake across the ground towards them. Nathan tripped and the vision of Alex disintegrated. He hit the dirt hard. Covering his head quickly, he waited for an attack.

●●●

"Dam it!" Alex gasped, "I almost had him!"

"What happened?" Charlotte asked, still shaken up by her connection. She had never been part of Alex's vision or powers before.

"I don't know!" He jumped to his feet and began to pace. "I had him in my hands. Who was that?! I was so close!" He continued to yell. He closed his eyes again, desperately trying to feel for any lingering presence of purgatory, but there was nothing. He had lost it—again. Turning to Charlotte, his legs weakened beneath him. He reached for her, but she didn't make it in time.

●●●

The screams increased as the wind picked up, circulating the area. All of a sudden, a burst of white light shocked the landscape—then faded just as quickly. Everything was silent. The sound of footsteps headed towards him. He felt a scuff of dirt tossed into his hair as the sound stopped right near his head. Nothing was happening. Slowly, Nathan opened his tired eyes, adjusting them up to the gray sky above.

"Are you alright?" Gabriel's voice said calmly. He then held out his hand for Nathan.

He couldn't believe his eyes as he reached for the Archangel. Gabriel pulled him to his feet. His eyes searched the area for spirits, but the only thing left was Serena.

"You can't take him from me," She said, sternly.

Nathan stared at her, he hadn't forgotten about the strangling.

"You misunderstand Nathan… it's not what you think." She replied.

Before Nathan could respond Gabriel stepped in front of him.

"I'm not weak anymore, and neither is he." The Archangel warned.

"I need him Gabriel, I'm on your side. Trust me." She said, changing her tone.

"You will never be on our side. Now be gone!" He insisted, stepping towards her. Nathan quickly grabbed his arm.

"Gabriel…" He then glanced to Serena, begging her silently to retreat for now.

She stepped closer, testing the Archangel's words.

"I wouldn't…." He warned one last time.

Suddenly, Nathan's light began to grow again around them both. He looked down at his hands as it casted brightly from his palms.

"What is this?" He asked, nervously.

Gabriel's eyes lit up.

"You're changing, Nathan. We'll figure it out together, if you come with me. Let me help you." Serena begged.

Nathan looked at her, then back at Gabriel.

"You know…don't you?"

"He doesn't know! He's working with Anna!" Serena panicked. "I'm on your side, Nathan. I promise! I was trying to help you back there. I was only trying to release you from the spirit's grasp. I would never hurt you!" She begged again.

"Enough!" Nathan shouted. The pressure of his new power and the two of them arguing was getting to him. He wanted to know what was happening and why this was happening to him. He needed a second to think.

"I just want to understand this all!" He yelled, looking back to Gabriel. "I need you to tell me what you know, please." Nathan's body was sweating now, an immense heat was radiating from his skin.

"Where have you been?" He asked, clearly upset.

Gabriel had left him again like he did before when Fate attacked Sophie in their room.

"I'll explain everything, but not here. Be gone Serena!" Gabriel warned one last time.

Stubbornly, she remained still. "Nathan please, I—"

Suddenly, a bright white light exploded from Gabriel's hand and blasted Serena out of site. He glanced back to Nathan.

"I know you have a lot of questions," Gabriel began, "And I will answer them all. But first, we must move. It's too dangerous here."

"No, explain this now!" Nathan shouted.

"Not here," Gabriel repeated. "We need to find a safe place first. Calm your energy, or we will have another battle on our hands very soon. They can feel us. Now let's go."

Nathan growled under his breath, frustrated. He didn't know who to believe. Eventually, he took a breath and slowly let the red energy fade away. He knew Gabriel was right. They needed to get out of there, fast. He then followed the Archangel further into the dark woods.

When Gabriel finally stopped to rest, he took a seat and motioned Nathan to sit down next to him. Nathan fell to the ground completely exhausted.

"Well?" Nathan said, still trying to catch his breath.

"Rest for a moment."

"No, I don't want to rest. I want to know what the hell is going on inside of me, Gabriel! And where have you been lately? I could have been killed numerous times. Did you forget about me? Or were you just too worried about Anna that you—"

"I did not forget about you, Nathan." He interrupted. "I knew Serena wouldn't let anything happen to you. I knew I had some time to try for her."

"What are you talking about? Did you not see what just happened? She strangled me, then chased me alongside at least fifty or so spirits!" He coughed a bit choking on his dry throat.

"She is not on our side Nathan, that is for sure. But she wasn't trying to kill you."

Nathan looked at him confused.

"She was linking on to that spirit that was strangling you. You see, if she connects with them, then she can control them. That's why it looked like she was strangling you. A moment or two more and she would have exploded it from you."

Gabriel dusted the dirt from his sleeve that was no longer white. Their garments were full of soot and barely holding together.

"So you knew, and we still abandoned her? This is ridiculous, I have no idea who to believe now." Nathan slammed his fist to the ground, then dropped his head between his knees. Anxiety was building inside. He had never experienced this before. In fact, he couldn't remember a time he'd ever had anxiety in his entire life.

"Serena would not have killed you, but because Anna still controls her—we need to be cautious. Anna..." He paused sadly. "She is a loose cannon, I tried desperately in the moments I had with her to talk and explain everything. I wanted to clear her mind and set things straight about our past. But she is still angry with me for her death. I know she deeply loves me, but her emotions are blinded by rage." He said, taking a deep breath. "She tricked you Nathan,"

"I know," He responded quietly.

"She knew what she was doing when she contacted you in your dream. You know that item she gave you, the bead?" Nathan nodded.

"I hold the replicate." Gabriel then pulled a thin black string out from under his shirt. Hanging in the middle of it was the same bead. "She knew you wouldn't get pass me, and she couldn't have opened the portal without that bead—without me."

"If you recognized the bead when you saw it, why didn't you say something?" Nathan asked, frustrated.

"Because no matter what I said, your mind was set. I knew at that moment, this was not just your problem, but my own as well. We both needed to go. As I said to you before, I have to protect you."

Nathan closed his eyes, it was too much information—too much to deal with.

"We must keep our heads on straight." Gabriel spoke again. Nathan's eyes opened slowly.

"I just don't know what to do anymore. How do we help them?" He paused. "Should we still help them?"

"I'm not sure yet, but we must be prepared for the worst. If it gets out of hand, we will end it quickly or abandon the idea completely. There are bigger things at stake here. Our future, and—"

"Speaking of that..." Nathan interrupted. "What the hell is happening inside of me? This red light, what is it?"

Gabriel smiled, slightly, "I had hoped this conversation wouldn't happen until much later, but it seems I have no choice now."

Nathan looked at him oddly. "You don't seem too nervous about it. Tell me Gabriel, please. Is it Angel powers? I mean, I know I'm human now, but why is this coming forth? Is it something to do with being a guardian in the past? Do I still have some power left?"

"Sort of," Gabriel replied, vaguely.

"Sort of? That's all you have to say? Come on, I'm serious. Quit stalling, what is it?!"

"Calm down, do not make a scene." Gabriel's voice rose, then quieted again. "It is part of your fate, Nathan. Yes, it is a type of Angel power."

Nathan sighed in relief. "So this is good, right? What does this mean for me?"

"Your soul has lived three separate lives now. Human, guardian, and human again. Which we all know is very rare. An abundance of power has built up around the rare soul inside you. It's unlike anything we've ever seen and it's been lying dormant until now. A soul that's crossed through so many time-frames begins to collect and store fragments of each life. So even though you are human now, you will always have a piece of us inside of you after being a guardian, and this new heart of yours is strong—very strong and protected by that powerful soul and capable of many things. We've heard stories of a power like this, but only now am I truly understanding it."

"Did this happen to any of the others that got a second chance? What became of them?" Nathan asked, still trying to make sense of it all.

"No. You are the first."

"But how?"

"It ignites when your emotions hit their peak. Those feelings are driven from your heart and your heart is the flame inside of you. The core of the energy eventually erupts into a powerful orb that pushes its way out of your body protecting you and ultimately killing or diminishing the threat around you. It can also act as a shield, as you saw when protecting Sophie back in your apartment."

Gabriel rotated his shoulder that was a little sore as he continued to speak. Unfortunately in purgatory, everyone could feel pain.

"It is a very rare thing that is happening to you Nathan. I wondered for quite some time if these tales could possibly be true. Everything added up with you, all of the stories, and it makes sense that it happened to you. But what doesn't make sense is why it's happened so early. Your soul was on the path to this eventually, but what I didn't add into the equation was your love for Sophie and how powerful it was. For in all the three lives your soul has lived, you had never loved something as much as you do right now. It must have been the reason it sparked early. The amount of love you two have for each other…it's no wonder it ignited from you when Sophie's life was threated." He wanted to leave it at that, in fear of giving too much away.

"Okay, so… this power. It's kind of like the orb that you Archangels generate when fighting, right? How long will I have it? Can I learn to control it?"

"Yes it's very much like ours, and yes you can control it." Gabriel stood up and faced him. "Like I said, it's generated from your heart. So when you act from true love for someone or something you're passionate about, it will ignite. Sophie is something you truly love. Your heart couldn't face the idea of losing her. It chose to protect you both. The same thing happened just moments ago when you were attacked and Alex showed himself to you. The feeling of your friends around you, people you love—sparked it again. To control it, all you need to do is concentrate on those that matter to you most. It will then ignite for battle or for protection. But you must also learn to contain it. You must only use it for good. It is very powerful Nathan, more powerful then you, and more powerful than any Archangel."

Nathan's eyes widened.

"If used the wrong way…" He paused, nervous to even mention it. "It can take over your soul."

Nathan swallowed, nervously.

"More powerful than the Archangels? How is that so?" He asked, getting up from the ground. "Am I—I mean, am I an Arch–"

"Possibly, I'm certain that after you pass on from this new life, you will become one of us." He said, stepping closer to

Nathan and placing his hand down on his shoulder.
He couldn't say anymore.
Nathan then smiled, "So you saw him too…Alex, I mean."
Gabriel nodded.
"He's trying to save us, I know it."
"He's very loyal." Gabriel smiled. "Sometimes a little reckless… but loyal."
Nathan smiled again at the thought. He was thankful for Alex's recklessness.
"You are truly a remarkable being, Nathan." Gabriel spoke again. "Everything that you have experienced and survived, everything that you have seen and learned is past anything a normal human will ever experience. I'm sure there is much more to come for you."
Nathan smiled again. Then slowly, he slid Gabriel's hand from his shoulder.
"But this life I'm living right now, with Sophie…" Nathan began, "It's the last one I want to live, Gabriel."
The Archangel looked at him surprised and before he could speak, Nathan continued.
"I want nothing more than to live a full life with her and then… I want to pass on. I want us to be side by side in a grave—together forever. Like a normal couple who has completed their life here." His face lit up with thoughts of their life again. "Of course, before that, I want us to get married, possibly have children, then eventually grow old together. I want us to have a normal life and experience every stage of it together. But that's it Gabriel." He repeated. "That's all I want. I don't wish to be an angel again, or an Archangel. Nothing. I want it to be over. I hope you understand."
Gabriel stood silent for a moment, carefully choosing his next words. Nathan spoke again.
"I will use this power to finish what we came to do, but after that… I don't want anything else. I just want her. So could you maybe take the powers from me and make me fully human, so I can't come back?"
Nathan looked to Gabriel with pleading eyes. The Archangel

could say no more. He knew he had to let things fall into place.

"Of course, if that is your wish." He sighed. "I will relieve you of all powers when you are ready, but can you promise me something in return?"

Nathan nodded, feeling confident that anything was worth this promise.

"While we are still in Fate's hands, and until we have straightened out our situation, will you let me help you control this power? Will you welcome it, and use it to—"

"Of course, Gabriel." Nathan interrupted. "I will fight by your side until the end. But Sophie must be our top priority—always. If anything happens to her, I am nothing."

"Agreed." Gabriel said.

"Alright then, now what?" Nathan asked, looking around the wasteland that surrounded them. He hadn't got use to the smell yet. It constantly reeked of death.

"I believe that Alex might be our key. Now that you have connected with him, he has a better chance of reaching us a second time. You've become stronger, Nathan. Alex can feel it and so can I. That's why he was able to connect with you and that's why I have the powers I do in here. Somehow, what you are igniting is keeping us both alive. Although, I worry about Alex. For if he is reaching us in here, he is surely tampering with the darkest of arts. Forbidden magic to spirit guides, angels and all that follow Him. The angels believe that dark arts have the power to turn any soul evil. He won't have much time left until they figure out what he's doing, then they will come for him."

"Evil? Alex? That's impossible." Nathan responded.

"I agree, and I have faith that he can make it past that darkness as long as he uses his new strength only when necessary." Gabriel then paused, nervously.

"But it is taking a toll on him. I could feel it when I saw him earlier. There was something dark lingering alongside him—powering him onward. Which is to be expected when dealing with that kind of magic. Thankfully, Charlotte's warm light

beside him was keeping him grounded. I believe as long as she
is by his side, he will be fine. But he puts himself, as well as
her in great danger the further he dabbles in it."
"Then we better find a way out of here fast." Nathan replied.
Gabriel stepped back from him.
"I want to try something, although I fear we will expose
ourselves too much."
"Try what?"
"If we were to connect our powers… I think combined, Alex
could find us much faster."
"Makes sense, let's try it." Nathan said, eager to get out of
there.
"It's not that simple. If we do it, it will take a mass amount of
energy which will light up this entire place and also make us a
sitting target for every spirit in here. They will find us fast and
I fear there will be too many of them for us to fight. If Alex is
not prepared, if he is not powerful enough to pull us out at the
exact moment—then we are certain to be defeated."
"But you said you had faith in Alex, right? Do you think he
can do it?"
"Yes, but I also fear what it will do to him if we succeed."
Gabriel replied.
"Then what do we do? I don't get it?"
"We wait for Alex to make contact again and when he does,
we can only hope he is ready for what we have planned."
Gabriel responded. "I only hope that if something goes wrong,
I will able to heal him. Or if not me, then…"
"What Gabriel?"
"Let's just hope for the best," He said, with a slight smile.
Nathan's eyebrow raised to him.
"For now, we wait. It's all we can do. Let's concentrate on
controlling your power until contact, alright?"
"And what about Serena and Anna?"
"We deal with them, try to make them understand if we get
another shot, otherwise…" Gabriel sighed at the next thought.
"If Alex makes contact before we get that chance, I say we
retreat and do what we can from the other side. Do you not

agree that this world may be too much for us?"
Nathan nodded this time, without argument. "We're sitting ducks." He replied. "And Serena, I've tried to reason with her but…I need to get back to Sophie. We'll think of something else, I know it. This isn't over yet."
"Then we wait." Gabriel repeated.
After taking a moment to clear his mind, Nathan glanced back at Gabriel. "He can do it," He said, confidently. "I know it."

4

The Ultimatum

Alex slowly opened his eyes as the sun peaked through the blinds in their living room. He rubbed his face trying to remember what happened last. Everything was fuzzy. He sat up, searching the room for any lingering energy. Hoping secretly, that he had made enough of an impact to return easily again when needed. Everything was in its place and seemed to be normal. Rolling his shoulders back, he cracked his neck that was stiff from sleeping on the couch. He wondered where Charlotte was.

A little light headed, he rested his head down into his hands sitting on the edge of the couch now. He had gotten so close—too close, from what he remembered. If only he had a few more seconds. What had gone wrong? What had he missed? The connection broke so quickly. He began to rack his brain with all of the things he had studied. There had to be something he wasn't doing right. Why wasn't he strong enough to stay in there longer? He had been successful with finding Sophie, but that spell was a one-time deal as most were. There had to be another spell, one that was just as strong, if not better to keep him in there long enough to pull Nathan and Gabriel out.

Suddenly, he thought of Charlotte again. She had seen into his vision and felt Nathan too. Her purity, love for her friend,

33

and for himself shot her instantly into that world. But how? Charlotte didn't practice any magic or prayer? How had she connected so deeply? Was it truly as simple as the act of love? Was it the same as in the kitchen, when he had casted the relaxation spell on Sophie. The moment Charlotte knew Sophie was in pain, her heart went out to her friend and she felt everything Alex was radiating. His mind began to race. This was something new. Something he hadn't thought of. Which made him think back to reading an old spell book he came across when he was looking for ways to connect with the purgatory the first time. Before deciding on using the bridge spell, Alex had seen a spell about connecting hearts—loved ones, to find one another. But because Nathan's mind was all over the place with Sophie being gone, he didn't want to involve him in the spell, in case it failed and caused him more grief. But it might have worked, and it could still work with Sophie. Sophie could locate Nathan. He was sure of it and if Nathan's energy connected with his and Charlotte's for that brief moment, there's a possibility it would do same, if not more if he felt Sophie's energy. His love for her could link them and possibly bring him back—Gabriel too.

Alex stopped for a moment, and wondered if it might be too much for Sophie with the current state she was in. Was it too big of a chance to take? Would she even go for it? She was so angry at him, at everyone. He worried if she was pushed too far, too soon, that she might lose her mind again to the unruly world of purgatory. It was something he needed to think about carefully. But on the other hand, there was always the option of erasing Sophie's mind if things went horribly wrong. If she did react too much to the spell, he could take it all away and make her forget about everything. But there was one thing he secretly worried about. Something he hadn't mentioned about that kind of spell. If he attempted to erase Sophie's mind, he wasn't sure how much memory it would take from her. Of course, he would try and guide it to just erasing purgatory thoughts, but spells were never guaranteed. There was a chance it could erase too much—meaning Nathan, him and possibly Charlotte too. He needed to research more before attempting this, but it was definitely an option.

"Hey you…"

His train of thought broke when Charlotte entered the room. She slid in behind him on the couch. Her hands began to massage his tense shoulders.

"I'm glad you're finally awake. Are you feeling better? You've been asleep for a day and a half. You had me worried."

"A day and a half?" He repeated. "I felt like it was just last night…" He said, rubbing his forehead.

Her hands slid down his back and around his waist, she then rested her chin on his shoulder. Slowly, he slid out from her grasp and stretched a bit. He then turned and smiled.

"You helped me, you know that?" He said, softly.

She smiled.

"I couldn't believe what I saw, Alex," She paused. "Nathan was horrified. We have to get him out of there."

"I know." He agreed.

"How was it that I could see him anyway?" She then asked.

Alex sat down next to her and touched her cheek gently.

"Each human has an energy force within them. I can feel it every time I'm around you. It tells us who you are inside." She touched her hand to his.

"You have a good soul within you. It's bright and warm, and I'm guessing when you touched me, it connected with mine which opened your third eye into our supernatural world."

"Third eye?" She asked, confused. "I'm not sure if I like that."

"No, it's a good thing, I promise." He brushed her hair back behind her ear then moved in closer.

She held his hands tight. She was nervous and he could feel it. He then rested his head against hers, breathing in her sweet perfume that smelled of sugar. His lips hovered closely to hers before she impatiently leaned in and kissed him. Her hand slid down his chest and slowly pushed him back down to the couch. She moved herself over him completely, kissing him carefully as he wrapped his arms around her.

"Your energy is what keeps me grounded, Charlotte." He said, pulling her in close.

She smiled again at the thought.

"Char…" He spoke, quietly.

"Yes?"

He paused.

"I love you."

"What?" She stuttered, a little shocked.

He could feel her energy rippling inside of her, nervously.

"I said, I love you silly." He repeated.

"Um… thank you." She responded.

"Thank you?" Alex laughed a bit. "Well that's not… um," He paused again, looking back at her. It was not the reply he was hoping for. He worried for a moment if it was too soon. When she still didn't answer, his hands moved up her arms gently.

"Charlotte? Are you alright?" He asked.

"Yes. I'm fine," She whispered, then bit her lip.

"Should I take it back? If it's that uncomfortable for you, I can take it back…" He began to say.

"No." She answered quickly—surprising him. "I'm sorry… I'm just thinking." She said. "I didn't expect it—ever…. I mean, from you."

"Ever? Wow, that's a long time." He said, sitting up a little.

"I mean, I feel like we are at that point, or at least I felt I was. Do you not agree?"

She didn't answer again.

"Oh… okay, clearly I was wrong. I'm so sorry." He ran his hands through his hair, a little embarrassed now. He was about to get up when she quickly grabbed his shoulders and pushed back down. Her energy shifted again and a soft smile grew on her face.

"No, you're right." She said, touching his chest again. "Of course I feel the same. I mean," She blushed at the thought. "I love you Alex, I do. I just didn't expect it, any of this. But I love it—all of it."

He sighed in relief, then leaned up to kiss her again. A huge weight had been lifted from his chest.

"I knew you did," he smirked.

"Oh really?"
He nodded, then kissed her again.
"I also knew you would never say it first." He then said.
Her eye brow rose, she then frowned a bit.
"Alex, it wasn't like I was afraid, it's just…." She paused.
"What?"
"We're different, you and me."
"And?"
"Well, I mean… You're a supernatural being and I'm—
human." She stared at him for a moment. "It's just, I'm
eventually going to be…well—old!" She said, crossing her
arms like a child.
Alex exploded in laughter.
"Old? That's what your worried about? Being old?" He
continued to laugh.
"Yes, and it's not funny, Alex! You're going to stay young
and handsome forever and I'm going to age and get—old!"
She shuttered at the thought. "You won't want me then. How
can we be together without this looking weird? I'll look like a
cradle robber!"
Alex couldn't stop laughing no matter how serious she was.
"Stop it!" She said, shoving his chest. "It's not funny! I want
to be with you Alex, more than anything, but I also want to
grow old with someone, have kids, and …"
He quickly grabbed her, pulling her in for a kiss again. She
struggled at first, then eventually gave in. When he was
finished, he looked back into her eyes and said,
"Charlotte, no matter how you look, I will always love you.
And I too have thought of that, but… we spirit guides are not
attracted to looks." He then touched her chest gently with his
hand. "We're attracted to your energy and your heart."
His smiled faded a little, "It's funny…"
"What?" She asked, worried again.
"It's just, now that I think about it. No spirit guide has ever
fallen in love. Not that I've heard of anyways."
"Really?" Charlotte asked, surprised. "But you have a heart,
and your own feelings. You're here living a life with me, so

why not, right?" She asked, looking down at his chest.
He shook his head back at her.
"This body has a soul alone. It's made up of energy. That's all—no heart..." He said, sadly.
She stared at him, her fingers tracing his chest. "How can that be..." She whispered.
"The Archangel Chamuel created me as a gift to Gabriel. I was specially made for him." He stopped and thought some more, "Chamuel is the angel of love," he smiled. "You'd think a heart would be the first thing he'd put in me." His hand touched hers.
"Alex, then how do you know it's love, if you don't have—"
"It has to be," He said, very seriously. "We spirit guides still understand what love is because we feel it for the Archangels we were created for very deeply. It's just different, it comes from our soul. Most people don't understand how much love a soul can carry. It's much wiser then a heart and this... you and me," He paused looking at her. "It's unlike anything I've ever felt in my entire existence."
"You really love me?" She asked again, staring back into his eyes.
He nodded.
"Then that's all that matters." She reassured him with another kiss. It was good enough for her. It was also kind of beautiful to think of the soul that way. She hugged him tightly.
His hands slid down her sides, tickling her slightly, trying to lighten the mood from their serious conversation. She wrestled him back, making them slide off the couch and fall to the ground.
"Very cute..." The voice startled them.
Alex pushed Charlotte off and immediately put himself in front of her as the Archangel Michael stood towering over them.
"Disgusting if you ask me. Why is a spirit guide playing around with a human?" Uriel asked, from the other side of the room. Charlotte and Alex scrambled to their feet.
"What do you want?" Alex spoke, nervously.

"Although, she is kind of cute." Uriel teased, appearing behind Charlotte and flicking a piece of her hair with his finger. Charlotte quickly gripped onto Alex's arm.

"Enough Uriel…" Michael spoke, stepping closer to them. Uriel returned to his side.

"Where is Raphael?" Michael asked, changing his tone.

Alex was a little thrown by the question. He assumed they were here about Gabriel.

"I'm not sure, I haven't seen her in quite some time." Alex replied, honestly.

"Alright, then where is Gabriel? I've felt nothing of him for the past few months, nor your little friend, Nathan." He waited patiently for answers.

"I don't know." Alex repeated. "Look, we've done nothing wrong for you to be here in our home."

"Sophie walks alone now," Michael said, calmly. "Why is that? Where is her Nathan?" He asked again. "Or more importantly, where is the darkness that followed her before?"

Uriel's body fidgeted impatiently, waiting for an answer. He had different ways of getting information out of someone, and it was hard for him to stand still while Michael spoke so calmly.

Michael walked around them, trying to read their minds but Alex had already thought of that and casted a spell over them after Nathan left—protecting them from anyone trying to get in their heads.

"You're still playing with magic," Michael said, a little upset with the spirit guide. "You're blocking us from entering your thoughts. Very clever Alex."

"You know the rules... You're dabbling in the dark arts!" Uriel's voice interrupted.

"I'm grounded. I have complete control over all of it. I, like you, am looking for them too." Alex finally admitted, thinking if he gave them something they might back off. "But I have no idea where anyone is."

Michael stood directly in front of the spirit guide.

"You lie." He whispered with a smile. "What are you hiding?"

"WHERE IS RAPHAEL?!" Uriel howled, appearing behind them and ripping Alex away.

Charlotte was thrown back against the couch as the two struggled against each other. Michael stood silently as Uriel lifted Alex from the ground, his cold hand clenched tightly around Alex's jaw.

"Stop it!" Charlotte screamed in fear.

Michael's glance quickly turned to hers.

"You can stop this right now by telling us what we want to know. Then, we will release him." He said, sharply.

Charlotte looked back at Alex gasping for air.

Uriel's hand began to light up a bright ruby-red, it burned Alex's skin quickly.

"Don't say anything, Charlotte!" Alex begged.

"Wrong choice of words my friend." Uriel warned.

His hand grew brighter, continuing to burn the skin on Alex's face. The spirit guide screamed in pain.

"Stop!" Charlotte begged, "Please!"

Michael walked slowly around to her to whisper into her ear.

"You're killing him, he has only moments left…"

Suddenly, Alex's eyes grew black and Uriel's light started to fade with the cold that was generating from Alex's skin.

Charlotte knew what he was doing. He was tapping into the dark arts right there in front of the Archangels. She couldn't let that happen. If they saw how powerful he had secretly become they would surely end him.

"There in purgatory!" Charlotte blurted out.

Uriel dropped Alex immediately and turned to her.

Michael's face had the same expression as his brother's—completely shocked.

"What did you say?" Uriel asked, unsure if he heard her correctly.

"Charlotte no!" Alex cried, as his eyes faded back to normal.

Charlotte dropped to the ground before them.

"They're in purgatory." She repeated. "Nathan went after Serena. To try and help her, and Gabriel, he went in after him. We haven't seen them since. We're trying to locate them, that's why Alex is using witchcraft, to save Gabriel and Nathan."

"Gabriel is in purgatory?" Michael repeated in a worried tone. "What about Raphael?"

"No, she didn't go with them. We haven't seen her since the day they left. She looked over at Alex on the floor as he covered his face.

"Charlotte…" He whispered.

"I'm sorry Alex," She said, sadly.

Michael paced around the room as Uriel stared at him.

"How are they in purgatory? How did an Archangel get in there without being banished through our portal?!" Uriel asked, still shocked from the news.

Michael stopped and turned to Charlotte who began to pick herself up from the ground.

"How do you know all of this?" Michael asked, again.

"Stop Charlotte… don't say another word!" Alex begged again.

She stood in fear as Uriel turned to Alex once again, his hand lighting up as it did before.

"Fate!" She shouted. "She told us!"

Uriel's hand unlit. Alex sighed again.

"I'm sorry." She cried.

"She's lying!" Uriel yelled to his brother. "Why would Fate allow an Archangel to just walk into purgatory? There's something she's not telling us. She must know where Raphael is, let me force it out of her!" He turned to grab Alex again, but Michael appeared in front of him.

"She's speaking the truth." He said, "Her energy is glowing bright. It is not tainted."

Charlotte pushed past Michael to Alex's side and wrapped her arms around him.

"I'm sorry. I'm so sorry, Alex. I had to."

She then pulled his right arm over her shoulder and lifted him from the ground.

He was mad—not at Charlotte, but at how the Archangels were treating them, especially an innocent human. It wasn't right. The power began to fuel inside of him once again, Charlotte could feel his body getting warmer.

"No..." she said. "Keep it hidden, stay calm." She whispered. His energy slowly faded back.

"I don't trust this one," Uriel spoke quietly, keeping his eyes on Alex. "They are of no use to us anymore, they will only interfere. Spirit guides are not permitted to play with dark magic. This guide is tainted. I can feel it. We should—"

"I feel something too..." Michael said, cutting him off. "Although, it is confusing to me, perhaps it is the girl." His eyes then linked with Charlotte's. "He is using her as he said. This is remarkable..."

Michael walked closer, then reached out to touch Charlotte.

"Leave them be, I'm here." Raphael's voice chimed.

Uriel disappeared quickly and reappeared in front of her, slamming her hard into the wall.

"Where have you been, Raphael?!" Uriel shrieked, but Raphael did not fight back.

"Release her," Michael said calmly, turning towards them.

"I was not hiding from you. I've been working on my skills, my soul and trying to find Gabriel as well. We cannot leave one of our own in purgatory to parish. Especially not Gabriel. Do you not agree, Michael?"

Michael smiled at her, impressed with her new found confidence. "Indeed," he replied softly. Michael took a step closer. "I can see the work you're doing. It's good. I can feel your soul. It's different—clean."

She smiled slightly, hoping her days of hiding were over. She was ready to face them, to beg for her place back alongside her brothers.

"But on the other hand," Michael went on, "Gabriel went in there of free will. Why should we risk our lives to save him?"

"Because it's not just him we are saving, but Nathan too." Raphael replied. "He is... what we've been waiting for. It's true. I've seen it with my own eyes. That's why we need them both back here—alive."

Michael looked deeply into her eyes, taking another step

closer. He was right in front of her now.

"You truly believe he is the one?"

She nodded.

"Alright." Michael replied, staring at her silently for a moment. "How does it feel to be back here amongst us?" He then asked, changing the conversation. "It must be intimidating, knowing what you face and how much must be forgiven for you to stand by our side once again."

"Of course." She spoke, quietly. "I wish to please you. I wish to do whatever it takes to be by your side."

"It's a trick Michael! She's not one of us anymore. She can't be trusted." Uriel interrupted. "We should have killed her back when she reappeared from purgatory in the first place!"

"Quiet down!" Michael's voice rose, then calmed before speaking again to her. "Raphael?"

"I'm doing my very best to prove my loyalty. I want only the best for all of us. I too, want the prophecy to come true. I have learned my lesson. I promise. I am on your side and I will spend the rest of my life proving it to you, if need be. All I ask is for a chance,"

"A chance?!" Uriel huffed.

"Quiet." Michael repeated staring into Raphael's eyes. "You truly want to prove yourself to us?"

Raphael nodded.

"Then I shall give you this one chance."

Uriel looked confused as Michael turned and motioned for Alex to join his side. Charlotte held tightly to his arm.

"No," She begged.

Suddenly, Uriel appeared beside her and pulled her from his grip.

"Charlotte!" Alex shouted.

"Do not worry, no harm will come to her. Come here, please." Michael asked, politely.

Alex kept his eyes on Charlotte as he walked towards Michael and Raphael.

"You too, have personally experienced the wrath of purgatory. You understand it and have the best idea of how long each of

them will last in there, don't you?"
Raphael looked to Alex, who suddenly had fear growing in his eyes.
"Do you still fear purgatory?" Michael asked in a more pleasant tone.
Taking a moment to understand where this conversation was going, Alex finally replied, "More than anything,"
A smirk grew on Michael's face as he turned back to Raphael. "How about you my lost friend? Now that you've pulled yourself back together…" He paused as her look became more fearful. "You want to prove yourself to us, don't you?"
She nodded.
Michael stood in silence as the two of them waited for the words they had hoped to never hear.
"Then you shall both go into purgatory and bring out Gabriel and Nathan, alive."
"NO!!!" Charlotte screamed hysterically. She ripped from the Archangel's grip and ran towards Alex, but she didn't make it. She was quickly grabbed again by the back of her head, before Uriel tossed her to the ground.
Alex was ready to lunge at him, but stopped suddenly by Michael's hand against his chest.
"Bring me Nathan and Gabriel, then I shall let you and the girl live your life." He looked at Raphael. "And you. You will have proven your loyalty to us and will be welcomed back fully to the angel realm."
Alex looked at Raphael nervously. They both knew they had very little chance of surviving purgatory a second time, but what choice did they have? Go forth, or be killed now?
Charlotte cried from the floor where Uriel held her down.
Michael waited patiently.
"I will go," Raphael said, quietly.
Alex looked to Charlotte again, tears running down her face.
"I'm sorry," He whispered, then glanced back to Michael.
"I'm in." He agreed.
"Alex no!"
She couldn't believe what he was saying.

"You have no chance in there, Alex! You barely got out alive last time. You'll be lost! I know it!"

"He won't be lost," Raphael spoke confidently, then stepped forward. "Release her, she did nothing wrong." She demanded. "Angels do not act like this, nor treat His creations like so." She waited for Uriel. He made a face, disgusted with her words.

"Let her go, Uriel." Michael agreed.

Uriel shoved her down, then appeared by Michael's side.

"Stand up, Charlotte." Raphael requested, touching her shoulder gently.

Charlotte wiped the tears from her eyes as Alex stood still in front of Michael. Eventually, she reached for Raphael's hand and was lifted to her feet.

"You won't make it, I know it. Please, stay here. We are so close to finding them. There has to be another way, I know it." She pleaded. Raphael held her hand tight.

"I will not let anything happen to him, I swear." She promised. "He is stronger than you think, Charlotte. You have to believe it."

Charlotte stared quietly back at her, and then glanced to Alex sadly. She wasn't prepared to feel what Sophie felt after losing Nathan. She knew it would be too much.

"You are what keeps him grounded, Charlotte. You can help us from here. I will teach you." Raphael requested pleasantly. "I too have studied what he has…" she then whispered.

"But how will we get into purgatory?" Alex finally spoke, his voice a little shaky.

"Through the portal doors. The same one we use to—"

"Banish angels and evil spirits…" Raphael quickly finished his sentence. The same ones she had been banished through years ago. Uriel smiled at her.

"But how will they get back?" Charlotte asked, trying to hold herself together.

"We shall bless upon them a protection light. It will protect their powers and keep them strong for a limited amount of time. Just enough to get in, find them, and get out."

Alex paused in thought.

"But purgatory isn't that easy Michael," he began. "It took me forever to find Sophie. What if we don't get out in time?"

Michael turned from them, crossed his arms, and looked out the window.

"Then I suggest you be quick, or you both will be lost forever."

Charlotte's heart stopped at the thought.

"Prepare yourself for your journey. I'll give you forty-eight hours, then we will return." Michael said, nodding to Uriel. "Let us go, brother. You need to prepare the portal doors."

He then glanced back at Alex. "Get some rest."

Then they were gone.

5

The Ones That Linger

"Anna!" Serena yelled, repeatedly. "Anna, where are you? He took him from me! Anna help me!" She continued to yell. Her hands shook from rage as she pulled the green bracelet from her pocket and laced it around her wrist. It had brought Nathan back to her, but seemed to be useless now. Gabriel had snagged Nathan right out from under her. Serena raced through the trees, tearing dead branches off along the way. "Anna! Answer me!" Her voice demanded, echoing throughout the woods. Thoughts burned through her mind, making her more upset as she came to a sudden halt.

"My, my, you're a noisy one aren't you?"

Serena shot around to Fate.

"What's wrong? Can't find your little friend?"

Serena stood silent. Fate disappeared, then reappeared beside her before she could run.

"Gabriel again, huh? He's a tough one, isn't he?" She joked, crossing her arms.

"What do you want?" Serena finally said.

Fate smiled maliciously at her.

"Look, we're all playing your stupid game. Can't you just leave us be?"

"My games aren't stupid, Serena." Fate replied. "Sure they're challenging, but definitely not stupid."

Serena didn't answer.

"Every time you get close to something you want, I put a wrench in your plan and spin the playing board again, don't I? This is really getting complicated, isn't it?" She continued to tease. "To be honest, I'm having a hard time keeping up with you all. You're such good little players."

"Why can't you just leave us alone?!" Serena cried.

"Because I control you! All of you!" Fate shouted, then paused to calm herself once again.

"Your friend Anna, she's scared of me—more than you." Fate smiled. "She's also weakening, have you noticed? She needs you to keep going, you know that right? She's been in here a long time and until she found you, she didn't have the power or any chance of getting into the real world to seek her revenge on Gabriel."

"What do you care what we do? We both didn't deserve the life you designed for us. We had our bliss, then you stole it from us! It's not fair!"

"Life isn't fair dearie! You were weak—both of you. Barely hanging on. You both had no life skills, no hope for the future and no real drive. You were a waste of space on this earth and I tested you like everyone else, and you failed." Fate stepped closer, face to face with Serena now. She touched her hair gently.

"When faced with tough challenges in life, most humans will fail. Most don't have the drive to keep going. To keep trying. To handle things with a level head. They're driven by emotions which in time, drives them insane—to where they then become their own worst enemy."

Lacing a single strand of Serena's hair around her finger, Fate watched as it darken, until it was black. Serena's eyes grew wide as Fate's grip tightened.

"What are you doing?!"

"Your time is coming soon. I can feel it." Fate then released Serena's hair. It fell slowly to the left side of her face.

"You're fading—like her." Fate spoke again. "If you're not careful, you might get yourself killed."
Then she was gone.
Serena looked down at the pitch black hair blowing in the wind across her lips.
"We'll see about that." She said, tucking the tainted strand behind her ear.

The sounds of purgatory surrounded her. She continued to pace impatiently. Spirits lingering in the shadows, listening in on her thoughts—anxious for another taste of life again. They had missed out on Nathan. They were hungry and angry with their failed attempt to catch him.
"You fools!" Anna screamed. "How could you let him slip through your fingers? He was right there! That was our chance!" She pulled at her hair violently.
"Serena is too weak around Nathan! Without Sophie here to fuel her, she acts like nothing more than a silly human!" She growled. "If her power doesn't increase soon, I'll surely vanish."
Anna let out a scream that pushed the spirits back a bit. She then took a breath and tried to calm herself.
"Perhaps it was a mistake bringing them here. We had much more power when Nathan and Gabriel were in the real world." Anna came to a halt in the middle of the cave, the sounds of spirits began to grow again.
"Shut up!" She screamed, trying to concentrate.
She continued to think. Her original plan was to take down Gabriel while he was in here... but now, there was no way. She was becoming too weak, all because of Serena.
"Should I release them back into the real world again and plan my attack out there?" She pondered.
The spirits growled loudly, upset with the idea.
"Shh!" She said, continuing to think. "I need more power, more emotions to feed off of—more...." She paused as another thought entered her mind. "Sophie,"

A smile grew on her face at the thought, it was perfect.
"But how..."
The spirits around her snarled at her thoughts again—they
didn't like it. They didn't approve of anyone leaving this
place.
"Don't worry, it's not the last you will see of them." She
assured them out loud. "Your time will come. Once I gain full
control, I will open the door into the real world indefinitely.
Not only will I get my revenge on Gabriel... but we will have
our revenge on Fate and the Angels that casted us away."

   Gabriel stood directly in front of Nathan, he watched as his
weak body fought to stand upright. He wasn't the same as he
used to be as a guardian. Purgatory was taking a toll on him
fast.
"This light inside of you is very powerful," Gabriel began,
"and you haven't even tapped into what I believe you can do."
He then walked around behind and placed his hands down on
Nathan's shoulders.
"Breathe slowly. Calm yourself, we mustn't make too much
of a ruckus or the spirits will sense us. Always try to remain
calm, it's the best way to control your power."
Nathan took a deep breath in and relaxed his shoulders.
"Close your eyes, think of what is most important to you.
What do you want the most?" Gabriel closed his eyes. "Think
of her, think of the good times you had together. Think of what
you promised each other. For no matter what she says aloud,
she needs you desperately. She is heartbroken now, but still
longs for you, Nathan. You must protect her. You must fight to
have the life you wish for. You must fight to protect all of your
friends..." Gabriel continued to motivate Nathan's heart and
mind.
Nathan closed his eyes. His body began to tremble beneath
Gabriel's soft grip.
"Relax, do not let yourself get carried away with doubts. You
can do this."

Nathan thought of Sophie, and how he missed lying next to her. He missed her laugh, the touch of her lips and the warmth she brought to his heart when she was close. It was colder now that she wasn't around.

"I miss you, crazy girl…" He whispered as a tear fell from his eye. His palms began to sweat as he clenched them tightly.

"Feel that strength—the heat building inside of you. Light that fire within. Let it grow. Let it fill your body and flow throughout your veins. Picture it pouring outward from your heart…" Gabriel went on.

Suddenly, a red energy began to illuminate from Nathan's skin.

"That's it, do you feel it?" Gabriel's eyes opened.

"Yes." Nathan replied, swallowing hard. His throat was suddenly dry. The air around him was changing, it became thick and hard to breathe. "It burns,"

"Do not let go." Gabriel urged. "Hold on tight to that feeling. Let it grow." He then stepped around to face him.

"It's too strong Gabriel, it burns… inside." Nathan began to sweat profoundly.

"Don't stop, you will lose Sophie if you cannot learn to control this. Take a breath and picture your skin absorbing the light, let it flow evenly throughout your body. Then gather it in the center of your chest. Do it now, Nathan!"

Gabriel could feel the heat penetrating off of him.

"I can't! It's too much… I…." Nathan's whole body began to shake.

"Think of it as an adrenaline rush, let it take over. You must guide it. You have the power to tell it where to go. Pull it towards your center!" Gabriel took a step back as the light became brighter. "This light will protect you and Sophie from anything. You need it!" He yelled as the wind picked up around them. "Hurry Nathan, collect it in your center."

Gabriel kept his eyes peeled, worried the spirits nearby would feel the energy that was growing around them.

Nathan thought of the attack back in their apartment, and the moment he thought he might lose her. That feeling horrified him more than anything. He pictured the fire inside, rushing through his veins to his center. He felt his heart burning brightly. The feeling was overwhelming, stronger than ever before. He fought hard to hold onto it, even in his weakened state. He would do whatever was needed to get back to her—even if it killed him.

"That's it, Nathan! Now release it!" Gabriel heard the screech of spirits in the woods behind him.

"It's so strong… I don't know if I can…." Nathan felt his heart thundering inside his chest now. Pounding, the pressure felt as if it was going to burst from within. Suddenly, his arms grew stronger, his legs were not as weak as moments before, and his eyes shot open. They were pitch black.

Gabriel took another step back nervously. The screams around them grew closer, then instantly, they were surrounded by hundreds of spirits. Their howls barreled around them. Gabriel turned in defense, ready to protect Nathan as they drew closer—they growled with hunger and rage. The energy around them suddenly shot up into the dark sky above. It was attracting too much attention now. Gabriel's eyes darted around the area, trying to stay alert.

"Nathan," Serena whispered from a distance. She could feel him. She quickly raced towards the light in the sky.

Also nearby, was Anna who stood quietly, awaiting this very moment. She too, had felt the sudden burst of energy.

Nathan was now radiating a force that none of them had ever seen. Even the spirits surrounding them lingered with a little distance—unsure of what it was. Gabriel stood guard, waiting to see who would attack first.

Serena suddenly arrived at the scene, followed by Anna. Her finger shot up to her lips, insisting Serena stay quiet. They hid behind a tree, watching Nathan's power grow.

"Where have you been? I've been looking for you," Serena whispered, then looked back at Nathan and Gabriel. "He's in the way again. You have to help me." She pleaded.

"I will, let me distract him." Anna insisted. She then stepped past Serena, whispering something into the wind as she made her way through the woods towards them. The smoky spirits now had Nathan and Gabriel surrounded.

"Make a path, let me speak," She said aloud, and like that, the spirits parted as Anna floated across the ground, entering the circle to face the Archangel. Serena watched on, impatiently.

"It's too much for him, Gabriel." Anna spoke, calmly.

He turned to the sound of her voice.

"Where have you been? Don't step any closer or you could—"

"He won't hurt me," she replied calmly. "He won't hurt me because you will not let him." She continued to walk, but just as Anna reached the Archangel, Serena rushed through the circle of spirits, towards them. Anna shot her a nasty look.

"Nathan stop! Let me help you." She called to him. "This power, it will surely kill you. It's too much!"

Nathan didn't react. His eyes were black as night now.

"It's taking him over Gabriel, stop it!" She pleaded, turning to the Archangel.

"Go, the both of you, before you get hurt." Gabriel repeated as Anna stepped towards him again.

When close enough, she gently touched his arm.

"I'm here to help. Trust me, please." She whispered.

"Anna, not now. I want to help you, but you have no idea what you're dealing with here. Please go." Gabriel begged again.

"You don't understand. I've found a way to stop this all. I'm going to get you out of here Gabriel. Nathan too."

Gabriel paused, confused.

Serena face became tense, she didn't like what Anna was saying. She knew nothing of this plan.

"We came here for you, to help you both." The Archangel snapped. "But you resisted us the entire time. Why help us now? Why not offer before? You could have made this journey much easier on all of us. I don't understand." He said, upset with her.

"I see now that you were only trying to help us, and I apologize. I've been blinded by our past." She spoke, quietly. Serena strained to hear her their conversation as the wind picked up around them.

This conversation didn't make sense to the Archangel. Why was Anna having a sudden change of heart? Was she trying to trick him? He glanced back at Nathan who was struggling now. He didn't have time to think about her, Nathan was changing right before his eyes. His priority was to get him out of there as quickly as possible. This place, would not do well for him if he fully manifested inside of here. He needed to get him back to the real world, back to Sophie and all that was positive before it was too late. He couldn't worry about Anna, or Serena for that matter. As much as it pained him to leave her again, he had to—for everyone's sake.

"The bead…" She then said, "Nathan has my bead. I can channel it for you and open a portal. I just need to get close to him." She began to step past Gabriel, but he quickly grabbed her arm.

"No. I'm sorry. I can't let you—"

"All of you, be gone!" Nathan suddenly shouted.

But it wasn't Nathan's normal voice. It was deeper and dueled with something else.

Gabriel eyes stared in fear, still holding on to Anna.

"I must get to him now Gabriel, please let me go!" She insisted.

"No." He repeated, shoving her away. "Get out of here!"

He then quickly shot a white orb from his hand. It tossed her back like a doll. Serena appeared behind her and caught her quickly. Anna turned to her, frantically.

"He's going to take Nathan back to Sophie…" she said.

Serena's eyes shot back to Nathan, her body instantly filled with panic and jealousy. It grew quickly and the energy poured out and into Anna—refueling her.

"He's going to take him from you. You're going to lose him, again!" Anna repeated.

Serena ripped from Anna's side towards Gabriel without another second to think. She was going to fight for him.

Gabriel's eyes returned to Nathan's as Serena charged.

"Now Nathan! Let it go with everything you have!" He shouted, lighting a protective white orb around himself just as

Serena reached him. It jolted her back hard against the ground. Nathan's hands clenched his chest. He could almost touch it, the fire inside him. His hands began to shake as the light ignited through his chest and into his palms. It burned bright, blinding him and the others.

Fate secretly appeared in the trees above.

Nathan's eyes closed as everything went silent—to everyone. It was the most horrifying sound, having the world muted— even to Fate. Then, just as quickly, a thunderous roar like no other, tore out from Nathan making everyone cover their ears. The energy blasted from within him and shot straight up into the sky. It then trickled down around them, lighting everything on fire. The spirits screamed as they disintegrated quickly. Serena and Gabriel were thrown back into the trees that now burned a fiery red. Gabriel, still shielded from his power, snagged onto a single tree to stabilize himself. It cooled immediately from his angelic touch. He looked to his left, Anna was clenched to a tree as well, screaming in pain, burning up right before his eyes. The wind howled around the woods causing the flames to spread. Gabriel launched himself towards Anna and grabbed her hand tight. The flames cooled from his touch.

"Hold on to me!"

She stared at him, nervously.

"I can't. I can't trust you," She replied, pulling her hand from his. Her body blew away with the wind into the darkness.

"Anna no!"

But she was already gone from sight. Gabriel turned back to Nathan and shouted, "Control yourself, you have the power!" He reminded, watching everything around them quickly burn into dust. In the distance, his eyes caught sight of Fate. Suddenly, she vanished and reappeared beside Serena on the ground. Her hand grabbed Serena's mangled arm, then tossed her towards the large flames surrounding Nathan. Serena screamed as the fire lit her up instantly. Her voice shot through Nathan like an arrow to the heart. Suddenly, he blinked, and his eyes returned to their normal shade of

brown. The flames continued to burn bright as Serena tried
desperately to get away from the fire that was eating her up.
"Help me, Nathan! Please!" She pleaded.
Nathan dropped to his knees. His body was exhausted.
"Serena…" He called out weakly, attempting to reach for her.
He then dropped like a dead weight into the dirt and as quickly
as Nathan went down—so did the flames.
Fate smiled as ashes floated to the ground around them now.
She then disappeared from sight.
Gabriel hurried to Nathan's side. "Nathan…" He shouted.
"Nathan, wake up…" His hand touched Nathan's face gently,
there was no heat to his skin.
Serena stumbled to her feet in tears. She could barely stand,
until Fate appeared behind her. Her grip was tight as she
vanished again, this tine with the ghostly girl in her arms.
Gabriel had no time to worry about the two of them or Anna,
his attention was on Nathan. What Nathan had just done,
surpassed anything Gabriel believed he could do and it scared
him. He had managed to hold onto his protective orb just long
enough to survive Nathan's blast, but any longer and he would
have perished too. He calmed himself, collecting what energy
he had left and built up a white light once again from within.
His hands hovered Nathan's lifeless body as the pure energy
began to rain down from the palms of his hands.
Moments later, nothing had changed. Nathan's body was still
lifeless on the ground before him. Gabriel carefully lifted
him from the dirt and threw him over his shoulder. He needed
a safer place to be while Nathan healed. More spirits would
surely come and they were a sitting target out in the open like
this. He had no choice but to wait it out. He needed Nathan to
heal. He needed Alex to find them sooner than later.

6
Last Kiss

Charlotte scrambled to the front closet to grab her jacket. Raphael stood silently as Alex sat on the couch going over in his head what had just happened, pondering how he and Raphael were going to survive this journey ahead of them.
"I can't do this, I can't watch you go…" Charlotte cried, pulling her jacket on.
Alex quickly snapped out of his thoughts, got up from the couch and hurry to her side.
"Charlotte no, please, just listen to me. I'll be fine, I promise." He pleaded, pulling her jacket from her arms. Never was he so forceful with her than he was in this very moment.
"No, this is just like Nathan…" She said, short of breath.
"Poor Sophie had to go through this and it destroyed her. He promised her he wouldn't leave and he did—and he hasn't come back. He won't and neither will you. I know it! We both know it." She said, pulling the jacket back from him.
"No, we're different, Charlotte. I'm more powerful than he ever was. I can do this. I've already done it and I'll do it again. I swear!" He said, forcing her into his arms. "What about everything we just said, moments ago? I meant every word. I love you and this will not change a thing." He spoke,

holding her tight.

"I need you. I need you to ground me. I can't do any of this without you." He pleaded as Charlotte cried into his shirt.

"It won't happen to us." He repeated. "We will always be together. You believe me, don't you?"

She didn't answer.

"Charlotte, I love you." He whispered in her ear, then kissed her on the forehead. He let his lips linger on her skin for a moment as his breathing deepened. He tried to get control of himself. He needed to stay calm, he needed to sound confident in his words.

"It's true. We have a much better chance than Nathan and Gabriel ever did," Raphael spoke up. "Alex is strong, and he's right. We have both made it out before—alive. You must have faith in us—in him, because you are his rock. He needs you as much as you need him." She said, stepping towards them.

Charlotte looked up from Alex's chest, her eyes red from crying. She didn't believe a word they were saying.

He looked down at her again.

"I love you, Charlotte. I will be back sooner than you think."

Her eyes closed as he leaned his forehead against hers. She took a deep breath in, then finally spoke.

"I'm sorry, I just can't."

It was silent for a moment until Alex opened his eyes, clearly upset by her words. She then stepped back from him with her eyes locked on his.

"I can't," She repeated, then looked at Raphael. The fallen angel smiled at her sadly with forgiving eyes. Charlotte then pulled from Alex's grip and quickly hurried out the door.

In shock still, Alex didn't flinch when Raphael's hand touched his shoulder. She could feel him. His energy had become very heavy.

"I know it's not what you thought she would do, but you must remain calm. We need to hold ourselves together to make it through this alive." Raphael spoke clearly. Alex didn't react.

"She still loves you, it's just been too much at once. She's scared of losing you. As Sophie was for Nathan. Surely you

understand?”
“What if she doesn’t?” He said, his eyes still on the door.
“What if she hates me now, like Sophie hates Nathan.”
Raphael sighed, “I don’t mean this rudely, but we can’t worry
about her right now. You need to think of the task at hand. We
are about to walk into the biggest battle of our lives and we
need to prepare ourselves.” She said, sternly. “I’m confident
we will make it back and you can work on her then. She will
forgive you, I’m certain. Prove her wrong Alex. Show her you
can do it.”
Stepping away from her, Alex quietly walked down the
hallway towards his bedroom, then slammed the door behind
him.

Charlotte wiped her eyes repeatedly as she hurried down
the street. As beautiful of a day as it was in Vancouver, it was
nothing but darkness inside of her. She needed someone, she
needed her best friend—no matter the state she was in. As she
hurried through the park towards Sophie’s apartment she only
hoped that she would be home and not on set today.
The sun continued to shine as she approached Sophie’s place,
scanning the buzzer options she found the apartment number
and held the button down. It buzzed once, twice, a third time,
then finally a forth, but no one answered. Charlotte collapsed
against the wall, she began to choke up and just as she was
about to leave a deliveryman walked up and unlocked the front
door. Charlotte quickly held the door for him as he attempted
to pull his cart inside. She then hurried past him towards the
steps and up to Sophie’s floor.

Hearing the front door slam, I pulled myself from his lips
just as Charlotte entered the living room.
“What are you doing here?!” I yelled, but Charlotte’s eyes
were glued on my guest. The young man got up from the

couch feeling a little awkward. I sighed, tossing my script down onto the couch before getting up.

"Sorry Ben, can we finish this later?" I said, crossing my arms at Charlotte.

"Sure Soph," he said, uncomfortably.

"Sorry again," I repeated, "I promise we will finish the rehearsal before we shoot this weekend. I'll call you later, okay?"

"Okay, talk to you then." He then gave me a hug, and smiled as he passed Charlotte on the way out.

We stood in front of each other, silent for a moment. When she didn't speak, I headed past her into the kitchen. I knew she was upset and I knew what she was thinking, but I didn't care. "Want some tea?" I said, filling the kettle with water.

I heard Charlotte enter the room.

Plugging in the kettle, I watched as Charlotte looked around my apartment. It was the first time in a long time since she had been here. I never had anyone over—not even her and Alex. They had only been here once, when I first moved in. Things were much different in this apartment. It was bare, as if I just moved in—but I didn't. There were no signs or reminders of my friends, or him. Not a single picture or item on the wall. Charlotte wiped her eyes and cleared her throat.

I spoke before her. "What do you want? I'm kind of busy today." I said, placing a tea bag in each cup.

When the water finally boiled, I filled the cups and placed one in front of her. I then sat down across from her at the kitchen table.

"I'm sorry to barge in on you like this… it's just," She paused. I knew again what she was thinking and she knew our rules very well.

"I have no one else to talk to and this is huge, and… I don't know what I should do. I just need–"

"You know the rules, Charlotte," I interrupted. "If you're going to speak about anything from my past or of the supernatural—"

"Alex and Raphael are going into Purgatory to find Nathan

and Gabriel!" She blurted out.

I stared silently for a moment.

"That's none of my business, Charlotte. I don't care." I said finally said, trying hard to not let it affect me.

"You don't understand, Michael is making them go and I know, I know Alex won't make it out alive this time. Even if he finds Nathan and Gabriel, he will sacrifice himself to get them out."

I felt my hand twitch a bit.

"That's enough, Charlotte, I don't care what—"

"Yes you do, stop saying that!" Charlotte shouted.

I felt a heaviness building inside of me, I was growing angry from her uninvited presence.

"Listen, Alex was so close to finding them just recently. He can do it, but this isn't the way. He's leaving tomorrow night, Soph. I can't watch him throw his life away!" She pleaded.

I started to get up from the table but Charlotte grabbed my wrist and pulled me back down.

"I remember how painful it was watching Nathan leave, but now I feel it too, Sophie. I do, I get it and I'm so sorry for your pain and everything you've been through. But we can stop this, together." She begged. "Help Alex, he's always been good to you. He went into Purgatory and risked his life to save you! Now you can save him!" Her voice continued to rise.

She clearly didn't care what this would do to me, what it was already doing to me. I bit my lip, trying to force the emotions back down. I wanted her out. I pulled my wrist from her grip, but she reached for me again.

"Sophie if you just—"

"Shut up!" I snapped. "I don't want to hear it! Don't you get it? I don't care what anyone does anymore. I don't care about them—none of them!" I yelled.

"Sophie, stop this please!" She cried, slamming her fist down to the table. "You can save Alex and get Nathan back, I know it! We can make this right. Please trust me, you need to try again. You need to care. They need you to care! I need you! I'm begging you as your best friend. Help me! Maybe we can

find a spell that can help Alex find Nathan before he goes and—" Charlotte shuddered back in fear as I tossed the tea cup past her head. It shattered against the wall behind her.
"I said SHUT UP!" I screamed again. "I don't want Nathan back! He's never coming back! It's over Charlotte! Why do you insist on taunting me about this over and over again?! I mean, do you hear yourself? Dabbling in magic too? You've changed. Don't you see what they do to us?" I stared back at her in rage. I could feel the hole inside of me expanding.
"They create this wonderful thought of a world and they make you think that they love you, but it's all an act because they can never have what we have—a real life! They will always be attached to that world." The words poured from my mouth. But they were true. They had to be. It was why nothing ever worked out. I clenched my chest as my friend stared back at me.
"They will rip everything out from under you. If you don't get out now, you will surely end up like me. Don't you see that? It's already happening. You're changing. Don't lose yourself, Charlotte. I'm still trying to put my life back together... Can't you see that? Can't you respect that?"
She didn't respond.
I slowly made my way past her, leaned down and began to pick up the shards from the tea cup.
"You still love him. I know it." Charlotte finally said.
I stopped for a moment and took a breath, trying to contain myself, but she went on.
"You love Nathan very much and that will never change—no matter how hard you try to ignore it. No matter how you try to move on, or meet new guys... or change your life completely. You two are meant to be, I know that now."
Charlotte then stood up and walked over to me. Slowly, she knelt down. I felt her hand on my back.
"I know this isn't the life we chose, but Fate has given us this road. We have to survive it. We have to face it head on, and you have to know that there must be something great at the end if we make it through, don't you? Don't you believe that,

Sophie?" She asked again. "This is what we've been given, and there are some pretty amazing people in our life compared to others. I mean yes, ours is much more difficult and a little more dangerous at times, but what an adventure it has been so far, hasn't it?"

I knew what she was doing, but no matter what she said, she was just as scared as me inside. It would take her eventually, just like it took me. It was only a matter of time. There was nothing I could do for her now. I let the shards of glass fall to the floor as I stood up. Charlotte rose with me.

Staring into her eyes, I saw my friend smile back at me.

"I know you're scared Soph, but so am—"

"Get out." I said, sharply.

"What?" Her smile faded.

"I said get out of my apartment," I repeated.

"Soph… you don't mean that. This is important." She spoke, nervously.

"We are no longer friends. Don't come here ever again, or I'll call the cops." I said, very clearly.

When she still didn't move, I felt myself snap.

"Go on, get out!" I shouted, making her jump back from me. Slowly, she began to back her way out of the room. Opening the front door, she stepped into the hallway—facing me still. I could tell she was racking her brain for something else— anything else to change my mind.

"You're my best friend…" Was all she said.

I stared back at her, blankly.

"You have no idea what you're getting yourself into," I said, quietly. "Have a nice life." I then slammed the door on her face.

I stood still for a moment, trying to calm myself. My body was twitching, trembling, reacting from her visit. The thoughts raced through my mind. I scratched my head that began to burn on the right side, then gripped onto my hair tightly.

No...

Turning from the door, I quickly headed into the living room. I snagged my cell phone off the side table and searched the contacts. I waited as the phone rang only twice, then he picked up.

"Hello?"

"Ben? Are you still close by?" I said, scratching at my throat. "I'm done with my friend. We can finish our rehearsal if you still want to?" I said, my voice shaking a bit.

"Sure, that's fine. I have no plans today." He responded. "Is everything okay?" He then asked.

"Yea, it's fine. Just friend drama. Hurry over, okay?" I insisted, ending the conversation quickly.

It didn't take long for Ben to return. I let him in and led him back into the living room. I tried my best to contain the twitching happening inside of me.

"You sure you're alright?" He asked again, studying me.

"Yeah, every thing's fine. I just had to deal with her. I'm not really friends with her anymore. She causes me too much stress. I'm trying to stay on the right path, ya know? Only positive things in my life right now. I've got no time for games."

"Yeah, for sure." He replied, studying me still. "Well, shall we get started then?"

I nodded grabbing my script, then motioned for him to follow me into my room.

"Let's do the bedroom fight scene, okay?" I said, sitting down on my bed.

Ben pulled the script out of his bag and sat down next to me. I hated his expression. I didn't want him to look at me that way. It reminded me of everyone else. He was looking at me like I was a fragile doll about to break.

Ben had only been around for about a month now, but was a nice distraction. I met him on set of my drama series. It had really picked up this year and he was my new co-star/love interest on the show. We got to know each other very quickly. He's nice and very normal. Ben is an only child and doesn't speak much about his past—to anyone, which suited me fine because I didn't want to talk about mine either. We worked well together. We understood each other and never invaded each other's space. He was a quiet guy, strong and athletic with sandy-blonde hair that was always cut clean and perfectly shaped. His best feature was definitely his eyes. They were a piercing blue. Every girl on set had a crush on him, even I had to admit he was nice to look at. But I wasn't looking for anything, we were never more than just co-stars. I kept it very professional, even when most of our scenes were physically close and intense. I was very good with not getting caught up in it like a lot of the other actors do on set.

Ben cleared his throat and began to read.

"Okay in this scene, Becca and Scott have their first fight. Becca caught Scott kissing another girl at the dance, but it's actually not what she thinks. Scott tries to explain it to her, but she just won't listen."

My eyes didn't move from the paper as he began to read the script.

"Becca, will you just listen to me? She kissed me. I didn't want to kiss her. She just threw herself at me. I swear." Ben then waited for my response.

I dropped the paper down to my side.

"Why do they always try and say it's not their fault…" I said, rudely.

"I'm sorry, what did you say? I'm not sure that's in the script Soph, can I see?" He replied, leaning over to see my paper.

"No, I know." I said pulling it back from him. "I'm just saying, how come guys always say they aren't at fault when another girl is involved. I don't get it? You can't always get what you want in life, and sometimes you have to hurt someone's feelings. It's just life. Tell that other girl no, and keep your distance, it's as simple as that. Otherwise, you will lose what you have right in front of you. I mean, why do I have to suffer because you don't want to hurt someone else's feelings?"

Ben looked at me oddly.

"Sounds like you've been through a similar situation?"

"No…" I quickly replied. "I just mean, it's just—stupid."

"This scene is stupid." I said in a huff, then flipped my paper back up.

"Well, it's a drama series, Soph. Most of them are stupid." He laughed.

"Whatever, let's just do this." I said, scratching the right side of my head again.

"You sure? It seems like something is bothering you today." He paused, but I didn't look at him.

"I know we don't normally do this but, do you wanna talk about it?"

"No, I wanna practice. Let's go." I replied.

"Alright, no worries... Where was I?" Ben said, lifting his paper again.

"It's actually my line..." I interrupted, then tucked my hair behind my ear before speaking again.

"I don't wanna hear your excuses, Scott. You knew she was obsessing over you for the past little bit and you didn't say a word to me." I stopped again, losing my spot on the page for a second. "I mean, we've been together for a while now. If a situation comes up... we have to face it together. That's how relationships work, but instead, you decided to keep it a secret and look where we are now?" I got up from the bed, collecting my troubled energy and pushed it into the scene.

"I know, I'm sorry, but you don't understand. She's hard to deal with and I didn't want to hurt her. You know I love you, Becca. I just messed up, it will never happen again. I promise." Ben got up and touched my arm.

I flinched at his cool hand. Then looked into his eyes sadly, taking a deep breath. Ben waited for my next line, but my eyes didn't move from his. Something was stirring inside of me.

"Soph... it's your line." I heard him say, but I couldn't speak. I felt him shake my arm just a bit.

"Sophie, you have to forgive me now. Our characters have to make up—remember?" He said, slightly smiling at me.

My hand numbly reached up to his face. He stared back at me as my fingers brushed across his cheek. My body was weakening beneath me... those words. Those words were stuck in my head. I found myself moving closer to him. Why was he so calm? Why did those words affect me so much? "Sophie," Ben spoke again, but I suddenly found my lips connected with his. My hands then slid up and wrapped around his neck as I forced him back against the wall. He pushed back against me for a second.

"Hey, Soph,"

I kissed him again, and again. Until he pulled back a second time. "Sophie. Stop, we missed a line." He said, eventually pushing me off of him.

My eyes shot open and I stepped back immediately. I felt a tightening in my throat. My nails quickly dug into my skin as Ben stared back at me confused with what was happening.

"What are you doing? Stop..." His hand reached for mine but I pulled back from him, then snapped.

"It's all your fault!" I heard myself say. "You ended us! You ruined my life, Nate!" The words electrified my body and I bolted from the room.

I could hear him scrambling to collect his stuff as a I raced for the door. I needed to get out of there. What had I done? I frantically hit the lobby button inside the elevator.

"Come on… shut!" I shouted.

Then, just as Ben appeared before me, the elevator doors slid shut on his face.

"Sophie wait!"

When the doors opened again, I took off fast, out of the building and down the street towards the park. I could hear him close behind me. He was fast, but so was I now.

I dashed through a bunch of families having a picnic and past the swing set filled with children. He was right behind me every step of the way. I jumped onto a path and darted towards the trees. I could escape him if I could just make it to the woods. But soon enough, he tackled me to the ground.

The pavement scrapped across my skin as we rolled into the grass.

"God dam it! Why can't you just leave me alone?!" I screamed in pain. People stopped and stared, passing whispers.

I could only imagine what this looked like to them, but Ben quickly responded.

"Don't worry! We're just practicing a scene, it's all good." He laughed awkwardly, then waved with a fake smile.

He then turned his attention back to me as I continued to struggle beneath him.

"Sophie stop! Tell me what's going on." He insisted, but I continued to try and push him off me.

"Who's this Nate guy? Did he hurt you?"

The sound of this name stabbed my heart like a knife. I stopped suddenly, and for the first time, since that night in the park, I began to cry. I could feel his eyes on me, I quickly covered my face.

"I just want to forget it all, but they won't let me." I cried.

I felt Ben's hands pull me up so he could wrap his arms around me.

"He broke my heart, worse than anyone ever has." I whispered. "I don't know if I can survive this, I'm trying so hard to put it all in the past, but… it just keeps coming back." I gripped onto his shirt, I couldn't stop crying. He tightened his grip around me.

"I'm so sorry," he whispered.

He let me cry in his arms for a moment, then spoke again.

"But you will get past this. I promise."

I shook my head no.

I heard him sigh, then felt the warmth of his skin as his chin rested on the top of my head.

"Sometimes, you need to face your problems to truly get past them. I understand though, it's hard. I'm a lot like you. I have my secrets, but sometimes when you talk it out, people can actually help you. I also know how hard it is to trust people which is why I keep to myself. But it isn't always healthy."

I breathed quietly against him, listening to his words. I felt embarrassed now. This was too close for Ben and I. We didn't act this way and I worried for what it would cause between us.

He then leaned back from me. I felt his thumb brush a tear from my cheek. He then lifted my chin up to look at him.

"Trust me, okay?" He whispered.

I looked at him sadly. This was a side to him I'd never seen. Something about his presence right now made me feel safe and—loved. A warm sensation began to fill my body and I suddenly smelt a hint of lavender in the air around us. He spoke again.

"I can help you through this if you like, but you gotta trust me—fully. Okay?" He spoke kindly, waiting for me to answer. Eventually, I felt myself nod back to him.

"He was stupid to leave you, you're a great catch." He smiled, touching my face again. He then slid himself from on top of me and sat down next to me in the grass.

"Everyone messes up in life, Soph. Sometimes numerous times, and sometimes people need another chance. Even if they've had too many already." He smiled again, touching my hand. "We all need that person who never gives up on us. No matter what happens."

I felt my eyes begin to water again.

"He was my world," I said, sadly.

A smile grew on his face again from my raw and honest words.

"Then I'm sure your world is still here. He's just lost right now."

I felt his hands take mine. He then quickly pulled me up to my feet. His fingers carefully picked out a few loose pieces of grass from my hair.

"You're not going to believe me when I tell you my story," I said, nervously.

Ben gently took my hand again, then dusted some grass from his shirt.

"Try me." He said.

●●●

Charlotte wondered the streets for the rest of the day pondering over what to do next. She was truly on her own and had no one to turn to. She eventually reached the bubble tea shop that she and her friends had once gone to. It was Sophie's favorite. The memories of her past haunted her with every step. She wanted things to go back to normal. For everyone to be happy, but she just couldn't see that future anymore. Sadly, she went inside and got herself a medium sized berry slush with pearls, then continued her walk in the sunshine.

It felt as if she was avoiding the entire situation by staying out the entire day, but she wasn't sure what else to do. She couldn't go back and face Alex. She couldn't watch him willingly throw his life away by jumping into purgatory unprepared. How could Michael do this to them? It was unfair, all of it. She numbly sipped her drink.

"You're pretty confused in there, aren't you?" A voice spoke from behind.

Charlotte turned and immediately dropped her drink at the sight of Fate.

"Relax, I'm just here to talk."

"What do you want?" Charlotte responded quickly.

"What's your little lover-boy been up to recently? I see he's still dabbling in the dark arts, maybe more then he can handle?" She teased.

"Alex can handle anything,"

"Or so you think… He's growing weak you know?" Fate quickly responded. "That last one really knocked him out, didn't it? But you… You seem to keep him sane, don't you?" Fate spoke quietly, walking around her. She then stopped and turned to Charlotte.

"Alex is only trying to help, and I don't know much of what I do for him, but I'm sure it's not a lot. We're just trying to survive your game, Fate—like you said we should." Charlotte replied, trying to be smart.

"Yes, I did say that. Didn't I?" She chuckled, suddenly appearing behind Charlotte and flicking a stand of her hair as she passed by. She strolled slowly past her once again and smiled.

"But Alex also has Raphael, so… maybe you should step aside for a bit and let them do their thing."

Charlotte stared back at her worried, she needed to get out of there, but before she could, Fate reappeared behind her again and wrapped her arm around Charlotte's shoulders, her right hand gripped tightly to the back of her long sandy-blonde hair. Charlotte's teeth clenched in pain.

"I'm saying, we need to remove you from the picture for a bit," Fate's grip tightened.

Charlotte's scream echoed as they vanished from sight.

$$7$$

The Portal

ichael stood quietly in front of the large white doors in the portal room. Anyone sent through these doors should never return. But long ago, Raphael had pasted through these very doors and somehow return to them. He wondered if history would repeat itself. Could she make it back a second time? A gust of wind blew from behind as Uriel appeared.

"Are you ready?"

"Of course." Michael responded, turning to face him. "But first, we must protect the chamber and ourselves. Please hand me your sword."

Uriel carefully pulled a large golden sword from his back and placed it in his brother's hands. Michael turned back to the portal doors and lowered it to the ground before closing his eyes. It was silent for a moment before he began his prayer. The angelic words of protection.

"A thousand may fall at their side, ten thousand at his right hand, but they shall never reach us. We will observe from a far with our eyes and see true the punishment of the wicked—however it may play out. For He commands his angels and if they are true of heart, then He shall lift them up with his powers so that they will not strike their foot against stone.

Bind that world and protect us from any evil that may attempt
to break through. Hide us from the dark eyes that lingers
within and protect our guardians as you see fit. And if by
chance their hearts darken, let peace be with their souls in
whatever may come. For we shall close the doors to them,
forever."

Uriel began to smile as Michael lit up the ground before them.
The golden sword glittered off the walls of the chamber as an
energy began to grow from Michael's hands. A sheet of white
rose from the ground to the roof above them. It coated the
walls, oozing its way back down and over the doors in front of
them and eventually melted down to the floor below. Soon the
ground beneath them shimmered like diamonds. The room was
now sealed. Nothing could break through it.

The sword shined bright as Uriel approached. The single
weapon of the sole protector of the portal gates. Uriel was the
strongest, most agile angel of their realm. The one they trusted
to protect their world—to keep the unwanted out. Nothing
could stand against this weapon. Except maybe one.

Fate.

But it had not been tested. They only hoped that if the great
battle came… It would serve them well.

Eventually, the brightness faded around them. Michael then
respectfully picked up the sword and handed it back to Uriel.
"You know, it's almost certain that they will not survive
this journey. Alex's heart is darkening by the second and
Raphael—she will not last long before they destroy her mind
again."

"I know." Michael responded, sadly. "That is why I chose
this prayer. No one should make it back a second time, so
we must be prepared. We cannot afford for anymore slip ups
or openings from that world into ours anymore. It will only
worsen as time goes on if they remain here. It is best, if they
are removed from the picture indefinitely."

Uriel stood silently, a little surprised. This was a sensitive
subject for Michael. Although he didn't speak much of casting
Raphael away long ago, he hadn't been the same since and

every angel knew it.

"But what about Nathan?" Uriel spoke again. "Do you believe that he is the one Gabriel speaks of? You know… the—"

"I know what Gabriel thinks, but if he were the one, he would have broken himself free from purgatory already. Unless, he is having trouble with his new powers…" Michael paused. "There's just no way he will fully manifest into what we need him to be, even if he is the one." He paused again, deep in thought. "With the state he is in, he won't be able to handle it, those powers will surely devour him alive and this could end badly—for us all. There are too many scenarios at play here." Uriel stared at his brother, confused.

"I fear, he is of no use to us anymore…" Michael sighed.

"Let us rid that thought from our minds, brother." He then said, about to exit the room. He stopped suddenly, hearing his brother's internal thoughts. "He's too weak," Michael repeated. "It is up to us now. We must trust that He will guide us in the right direction."

Uriel nodded, "Of course brother,"

Alex continued to pace around his room. He hadn't slept the entire night. Pictures of Charlotte and their life that had just begun, began to haunt him from the walls of his apartment. Her photographs in frames, her clothes on the bed, the scent of her perfume on the pillows. He sat down on the bed hiding his face away in his hands.

"Charlotte, I'm so sorry for getting you mixed up in this…" His head hung low as he massaged the back of his neck. He soon sat up and pulled a small black book from his night stand beside him. He searched, read, and pondered over many spells that might help them on this journey to come. He wasn't sure if any of them would work, but he had to try. He had to make it through this. He couldn't let Nathan, Gabriel or Charlotte down. He believed like Gabriel did, that Nathan was the one and he would do whatever was needed to save him. To save

Gabriel. And as much as he loved Charlotte, Raphael was right, there were more important things happening. Things he was created for and others he was obligated to serve. His hands flew across the pages, writing note after note, studying everything he could. He needed a master plan, something that would protect him and Raphael while they were in there. Something that would bring them all out alive. His research in the spirit guide books were of no help, they had many protection prayers and healing techniques, but what he needed was something much stronger. For what he was going up against was not of the ordinary. He had experienced it before and this time it would be much worse. He needed the dark arts. He needed something to fight with. To fight them. Secretly, he had also begun to create a spell book for just this reason and he managed to keep it hidden away—from everyone—even Charlotte. For she would only be upset with him if she found out he had put this much time into magic. He scrambled around the room trying to remember where he left it last. Then he froze, hearing faint voices from the other room. Slowly, he walked towards his bedroom door. Carefully, he pinched the door open to listen. It sounded like Raphael, but who was she talking to?

"She is very damaged, barely holding it together. But I can keep at her," The male voice said.

"Good, watch her closely and don't leave her side. We must rip those thoughts from her mind and please, be careful. Fate is watching us." Raphael whispered as Alex crept down the hallway towards them. Who was she talking to? Whose mind were they trying to erase thoughts from?

He suddenly thought of Charlotte. He still hadn't seen or heard from her since she left. Worried now, he quickly turned the corner to catch them in mid conversation, but to his surprise… there was no one there. Alex searched the apartment, but found no traces of anyone.

"Raphael! Where are you?!" He shouted, but no one answered. Quickly, he hurried over to the couch and got down on his hands and knees. He reached underneath, feeling around for his book. He could feel it, calling out to him. His middle finger brushed across the edge of a piece of paper. He snagged it quickly and yanked it out. Sitting up on the couch, he scanned through the pages. He had written notes everywhere—it was complete rubbish with no order. It made no sense, and was meant to be that way. Only Alex could understand it. His plan was to combine the spirit guide prayers with spells from the dark arts. One to fight with, one to protect himself with and if need be, one to heal them all. He wasn't sure what he would be up against this time and now, he wasn't sure if he fully trusted Raphael. She was up to something. He was sure of it. What they were about to do needed full concentration and full trust, for he was about to go against everything they had been taught. The dark arts were forbidden to anyone that followed Him—no matter the desperation or situation. But what other choice did he have? Panic set in as he quickly took the book and raced back into his bedroom, locking the door behind him. Immediately, he whipped through the pages, then casted a protection spell to hide himself in his room from any supernatural being.

For the next twenty-four hours, he would plan his attack back into purgatory as well as a second plan—a protection spell—from the one he was traveling with. Just in case.

●●●

Morning came, slowly I sat up on the couch. My neck was stiff from the uncomfortable sleep. I had dozed off in front of the television, again. A regular occurrence for me since I'd been living on my own again. The sound of the TV seemed to help me sleep a little better. It was quiet in my place. I missed walking Bruce in the mornings. I hadn't picked him up yet—not since Nathan left. It would only remind me of our life together. I had told the people watching him that I was filming too much to tend to him for now. Luckily, they were more than happy to help care for him. I'm going to pick him up eventually, when I feel better—just not right now.

I stretched out and reached for the converter to turn off the television. Swinging my feet over the edge of the couch they brushed across something below.

"Hey, watch it…" Ben moaned, rolling over towards me and pulling his small throw blanket up around him.

"Why is it so cold in your apartment?"

I half smiled. "Ben, what are you still doing here?"

I carefully stepped over him.

"After we talked, we watched TV for a bit, then you dozed off. I guess I did too." He yawned.

I forgot. I forgot for a moment about what happened. I held out my hands to help him up from the ground.

"I thought you wouldn't want to be alone, so I stayed." He smiled, taking my hands.

I pulled him up towards me.

"After you fell asleep, I got addicted to some stupid reality show. Teen parents or something, don't tell anyone. I'll just deny it."

I laughed, it was kind of nice to not wake up alone for once. We then stood awkwardly for a moment. I haven't had anyone stay over at my new place yet, especially a guy. It felt wrong, but also… right.

"Okay, well… do you want some breakfast?" I then said, breaking our silence. "I mean, since you're here."

"I'd love some," He replied. "I wanna talk to you about some stuff today any ways." He then pushed me towards the kitchen.

"Talk to me about what?" I asked, worried.

"Nothing much. It's just you were talking in your sleep last night, about Charlotte and about that Nathan guy… I think I may be able to ease your mind,"

"I don't need you to ease my mind about anything, Ben. It's probably best if you stay out of it. I mean it." I said, sternly. I couldn't get Ben involved in my crazy life. I already felt awkward about yesterday.

After Ben tackled me down in the park and insisted I talk to him, I spilled—everything—right up until Nathan left me and

oddly enough, Ben entertained the idea and listened carefully. He was probably trying to be nice. Probably because we still had to work together. There was no way he actually believed me. He probably thinks I'm crazy now.
"Sophie, please." He said, grabbing my hand and turning me back towards him. "Let me just try. If it doesn't work, then at least you will get a good laugh out of it."
I looked at him oddly.
"You see, I have this secret obsession or hobby you could say, and I want to try it on you. That is, if you agree." He waited again, "Please, come on. It will be fun—I promise."
"What is it exactly?" I asked, a little intrigued with what his hobby could be.
"It's like a meditation type of thing. I'll explain later, okay? Let's eat first." He then shoved me back towards the fridge.
I opened it and looked inside. I was mainly a cereal girl, I never cooked breakfast like Nate—I quickly stopped my thought. I was doing it again.
"I can't really cook." I spoke.
Ben shoved me aside to look through the fridge. "Hmm… that's because you have no food." He laughed.
"Sorry." I replied, a little embarrassed.
"It's fine," He smiled. "Wait, you have some eggs and like, 3 strips of bacon." He laughed again.
"I like cereal," I said, feeling a little childish now.
"Of course you do. Let me guess… the ones with all the rainbow marshmallows in it?" His eyebrow rose at me.
I nodded.
"Okay well, do you mind if I eat this then and you can enjoy your cereal?"
"Works for me. I also have some bread for toast if you like."
"How about pancake mix? Most people have pancake mix." He then said.
"No." I replied, quickly. "Never pancakes."
The smiled on my face faded.
"No worries, this works fine," He said, taking the hint.
He then handed me the milk, and pulled the eggs and bacon

from the fridge.

"So," He said, grabbing a frying pan from under the stove. "Are you excited for our next episode we're filming?"

I reached by him to grab a bowl from the cupboard. He beat me to it. Our hands touched in the exchange.

"Yea," I replied, grabbing the cereal box off the counter.

"It's our first big fight on the show. Should make a few viewers pretty angry." He laughed cracking some eggs into the heated pan. "I love it when the fans write in all upset, it's hilarious."

"Definitely," I laughed. "I actually had a girl write me the first week you joined us. She said I was too mean to you. That I needed to appreciate the 'real man' I had in front of me."

"Well... you should." He agreed. "Becca's kind of a bitch." He laughed again. "Come on, admit it." He teased poking me with the spatula.

"What! No way! She's just misunderstood, it's mostly sarcasm." I argued. "It's like, eighty percent misunderstandings with her and—"

"Twenty percent bitch!" He interrupted.

I grabbed a marshmallow from my bowl and tossed it at him.

"Gross! It's soggy..."

"She's not a bitch," I said, getting ready to toss another at him.

"Fine, she's not a bitch." He paused, "She's partial,"

"Stop!" I laughed again.

"Poor, poor Scotty boy," He snickered.

"Oh my god. Fine whatever." I grabbed my bowl of cereal and headed over to the table to sit down.

When Ben was finished making his meal, he joined me. I had to admit, his presence calmed me. I was beginning to enjoy his company more by the minute.

After we ate, we continued to talk and he continued to distract me from my worries. But I couldn't help but think about that hobby he had mentioned. I wondered what other kind of stuff Ben did in his own time. He was much more than a co-star now. I almost felt like he was more of a friend. We had immediately switched gears in only a day. So I had to ask,

"Alright, enough of this. What do you want to do with me?"
He gave me a big smile.
"You know what I mean," I laughed.
"Okay, what I'm going to do is a little weird and most of my friends aren't open to it, but I really want you to be." He paused. "I actually really believe in this stuff,"
"Believe in what?" I asked, nervously.
"Well, this hobby…" He stalled.
"Yea, you said that. Cut to the point Ben. I'm losing interest." I said, impatiently.
"It's called, Reiki." He replied.
"Reiki? Isn't that some sort of Japanese spiritual crap?" I said, kind of rudely. "Like what Mr. Miyagi did to Daniel in the karate movie?" I had to laugh.
"Well, it's more like a healing technique, but yes. Some therapist use it instead of medicine. It channels energy into the patient by means of touch to activate the natural healing processes of the patient's body and restore physical and emotional well-being."
"Sounds like a load of crap," I smirked, but I did love The Karate Kid. Ben ignored my words and went on.
"You see, we each have within us seven chakras. Sometimes eight if we are lucky to connect with it."
"Chakras?" My right eyebrow raised.
"Just wait," He said. "The seven chakras are powerful energy centers within the body, each representing a different level of consciousness. Chakra means "wheel", a vortex of vibration— light and energy. A chakra point is where two lines of energy cross. Come here, I'll show you." He then grabbed my hand, and pulled me up from the table to lead me into the living room. Grabbing a purple pillow from my couch, he tossed it down to the floor.
"Lay down." He demanded.
"You want me to lay on the ground?"
His hands rested on his hips. "Will you just be quiet and trust me?"
I rolled my eyes, then walked over to the pillow.

Quietly, I lowered myself to the ground, adjusting the pillow under my head to get more comfortable.

"No funny stuff." I warned. I'm sure he thought I was joking, but I wasn't.

He knelt down beside me. His hand moved just above the crown of my head.

"I was always told that humans are made up of energy particles from the universe, like everything else in this world, and when we learn to align our energies we become healthier, more aware of our potentials and more in tune with our surroundings. It is said that Reiki can heal anything and everything, if you allow it." He smiled, looking down at me.

"Uh huh," I rolled my eyes again.

"This is the Crown Chakra. It glows either violet, white or even sometimes gold when activated. It's your consciousness and your brain. It encourages the growth of new ideas, peace, purity and can cut through mental confusion."

He then moved his hand down, directly over my forehead.

"This is your Brow or Third Eye, people call it sometimes. It glows violet-blue or dark blue when charged. This Chakra connects with the mind, intuition, insight and paranormal abilities…"

"Whoa, slow down. No supernatural stuff." I said, sharply. "I don't want any—"

"I know Sophie, relax." He begged. "This one is really important, it can cleanse emotional addictions. Release painful memories and heal the emotionally shattered."

"I'm not emotionally shattered, Ben—if that's what you're getting at." I attempted to sit up, feeling a little too vulnerable now. He pushed me back down.

"I'm not saying you are. Look, just humor me okay and let me finish."

I sighed, "Fine, go on."

"After this one is the Throat Chakra. Glowing a bright sky blue, this one is your creativity and self-expression. It's in your throat, ears, wind-pipe and upper lungs. Something an actress could definitely use." He teased. "It can bring peace,

look back into your past, and teach you to grow. It can also release you of mental confusion too.”
“Ooh…” I teased again. I wasn’t buying any of this.
Ben shook his head, “Poor, poor Scott, never taken seriously.” He sighed.
My eyes shot open and glared at him.
“Not being bitchy… just so you know.” I mumbled before closing my eyes again. “Continue,”
Ben slowly moved his hands down further to hover over my chest. I felt my heart begin to race as the heat from his hands warmed my shirt. I suddenly felt very nervous.
“This one, is the one I want you to listen to the most, Sophie. This is your Heart Chakra. The most important one for you. It glows Green when activated.”
“Green?” I spoke, opening my eyes again. “Shouldn’t a heart glow red or pink? Green doesn’t make sense at all,”
“Will you shut up!” Ben shouted. “Yes, sometimes it glows pink, but very rarely.”
“Sorry…” I said, embarrassed a little. “Touchy, touchy,”
I then closed my eyes again to listen to the rest of his rant. His hands returned to my chest.
“The Heart Chakra shows unconditional love, compassion and teaches healing techniques like learning to live in balance.
It also creates a bridge from the physical to the spiritual. It’s in your heart, upper back, your breasts, blood and general functions of the lungs. This Chakra can bring you clarity and stability. Healing both your body and mind as one complete package.”
By now, I had given up on teasing Ben about this whole thing. He seemed to be serious about this, so I listened carefully as he continued.
“The next is your Solar Plexus, a Chakra that glows yellow.”
I then felt his hand touch the center of my stomach, making me flinch just slightly.
“The storehouse of spiritual and physical energy. This one keeps the other Chakras healthy. It can ground us if we concentrate on it hard enough—a technique we could all use.

This one is located in your lower back, digestive system, liver, spleen and so on. This energy lets us learn forgiveness, it can remove depression, thoughts of suicide and help us build our self-esteem. It does this by releasing our fears and replacing them with the energy of joy and laughter."

The heat of his hand calmed my stomach that was beginning to turn a bit. 'Laughter' I thought to myself. I hadn't laughed or felt happiness in so long—not until today. There was no calmness or relaxation... Not until now. Not until Ben. Everything was so numb, so—dull. And forgiveness, it was a word I didn't want to think about. I didn't want to forgive anyone—especially Him.

I felt my eyes begin to water at the simple thought of Nathan. I swallowed hard trying to keep it in. Something was building inside of me. Something was creating a warm sensation throughout my body and it wasn't just Ben's hands. I suddenly noticed how tense my body was and took a deep breath in, trying to relax again. I felt the heat of Ben moving lower.

"Here, over your pelvis, kidneys, bladder and womb is the Sacral Chakra."

My heart was racing.

"This one gives off an orange energy, giving you an immunity from disease and also creates joy. It's your feminine energy that can break down barriers, help with mental breakdowns, depression and accidents. This is the best color for dealing with grief or loss of something... or someone." He hinted.

I felt the tears building up again. Why were these emotions coming up so quickly, they were almost overwhelming.

I tried my best to hold it in, but I felt a small tear slip down my cheek. I couldn't look at him.

"Finally, there's the Base. The Chakra that shines red in color. It's the root of the collective unconsciousness and controls stability and survival. It's in the body areas such as your teeth, bones and blood cells. It can renew enthusiasm and give strength to carry on, or power you to do something you dread. It can give courage for you to support yourself—or maybe a friend. It controls your willpower Sophie and ignites from the bottom of your feet." He paused.

I felt him gazing down at me, but I couldn't open my eyes. My fingertips began to tremble against the carpet as the tears continued to slip down my face. I felt Ben's hand slide into mine and close tightly.

"When you tap into these Chakras, there's no stopping you, Soph. They can help you with anything in life. Help you learn, grow and most importantly—heal. You need to heal Soph, and you know it. You have to face what you fear. You need to speak the worries you have out loud and let others help you. Know that all obstacles are beatable if you approach them correctly."

I felt his grip tighten around my hand.

"Don't run from your fears, they will only destroy you in the end. Please let me teach you how to do this, how to heal. I can see the pain in your eyes. I feel it," he said, softly.

What did he mean he could feel it? How was Ben suddenly so in tune with my inner self? Then he spoke again.

"You are a pure heart, everything you need is right inside of you."

My eyes shot open. *Those words...*

"You need to allow yourself to heal," He repeated.

My eyes adjusted to his. I broke down and quickly pulled my hand from his to cover my face. It was flooding through me. The pain, the regret and the sadness that I had managed to pack down deep inside.

"Breathe deeply, listen to my voice..." He said, "Picture a beautiful white light surrounding you. It's warm and very safe." He spoke, carefully bringing his left hand up to my chest again. He then placed it down. "Slow your heart..."

With tears streaming down to the floor, I tried my best to listen to his words. I didn't even care that his hand was on me, I truly felt the energy he was trying to push into me.

Moments later, my heart steadied to a normal rhythm and I felt calm once again. He smiled down at me.

"Now, feel each of the Chakras I spoke about. Picture them slowly energizing, lighting up one by one within. Starting at your crown, down to your third eye, making its way to your throat, and into your chest so that it can light your pure heart up. Let it push into your arms, down to your fingertips. Let it flow through your pelvis, legs, and down to your toes. Then let it pour out the bottom of your feet, leaving your entire body energized." He paused again.

I could feel it. I could see it in my mind. This energy was like water rushing through me, electrifying everything it touched.

"Now take a deep breath in again and stay relaxed, Sophie. Keep listening to my voice. Picture each of those coloured Chakras like a flower now. Open each one up, starting at your base. Let each flower open and move their way up past your heart and back to the crown again."

I hadn't noticed, but the tears had stopped running down my face and my hands were not shaking anymore. I was numb, in a much different way then I was used to.

"Help your friends, Sophie. It will help you in return." He then said. His words made me frown a little, but I couldn't speak yet. "Love him. He is still yours, as he always was. Let him be your world again."

My world...

Lavender. I could smell it again—everywhere.

Just then, a faint pink glow began to rise from my chest. My eyes were glued on it. I was fascinated by it. It felt... wonderful.

"Breathe deeply, relax. You're safe." He continued to whisper. "Think of what you miss. Think of what you truly want in life, Soph. Do not lie to yourself and do not be embarrassed or afraid. You deserve it all and you shall have it, if you choose to throw the fear away. Don't let that side of you that has been tainted control the heart within. You can do this. I believe in you. Let yourself love again. You deserve to love again."

I stared up at the ceiling, uncertain about what I really felt inside—what he was forcing me to feel again.

"Now, feel each of the Chakra flowers as they close. One by one, from the Crown down to your base. They have released the energy you need, but are always there—ready for you if

you need them again, should you be brave enough to ask."
My eyes closed again, sadly. I wasn't brave. I couldn't face it.
I was certain of it. I was just a scared little girl intimidated by
the darkness within. I couldn't... my thoughts began to race.
It was silent for only a moment, before he spoke one last time.
"Open your eyes, Sophie. Come back to me." He said,
removing his hands from my body. He was patient as I slowly
opened my eyes to him.
It felt like a dream. What just happened? I was suddenly
confused. Was it real? What did he do to me? It was too much,
too strong, too nice and... too soon. Suddenly the memories
flooded in. High school, acting school, the boyfriends, the
friendships lost, my Grandmother's death and worse—him.
Nathan infected my mind now. It made me sad again to think
of everyone and everything that had happened. It made me
miss them. It made me miss him—more than anything—as if
he just left yesterday. The pain had returned. But this time, it
was much stronger. I quickly shot up from the floor.
"Relax, everything's fine." Ben said, resting his hand on my
shoulder.
"What the hell was that?!" I said, suddenly upset with him.
"What did you do to me? Why am I having these thoughts
again? And how did you know about..." I paused, pulling back
from him.
How had he known about my pure heart? My hands began to
shake. Then one shot up to scratch at my neck.
Ben quickly grabbed it.
"No, don't let it control you." He said, sharply.
I stared back at him in fear.
"Your heart is stronger than what they have done to you,"
My eyes widened, he couldn't possibly know. My comforting
feeling about Ben quickly changed.
"How do you know about pure hearts?" I asked, "And don't
you dare lie to me!"
His hand released my wrist. "Do you trust me?"
"That depends..." I responded bravely.
"I'm your friend, Sophie. I swear."

"My friend?" I huffed.

"I know all about you. I know about your past, your friends and where they are now."

I swallowed in fear. No way. It wasn't possible.

"I know that they need you badly. I know that you've been through more than anyone ever could imagine as a human, but I also know how strong your heart is and what it can do. I know that he needs you—desperately."

I felt my eyes began to water again.

"Your world, you can have it again. I promise." He said. "And there are many others that should also be in your world Sophie, but you've closed them off. You're not living anymore. This act you're pulling, it will only destroy you. You must trust me. I will not let you down. I have only love for you and there are others that love you too—if you let them."

Ben's voice suddenly seemed different than before, especially in that last sentence. It was freaking me out now.

"Trust you, I've heard that before. Those words mean nothing to me, Ben… or whoever you are." I accused.

"I am Ben—to you."

I got up from the floor and backed away from him.

"To me?" I repeated.

"That's all that matters." He answered, standing up as well.

"Wow, way to get someone to trust you. What other riddles do you have for me?" I blurted out rudely again.

"Alex is about to go into something that he may not survive. He needs you—they all need you."

"Who needs me, and how do you know about Alex?" I began to shout.

"Sophie, you need to act now. There's no time for questions. You have to trust your heart."

"Trust my heart? No time? For what?" I snapped. "Look, I don't know who you really are, but I don't want anything to do with that world anymore. I'm not sure who sent you, but you can turn around and go home. I'm over this!"

I then quickly turned and darted off. I needed to get out of here.

Unfortunately, Ben beat me to the front door.
Placing himself between me and the exit. He spoke again.
"Charlotte is gone." He blurted out. "And if you don't change your mind now, you will never see her again."
I froze in disbelief.
"What are you talking about?" I asked. "Where is she?"
I paused. "On second thought, I don't want to know." I attempted to push him aside, but he pushed back.
"Fate has her, and she will use her as leverage. She's trying to pull you out. You can't fear her, you mustn't fear any of them Sophie. You are more powerful, please I beg of you. Help them." He shouted.
Fate–another name I didn't want to remember. The thought of her made me tremble inside. He couldn't possibly know about her too.
"I'm here to show you your worth. To show you how powerful and loving you truly are. How you complete others, just as some of them complete you. Nathan loves you more than anything. You can't be afraid of the greatness inside of you."
I had no idea how he knew all of this and honestly, a small part of me didn't even care. I just wanted to be free. Why was this stuff always following me? I couldn't escape it.
"How do you know all of this, you're just a human?" I stated, staring back to him.
"I have visions. I know it sounds crazy but…"
I shook my head, nothing sounded crazy to me anymore.
"Trust me, you can do this." He went on. "I know how strong you are inside. I've seen it before with you,"
I looked at him oddly, wondering what he meant. The only time we had spent together was on set or practicing in the trailers—and more recently, here.
"You smelt something earlier, right?" He then asked.
I stood silently, it was an odd question to ask.
"Lavender maybe?"
I nodded.
"You have greatness inside of you and around you. It protects you. When you smell Lavender, you're fully protected. For

me, I see energy… and visions. But you, the scent takes over.
It's wonderful, isn't it?"
I didn't know what to say. I had smelt lavender at many
random times in my life and I did wonder about it.
"I've seen visions of you before, in your past life. In high
school, when your best friend cheated on you with your
boyfriend."
"How could you possibly know that?" I asked, taking a step
back from him.
"You're extraordinary, Sophie Reid. You have more love in
your heart and more bravery then anyone I have ever felt or
met. You have within you such power, grace and loyalty that
will only continue to grow—if you let it."
How did he know about my life? None of this made sense.
"I'm just a stupid human, I have no power!" I shouted back.
"And… I'm not sure if I can love him again. He broke my
heart. You just don't get it!"
"You are not a stupid human. You have the purest heart I've
seen in a long time. Just as Gabriel told you,"
My eyes widened again at the Archangel's name.
"And do not worry about Nathan, save him as your friend…
then decide if you still love him. You will have your chance
again, and if you choose not to, you will still live greatly. But
you need your friends, Sophie. You need those familiar faces
in your life either way. It will help you heal, as awkward and
painful as it will be. Face your problems head on and you can
only end up on top. You will live a great life, but only if you
let yourself." He smiled again, then reached for me.
I didn't move as his hand took mine.
"Do you feel that I am lying to you? In your heart, right now?"
He asked. "Listen to it. Does your heart tell you I'm lying?"
I closed my eyes for a moment, my body was vibrating with
adrenaline, mixed emotions and confused thoughts. I tried
hard to listen—to really listen like he said. I wasn't scared
of Ben, and I didn't feel that horrible dark feeling with him
near. But I also didn't want to believe that Ben might be one
of them. He had to be one of them, right? Or maybe my mind

was playing tricks on me again.

No.

Ben had to be good. I needed him to be good. I opened my eyes and whispered, "You're not lying." My face then softened, I couldn't deny it. Ben wasn't bad. He couldn't be. "Everything you need is right inside of you." He repeated, touching my chest gently. His voice seemed to reach inside of me and hold my heart with such warmth.

"Who are you?" I asked, quietly.

Ben ignored my question again, then reached into his pocket to pull out a pink stone. It was in the shape of a heart and attached to a silver chain.

"This is for you." He said, placing it carefully into my hands.

"What is it?"

"It's Rose Quartz, a symbol of eternal love."

"It's beautiful," I said, carefully taking it by the chain and hooking it around my neck. It hung down gently against my chest and seemed to bring warmth to my body immediately.

"This stone will help you connect your Chakras to your pure heart. Hold it tightly when you feel fear, when it is dark, and when you begin to lose faith in yourself. It will recharge you and bring you back so you can see clearly with only love, trust and more power than anything you are facing. Trust it and it will trust you."

I held it tightly in my hands. For the first time in a long time, I felt my old-self lingering inside. I could feel the person I used to be very faintly. There was a lot of pain with it, but it was definitely me. It scared me. I still wasn't sure if I could be of any help to anyone, especially Nathan, and I wasn't even sure if I was ready to see him yet, but my friends... I secretly missed them. Emotions began to race through my body, scrambling my thoughts and attacking me all at once again.

"Don't let them overwhelm you," Ben spoke, taking my hand again. "When they race in like that, take a deep breath and remind yourself, one thing at a time. Love every emotion that enters your body, good or bad. It's all relevant to your healing process and your life ahead of you."

I did as he suggested and closed my eyes. Breathing deeply, I tried my best to collect my thoughts. It was working—a little. I opened my eyes again, staring sadly back at him. I then felt myself step forward so I could rest my body against his. Ben's arms immediately wrapped around me.

"Thank you," I whispered. "I'm not sure who you are, and I'm still not sure if I can do any of this, but something feels right here." I humbly admitted. "It still hurts—really bad, and scares me to death, but you're right. I miss them—all of them… I can't do this anymore."

His chin rested down on the top of my heard.

"I know, and don't be afraid of their response. They don't hate you. They will happily receive your help without question." He then pulled back from me.

"Charlotte is unreachable right now, so you must help Alex first." He warned. "He will surely lead us to Charlotte, eventually."

"Is she okay? What if it's too late?" I asked, nervously.

"Trust me, Soph. Alex is our priority right now. I will keep my eye out for Charlotte but for now, go to him. Help him with whatever plan he creates. Keep him grounded, keep him safe."

I was worried now that reality was setting in.

"Safe? Why? What's he doing?"

I then remembered Charlotte's recent visit.

"Purgatory…" I said.

"Now it's your turn to trust and follow your heart. Trust Alex. You need each other. Remember what I showed you. Remember what I said. When you need them, ignite the Chakras within. Now go, pack a small bag and hurry. There isn't much time."

I nodded, then raced into my room without another word. There wasn't enough time for me to think about what I was getting myself into or how I could even help. I just needed to get to my friend.

I grabbed a backpack from under my bed and threw a few clothes and essentials into it.

When I was finished, I hurried back to Ben's side.

"Head to Alex and Charlotte's apartment," he said, walking me to the front door. "Don't stop for anyone or anything. Every second is wasted time."

I nodded and then wrapped my arms around him one more time. I had no idea why my heart changed so quickly or why I trusted Ben so much, or how he was able to get through to me, but it didn't matter now. I had confidently decided I was doing this. I grabbed my keys off the hook and raced out the door.

8
Secret Doorways

I raced through the park, faster than I ever ran before. I felt stronger—more aware. I could only assume it was from Ben's treatment. I wondered how long it would last? I worried that my new found confidence would fade before I reached Alex. It took a few moments to register, but I was beginning to understand some of Ben's words from moments before. I was always worrying about my past, which is what I was doing right now and what Ben didn't want me to do. He didn't want me to be afraid or ashamed. He simply wanted me to learn from my experiences and grow—I think.

It was easier said than done, but I was aware of it now. Aware of what I was ignoring and what I was hiding from. I was also more aware now of those trying to help me. The ones I denied. I felt guilty for ignoring them—for being so mean. But I wasn't the same weak girl I used to be. I had grown in many ways in the past few months. I had to. Even if it wasn't all good. Ben had, for a moment, opened my eyes. He let me know how important it was to change. That I needed to try, and it had to start with Alex. Someone who had gone above and beyond to help me in my darkest times, and I couldn't worry about what might happen. I needed to take this first step and see where it leads. Again, I only hoped I could remain as confident as I was right now. I had to try and keep my mind straight to help him. It was hard though, my thoughts were racing... racing so fast. I didn't expect this today. I was supposed to be rehearsing. My mind frame from this morning to this very moment was like two different people. I didn't expect to change like this—and I was in no way completely healed, but the clarity of what I needed to do right now felt right. I suddenly thought of Charlotte and picked up speed. I only hoped she could hang in there, wherever she was. I hope she knows... I'd come for her. That we would eventually save her. I had to save her—somehow. Then I thought of him. *Nathan.* My stomach turned. My body reacted to his name inside my head. I wasn't sure about him yet. I tried quickly to change my thought. How had Ben and this Reiki stuff awakened so much inside of me? Was it witchcraft? Had he cast a spell? There was so much happening at once and there was much more to Ben than I knew. Eventually, I needed to know the truth from him. I needed to know who he really was. But for now, my friends needed me.

   As I reached Alex's apartment, I stopped at the front doors and took a moment to catch my breath. I was scared and nervous for everything I was about to face. My stomach turned again. "You can do this." I said.
Just then an old man exited the doors.
"Going in my dear?" He said very sweetly, holding the door for me.
I smiled at him. "Yes, thank you."
I raced inside and up the stairs to Alex's floor. When I reached the door, I knocked twice gently. My hands were shaking.
Come on Soph, you're here to help him. I reminded myself, then knocked harder the second time. He still didn't answer.
"Alex?" I heard myself call out.
My voice frightened me, it was confident and persistent.
"Alex! It's me, Soph. Let me in!" I shouted again.
Still no answer.
Carefully, I reached for the door knob and turned it.

Surprisingly, it was unlocked. I slowly entered the apartment. The smell of sandalwood filled the air. The apartment felt cold and abandoned as I made my way in. It was quiet—too quiet. There was a heaviness in the air as I made my way down the hallway. It was getting harder to breathe. I gripped the pink heart stone hanging around my neck nervously.

"Alex…are you here?" I called out again, standing in front of his bedroom door now. "Alex?"

I leaned in quietly against it to listen. I didn't hear a thing.

"Alex?" I repeated, "I'm here to help…"

Suddenly, I heard something from the living room. My eyes shot down the hallway. Another sound... Then silence. The silence was deafening. I could feel myself begin to twitch. Just then, the bedroom door swung open and I was ripped inside. It slammed shut behind me and locked as I tumbled to the ground. A hand grabbed onto my leg, making me scurry back in fear.

"Help me…" he cried.

My eyes shot up to the familiar voice. "Alex?"

He fell to the floor. He was worn and looked like he hadn't slept or eaten in days. I crawled over to him quickly.

"Alex, are you alright?"

His body shivered as I wrapped my arms around him.

"What have you been doing to yourself?" I asked, worried. "You're so cold."

I felt his hands slowly slide up my back and grip onto me.

"Sophie…thank god." He stuttered, weakly.

"It's okay, I'm here." I said, holding him tight.

He looked horrible. Was Alex really doing all of this for Nathan and Gabriel? For Charlotte? For me? He was giving too much of himself to help everyone else and it was destroying him. I had to help him. I needed to be whatever Alex wanted right now. I felt sick inside for letting this much happen.

"I'm sorry, Alex. I'm sorry I've been absent for so long. I'm sorry I was such a pain in the ass. I'm—"

"I forgive you, Soph." He interrupted. He then lifted his head.

"I've been horrible to you—to Charlotte..." I went on.
"She's gone... I can't feel her anymore." He said, sadly.
His heart was racing against me. I had never seen him like
this. He was sad and lost.
"I know, Fate took her." I said, "I'm so sorry. I should have
helped when she asked me too."
"Wait... what?" Alex said, adjusting himself upright.
"You don't know?"
"When? When did this happen?!" He asked, beginning to
tremble. I rubbed his arms, trying to calm him.
"She showed up yesterday at my place, asking me to help
you guys. I was horrible to her. I told her to leave." I paused,
feeling embarrassed for my actions and cruel words.
"I told her, we weren't friends anymore and to never come
back. But I didn't mean it, Alex. I was just upset. I haven't
been seeing things right or acting how I should."
Alex's eyes fell to the ground worried.
"But I'm here to help you Alex, whatever you need... I'll do
it." I waited for his response. "Alex what can we do?"
He took a few deep breaths—surely overwhelmed.
"There is something," He said, quietly.
"What? What is it? I want to help. Tell me what to do." I
repeated.
"There is a spell, but I can't cast it...without you."
I looked at him nervously. The thought of me being connected
to anything like that horrified me.
"You're connected to Nathan. If you let me, I can link you
to him and we just might be strong enough to find them and
bring them all back to the real world."
I sat quietly, staring at him. Link onto Nathan? Right now? It's
what I feared the most. I wasn't ready for him—not yet.
I wasn't sure what I wanted. I wasn't sure what I would say....
But what choice did I have?
"Is that our only way?" I asked, nervously.
"No, but it may be our strongest." He said. "And I'm not sure
how many chances we will have to do this. If we fail with
something weaker, we may not get the chance to try a different

route." He placed his hand on mine. "Sophie, I've been researching the Angel and Spirit guide books as deep as I can, but they're not enough. I started looking into the dark arts." He wiped his tired eyes and moved closer to me. "We need something stronger to fight what's in there. You and I both know that. Right?"

I nodded with hesitation.

"I know you're scared to think about that world again but you have to. You and I both know how horrible that place is and we both know how crucial time is for Nathan and Gabriel on that side. They've already been in there way too long. If we do this, I need you to be ready to face every fear you have inside of you, including the fear you have of seeing Nathan again. You need to push all of that aside and go in there ready to fight."

My eyes widened. What did he mean by going in there ready to fight?

"We can't fail Soph, this may be our last shot. It's a blessing that you have come to help me. We can do this together now, I know it."

I didn't say anything. My mind was flooded with the idea of going into purgatory and seeing Nathan again. He was all I could think of now. I felt a sharp pain in my chest.

"Sophie?" I heard him say, but I didn't respond.

"Sophie..." Another familiar voice whispered in my mind. It woke me from my thoughts. Ben.

I wasn't sure how, but it was definitely him.

"You're ready." He whispered.

"Sophie?" Alex repeated, "Will you do it?"

I sighed. Bit my lip nervously, then nodded.

"Whatever you need Alex, I trust you."

He smiled. "I'm so glad you're back, we've missed you." He said hugging me tight.

"I've missed you too." I whispered.

An hour later I was filled in on the master plan to get everyone back. Alex told me about his studies, but there was so much information, I felt I'd already forgotten everything by the time he was done. He had done so much on his own. I wondered why Raphael wasn't helping him? None of this made sense.

"Alex, when did you eat last?" I asked, changing the subject. "And why has no one from above come to help you?"

"That's something I still need to talk to you about," He replied, his voice more serious now.

"What is it? Where is Raphael?" I finally asked. "Charlotte mentioned that she was going with you. Shouldn't we fill her in too?"

"Listen, I need you to trust me and me only." His dry voice cracked. He cleared his throat before speaking again.

"I heard Raphael speaking to someone the other night, a man. She was talking about erasing someone's mind, but I'm not sure who she was talking about. Maybe Charlotte's? Or maybe even yours? I feel like she's plotting something behind my back. I hate to say it, but I'm not sure if we can trust her anymore." He paused. "I know it's hard to believe. "

I looked back at him. I was pretty messed up when Raphael was around, but I don't remember feeling like she was a threat. I remember her eyes being just as scared as I felt. I remember feeling connected to her in some way.

"Are you sure, Alex?"

He nodded.

"She's been distant lately. I don't even know where she is most of the time. Something is off. I think we need to be prepared, just in case—in case she turns on us."

I frowned at him. "Turns on us? Alex—"

"Soph please, trust me." He said, desperately. "I know it sounds crazy but if we go in there and something happens... I just—Nathan and Gabriel are our top priority."

"Okay. Calm down. I trust you." I sighed. "But, do we really have to go in there? I'm not sure if I'm—"

"You're not physically going in there, Soph." He corrected

himself quickly, "I'm sorry, I should have been more clear. Just your mind and spirit will go. Only Raphael and I will be going in physically."

I exhaled, but I still didn't like the idea of Alex going back. "If we can get Nathan to link onto your presence, I can cast the spell from within and bring us all out. But when this happens Soph, no matter what, you must not let your thoughts stray or..." His eyes locked on mine, worried. "Do you think you can do it?"

I swallowed in fear, "I can do it." I lied.

I wasn't really sure if I believed myself or not... the words just spilled out, but I had to comfort him.

"I know you can." He spoke again. "But we can't let Raphael know about our plan. We have to act like everything's the same, okay? I already have an idea of what I'm going to say when I see her."

"What's that?" I asked, worried.

"I'm going to admit that I've been studying the dark arts. I'll tell her that I accidentally let it take over me, which is why I locked myself in my room. There's a spell casted around us right now. No one can see us, hear us, or feel what I'm doing in here. It's like a barrier. It's the only way I could plan safely. So you must play along. We'll say that you barged in, waking me from a spell I was stuck in, alright?"

I nodded, "But what about Fate?" I asked. "Can she hear or see us right now?"

"No one can, Soph." He said, confidently. "What I've been studying...." He paused. "Trust me we're good," He then took both my hands in his.

"Okay, I need you to sit still for a moment. I'm going to release the barrier around us now that you know everything. The protective walls will fall and we will be visible once again."

He placed my hands back in my own lap, then adjusted himself to sit up straighter. I wanted to move back from him, but I didn't.

"I won't let you down." He said, then closed his eyes.

I grabbed onto my stone as he began the enchantment. It only took a moment or two, then it was over. I felt nothing.

His eyes opened to mine and he smiled. I smiled back.

"It is done." He said, then attempted to stand up.

I got up to help him and laced his arm over my shoulders to let him rest his weight against me.

"You need to eat." I said.

"They will come soon…" He replied.

I looked at him worried. "Okay, but you need to eat. You have no strength." I helped him out of the room and towards the kitchen. I wasn't an amazing chef, but we couldn't be picky right now. Alex needed to be strong if he was going to face what was coming. I sat him down at the kitchen table and immediately got him some water. I searched the cupboards and fridge before settling on cooked chicken, vegetables and rice. I hurried to make his dinner.

When I served him, Alex dug in immediately. I watched him shove piles of food into his mouth. It made me happy. I wanted to do more for him, so I decided to make him a little dessert. I knew he would still be hungry. When I was done, I placed down in front of him a baked apple with cinnamon and brown sugar melted inside—an old recipe from my Grandmother.

"Pretty impressive, Soph" Alex teased.

"What can I say?" I shrugged, "Gram's food always made me feel better."

He smiled. "Thank you."

"Thank you." I replied.

Hours later, no one appeared as Alex thought they would. By eleven thirty, we were still sitting at the kitchen table. I wondered why Raphael hadn't showed up yet? Perhaps Alex was right, maybe she did turn on us. I sat quietly, sipping the tea I made for myself. Alex was writing now in a small black book across from me. He must have felt me staring and glanced up.

"Thank you again, Soph. I feel a lot better." He said, trying to assure me that he was fine.

"You're welcome." I replied again.

"So, you've come out of hiding." A voice suddenly interrupted. Our eyes shot over to Raphael who stood at the edge of the kitchen, waiting patiently for a response.

"I did." Alex responded calmly. "Thanks to Sophie."

"Yes, thanks to Sophie." She repeated. "What happened to you?" She asked, making her way over to the kitchen table. As she sat down next to Alex, I did my best to act normal.

"I've been studying more of the dark arts, Raphael." Alex admitted as planned. "I had to. I know it's wrong but we're going to need it to survive purgatory. There's nothing in the Angel or Spirit guide books that can—"

"I know Alex. It's alright." She replied. "I understand why you did it. Although, I fear for you. I feel you are changing. You must be careful with that stuff."

"I know, like I said, thank god for Sophie. If she hadn't busted into my apartment and woke me—I might have lost myself for good."

"Yes, Sophie," Raphael repeated, turning to me. "It's good to see you. You too seem different. I can feel it as well. Why the sudden change of heart?"

"Well, you could say that a good friend got through to me." I answered, honestly. "I apologize for being so difficult."

"No need to apologize." She smiled. Her attention then returned to Alex. "How are you feeling?" She asked. "To be honest, I'm a little worried looking at you now. I'm not sure if you are ready for this journey."

"I'm ready." He replied.

"I had hoped to spend some time with you before we left, but no matter." She paused, "I must admit, I'm a little scared to do this. I may need to lean on you for strength."

He looked back her oddly.

"What do you mean?" I spoke quickly. " Are you not well?"

"I feel fine." She assured me. "I'm just a little worried about going back in there. I'm concerned about losing all that I have worked to become. I fear that my mind might race from me. I

will need you to keep me grounded, Alex—to keep me sane."
I worried for a moment. Was this was an excuse for Raphael
to turn on Alex. If she truly was against us, then this was
definitely a set up. I quickly changed my thoughts, worried
that Raphael would read them.
"Before now, I wouldn't be as confident in grounding you,"
Alex began, "But now that we have Sophie, I'm certain we
can succeed." He reached across the table for my hand.
"Sophie?" Raphael asked, confused.
"Yes, I'm going to help Alex link onto Nathan. He thinks he
can bring you all back in one piece through me." I felt I had
said it pretty confidently. Even I believed it.
"Are you sure she can handle that, Alex?"
"She can. She came to me, remember?" He spoke.
"It's true, I want to help." I cut in. "I'll admit I'm nervous.
I'm not sure if I'm ready to see Nathan yet, but… I have to
help them. They've saved me numerous times in my life. I
owe this to them." I said, sadly. "And Charlotte, she's lost.
Fate took her, so we need to find her too!"
"Yes, Fate paid me a visit." Raphael replied. "I assume to
tease me and get me worked up before entering purgatory. She
mentioned Charlotte." Raphael then paused and stood up from
the table.
"Did she tell you where she is?" Alex asked, releasing my
hand.
"No, and we can't worry about it." She scolded. "Don't you
see? She did that so that our minds would be distracted when
we enter purgatory. She's hoping we will let our emotions
take over, which will make us weak. You can't let yourself get
distracted Alex, your feelings for Charlotte will have to wait.
You will get your chance to save her, but now is not the time.
She will not harm her right now. Charlotte is leverage—for
everything. Promise me you will concentrate on the task at
hand." Raphael said in a polite, yet demanding way.
"Raphael is right, Alex." I agreed. "It makes total sense. She's
only doing this to distract you. We will get Charlotte back, I
promise."

"I know." He sighed. "This is why you're here. You'll keep me sane through this. Please, I need you to keep reminding me of what's important. I need you Sophie."
"I'm right here. I promise." My smile faded. "But Alex…"
I was scared to say what was truly on my mind. What I feared the most. I wondered if he could see it in my eyes, if he could feel my emotions begin to race.
"Don't let them take me back, okay?"
My eyes teared up immediately.
"Never." He assured me, reaching for my hand again. Just then, the walls began to shake.
"What the?" I rose from my chair and hurried to Alex's side.
"Come," Raphael said, guiding us towards the living room. We used the walls to stabilize ourselves as we entered the living room. This could only be one thing. I looked down at my watch. It was midnight now.
The air thinned as a strong energy began to fill the room. Alex's grip on my hand tightened as the lights began to flicker. Then it went dark.
"Alex…" I whispered, nervously.
"Don't be scared." He replied, squeezing my hand.
"They're here." Raphael spoke as a silver beam of light lit up the room in front of us.
For months I had managed to keep myself hidden from all supernatural beings. Hidden from the ones that brought negative things into my life—or at least—I used to think they did. Maybe it was all fear. When I thought about it now, if the supernatural beings had not been in my life, I wouldn't have Alex…or Nathan—even Ben. I wouldn't have survived my depression and everything else along the way. I had mixed feelings about it all. Although it felt nice to have a break from the craziness of the supernatural world, it also brought a lot of heartache. I could see that now. I had to face it. I had to face them. It was now or never. Before I knew it, they were here. Standing before us were the Archangels Michael and Uriel. Slowly, the lights came back on and a smirk grew on Uriel's face staring back at me. Michael's eyes locked on mine.

He approached slowly, "Well, well, isn't this a nice surprise. Good to see you again, Sophie." He stopped directly in front of me.

I stared into his eyes, gripping Alex's hand tight. I had seen them before, when I was confused and lost, but never as clearly as I saw them now. Their presence created a pressure within me, swirling my emotions around inside.

"Have you decided you want back in?" He spoke. "Or maybe, that hole in your heart is aching too much." His hand then lifted and gently touched my cheek.

I flinched a bit from the warm touch of his skin against mine. I was completely still as his hand ran down my check to my neck and finally, to the chain that hung low.

"I see there's something different about you." He smiled. "You've had a visitor lately, haven't you?" He pulled the heart stone from inside my shirt. Holding it carefully in his hand, a light pink energy began to glow around it. My eyes shot down to the beautiful energy that radiated from the stone heart. Alex's eyes met mine.

"There's only one person who could have…" He paused, and then smiled in relief.

I glanced over at Alex. The expression on his face said that he knew exactly what this stone was and more importantly, who it was from.

"Our little pure heart—so beautiful—so rare," Michael's eyes lit up.

Uriel stepped closer to see for himself.

"I bet you don't even understand your strength yet, do you?" Michael asked.

"No." I admitted, pulling the necklace back from him. "And I don't care, I'll figure it out eventually."

"Watch your words, girl." Uriel harped.

"I understand her strength," Alex spoke. "I will teach her." Michael's eyes adjusted to his, "Did you set this up? Did you ask him to come to her, Alex?"

I looked at him confused. Who were they talking about? Ben gave me this. How could Alex have set that up?

"You've been choosing new routes lately, haven't you?" Michael spoke again. "You're hiding something. I can't get inside your head. You're blocking me again, but for what reason? What have you to hide?"

Uriel stepped in front of Michael.

"He's been dabbling again." Uriel growled. "He has to be! We haven't been able to follow him for the past two days. He's been playing with the dark arts against our warnings!"

"I agree, something that could end up destroying him and everyone he loves." Michael added. "Your fate is changing, Alex. She sees it, as do we. I feel you may not survive this journey."

My eyes shot to Alex.

"He will." Raphael replied, immediately.

"You," Michael said, stepping towards her. "You have a new friend as well."

Alex looked at her worried, then back at me. I knew what he was thinking.

Michael's eyes noticed the expression on Alex's face.

"And you haven't told these two of this new friend either. Have you, Raphael? Why are you hiding it?" He urged.

"I'm not hiding anything. I'm doing what I feel will help us all. My actions are true. You must trust me. Please."

Alex was right, she was hiding something.

"This is getting interesting," Uriel teased looking around at us all. "Come brother, it's time."

"Agreed." Michael said, keeping his eyes on Raphael. "Are you ready?"

"Give us a moment," Alex requested, turning to me and pulling me aside. His hands gripped my shoulders tight as he stared into my eyes. "Stay strong Soph, remember our plan. When you hear me, do as I said, okay?"

I nodded.

"This may be our only chance, remember that. Don't let your feelings overwhelm you, promise?"

My eyes began to water. I quickly choked them back. I leaned in and hugged Alex as tight as I could.

"I won't let you down. Just come back to me, okay?" I
whispered.
"I will. I promise." He said, holding me tight.
I pulled back and turned to Raphael.
"Take care of yourself." I said softly. "You may not believe
this, but you deserve more—more than this."
She smiled, then stepped forward to hug me.
"Thank you," She spoke, quietly. "Same to you. You can still
have an amazing life, Sophie. I see it for you."
I went to let her go, but she tugged me back in to whisper in
my ear. "Know that there are others fighting for you as well,
even if you cannot see them."
I pulled back and looked at her oddly. I then watched as the
two of them stepped towards the Archangels.
"Goodbye," I said.
"No… see you soon." Raphael replied.
Alex touched his chest, motioning to my heart stone. "Use it,
let it guide you."
Emotions were building quickly as I watched my friends stand
nervously between the Archangels. I was scared—scared for
us all. Suddenly, a bright light lit up the other side of the
room, blazing from the floor to the ceiling. Two large doors
began to take form in front of us and a warm energy filled
the room. Alex looked at me once more. Tears began to form
in my eyes again, but I quickly wiped them away. I wanted
him to know I wasn't afraid. I wanted him to know I had his
back—even if I was terrified inside. The large white doors
slowly opened and a gust of wind blew from within. Alex had
once told of me of the great doors from the angel realm, but
to see them in person was beyond belief. I watched as Alex
turned to Michael. He nodded a goodbye, then stepped slowly
towards the bright light. Raphael followed.
"Good luck," Michael said, as they reached the doorway.
"You're going to need it." Uriel added.
I glanced at him, disgusted by his words.
I then watched as the light from the portal doors brightened
around my friends.

"I'll be right here, waiting for you!" I shouted. "Come back to me!" I wanted desperately for Alex to return—with or without Nathan. The thought gave me mixed feelings for a moment. Alex didn't deserve this—any of it. But did Nathan? I felt myself twitch again. I scratched my cheek nervously. *No* What was I thinking? I wanted everyone to come back—alive. No one deserved to be stuck in purgatory. We could survive this, couldn't we? All of us? I had to believe it. My thoughts paused as Alex glanced back at me once more. He smiled, then together with Raphael by his side they disappeared into the light and I felt a piece of me leave with them as the door slammed shut behind them. The sound echoed throughout the room. Everything went dark and silent again. I traced the walls for the light switch. When I found it, I flicked it on.
I was alone again.

9

City of the Fallen

"Hello?!" She said, painfully. Her throat was severely dry. "Is anyone there?!" She couldn't see a thing in the darkness around her. It was very cold and very damp.

"Somebody help me!" She cried again, this time her voice cracked. She was so thirsty and hungry too. She wondered how long she had been in there? Wherever she was.

"HELP!!!"

"Will you be quiet?" Someone finally shouted back. "Your voice is beginning to annoy me—seriously."

"Who's there?!" Charlotte replied, a little quieter.

She attempted to drag herself across the cold ground, but something snagged her. The metal around her ankles were bound to something in the cement. The chains scrapped across the floor as Charlotte tried to break free.

"Let me out of here! If you don't, my—"

"Boyfriend will come?" The voice teased, finishing her sentence.

"You have no idea of what he can do. You'll regret doing this when he appears." Charlotte warned again. "I mean it! Let me go! Before it's too late!"

"Before it's too late?" The voice laughed. "Oh you're entertaining. Trust me, I'm not too concerned about your boyfriend since he isn't around anymore."

Charlotte went silent for a moment. "What?"

108

A warm flame suddenly lit up in front of her face, it danced on the tips of Fate's fingers. Charlotte froze in fear.

"What? Are you afraid of the dark?" Fate whispered. "Let me light it up for you then."

She then snapped her fingers and the entire room lit up around them with hundreds of little candles. The yellow glow from the flames warmed their faces as Fate knelt down in front of Charlotte.

She smiled, "Come on, you know where he is…." Fate teased again. "Take a guess why don't you? You're a smart girl." Charlotte didn't respond.

Fate rolled her eyes, annoyed with her silence.

"He's with his friends on the other side all while that silly little girlfriend of yours is sitting in your living room, waiting for their return." Fate sighed. "She almost had her perfect life. Almost…"

"What?" Charlotte replied, confused. "Sophie's there?"

"Unfortunately yes. She thinks she can help, but she won't be able to. She's too weak and if this doesn't ruin her, the return of Nathan and Serena definitely will."

A faint smile grew on Charlotte's face.

"What are you smiling about?" Fate snapped.

"She came. I can't believe it." Charlotte said, happily.

Fate rolled her eyes again and stood up.

"She won't be of any help to either of you. Sophie is a human driven by her emotions and emotions ruin people—every time. Trust me."

Charlotte slowly shook her head, disagreeing.

"No. Not Soph. True, she is driven by her emotions and yes she may make some mistakes but deep down, she will always do what's right and follow her heart. She's stronger than you think."

"Ah yes… This whole idea of the pure heart. I've heard you all speak of her so positively, but listen to me very carefully…"

Charlotte looked up at her bravely.

"Pure hearts are rare, and you are very lucky if you find one, but the chances of them actually growing into their full

potential are one in a million. Sophie has no chance. Not with her background. No matter how much you believe in her."
Fate huffed and turned her back to Charlotte before speaking again. "Let's remember who controls everyone here. Have you forgotten already?"
"You're wrong." Charlotte responded.
Fate whipped back around and smiled at the smug human in front of her. "I like your spunk, but let me give you a little reminder..." She then snapped her fingers and every candle went out.
"No!" Charlotte shouted, her voice cracked again. "Please!" She cried, but Fate was already gone.
Charlotte closed her eyes in fear and thought of Alex. He would find her. She was sure of it.
"I believe in you," She whispered. "You can do this. I know it." Her body shivered against the damp cement floor as she continued to lay there in pain. The only thing she could do now was wait. She would wait, and hope that Alex and Sophie would find her.

With his eyes closed, his hands slid around the gloomy landscape. His fingertips traced across the dead tree branches, touching the black leaves here and there. They eventually crumbled and fell to the ground. He listened nervously for what could be around them. They had managed to enter purgatory without anything noticing them and they wasted no time beginning their search for Gabriel and Nathan.
"Anything?" Raphael asked, quietly.
Alex opened his eyes to the sound of her voice.
"They were here, I feel the lingering energy in the air and I don't mean the bad stuff. It's definitely, Nate."
"Good," Raphael replied, rubbing her forehead.
"Are you alright?" He asked, noticing the look on her face. Her hands began to tremble.
"I'm okay. This place, it—"
"I know. It's toxic." He said, cutting her off.

She nodded. "We need to hurry." Raphael said, walking ahead. Alex followed immediately.

"So what's our plan? Other than my spell?" He asked as they crossed the rotted land.

"When we reach them, go to Nathan. I will protect you as you cast your spell. If Gabriel is well enough, he too will help."

"And if Gabriel isn't?" Alex asked.

"Then I shall protect you both on my own. I too have some tricks up my sleeve."

Alex looked at her nervously.

"Don't worry." She assured him.

As they continued on, the overcast sky grew darker. It was only a matter of time before the spirits in there could feel the new presence—the presence of life.

Thoughts raced through Alex's mind. He hoped that nothing would happen to them before he got to cast his spell. He also hoped that Sophie was ready on the other end to receive it.

The air suddenly shifted, "We need to move." Alex warned. As they began to run, he reached into his pocket and pulled out a small stone. He held it tightly in his left hand.

"Is that Black Tourmaline?" Raphael asked, appearing beside him.

"I need it to put up a barrier, they're getting close."

"Agreed," She replied. "I can feel their energy much stronger now."

Just as Raphael said those words, screams barreled throughout the woods behind them. Raphael tripped but quickly caught herself. Alex grabbed her arm, demanding her attention. Her eyes began to wander in fear.

"Stay with me." He shouted.

The screams grew louder with every step they took. He could feel a strange energy coming off of Raphael now. He reached his left hand out in front of them, concentrating all of his energy on the stone. Then clearly and quickly spoke his enchantment.

"The darkness you have created here is bound to you. We do not own your darkness, so you may not share this darkness with us. As long as our hearts beat, your energy shall hold no evil or power over us.”

The sound of spirits now filled the area as an energy field grew from the stone in Alex's hand. He glanced at Raphael beside him, her eyes were falling again. He quickly squeezed her wrist and spoke again,

“I call upon the powers from the West, bring us your speed. Powers from the North, bring us your energy as the powers from the South, bring us their strength to fight.”

Alex stumbled as Raphael began to slow. They were getting to her, he could feel it. They were calling to her soul that was still tainted deep inside.

“I finally call to the East, bring us the fire! Fire to protect, fire to bind us from these spirits!” He shouted, desperately.

Suddenly, the stone in his hands erupted into flames and shot up above them, then rained down into a cage-like ball around them—protecting them from everything. The spirits tested the flame barrier, but their nails disintegrated the moment they made contact. They screamed in rage, keeping their distance now.

“It's working.” Alex said, pulling Raphael alongside him.

“Alex…” Raphael mumbled, pulling from his grip.

They stopped only for a moment before Alex grabbed her again, urging her to keep going. The spirits raced alongside them, awaiting desperately for the force field to drop.

Raphael pulled at his hand again.

“What are you doing? I can't keep this up forever! Come on!” He shouted.

The flames began to spark, any distraction from his concentration could break his spell at any moment.

“I can feel them in me, Alex. Their hands are gripping my soul. They remember me. It's like they're squeezing the life out of me with every breath I take.” Raphael cried.

“Shut them out of your mind. You have to!” Alex begged.

Raphael gripped her hair tightly, “I can hear their voices, taunting me…. I can't stand it.” She said, dropping to her knees.

"Yes you can! Get up! You have to!" He shouted, grabbing her arm again. This time with more force.

Raphael screamed. Her voice echoed as the barrier faded around them.

"No! Raphael you're going to get us killed!" Alex begged, holding his stone tight in his left hand. He pushed the energy back down his arm, every last bit to light the stone back up. The barrier exploded again into flames around them just as the spirits reached them.

"I need you Raphael, please."

She looked up at him sadly, then closed her eyes.

"Shut it off Raphael, shut it off and concentrate on me. Do it for Gabriel. He's counting on you."

"Raphael..." a voice whispered in the air around them.

"Remember what I said. Remember your promise...."

Alex jumped. "Who's there?!" He shouted, then glanced back down at Raphael.

"We are a team... you and I." The voice spoke again. "You aren't finished yet..."

Alex grew nervous, this was the same voice he heard down the hall from his room that day. Who was she working with? He backed away from her nervously as her eyes opened once again.

"Please, don't do this..." He said, prepared to fight.

Slowly, she raised herself from the ground.

"You may use what I taught you... if you truly cannot take it anymore." The voice chimed above the spirit screams.

Raphael's eyes shot to Alex as the ground beneath them began to shake.

"Raphael, don't do this! I'm on your side!" He begged, again.

Raphael's eyes rolled back in her head as she touched her chest with her right hand.

"I bring forth the power within, let it take them. Let it devour them all!"

Underneath her hand, a faint purple light started to glow through her fingers. Alex prepared himself for the worst.

"Gabriel!" He shouted. If this was to be his last moments,

he had to try anything. "Gabriel! I'm here! Help me!" He screamed, hoping his connection to the Archangel was stronger now that he was in here with him.

The purple energy ignited from Raphael and shot straight up into the sky above them, breaking down Alex's fire barrier on the way. Immediately, the spirits took their chance and jumped him. Viciously, they tore at his arms and ripped at this legs. Alex screamed in pain as he pulled an arm free, then scrambled back to his feet.

"No, not again! Not this time!" He cried, lighting another magnificent flame from his hand that still held the black stone. It singed the spirits, freeing him for a moment to run again.

The purple energy filled the sky and lit up Raphael as if she was on fire. Evil spirits surrounded her, waiting for their moment to finish her off from the last time she was there.

Alex didn't look back. He continued to run, scrambling frantically through his pockets. His body dripping blood like the last time he was here. He tried desperately to hold himself together. He couldn't let fear take him over.

The spirits followed close behind as Alex pulled a small white feather from his pocket. His hand shook tremendously as he tried not to drop it. He cleared his throat then shouted into the dark purple burning sky above him.

"One magic, one power. One spirit, one might... shatter the darkness and bring only the light!" His words lifted the feather from his hand. It lit up with such power that the Archangels felt it back in their own realm.

"What is he doing?!" Uriel shouted to Michael feeling a tug of energy from inside.

Michael stepped towards the white doors in front of them, their realm glowing bright with the golden protective barrier placed around them. Michael didn't speak for a moment. His eyes continued to stare at the closed door.

"Michael! I can feel him, it's like he's digging around inside of me!" Uriel shouted again.

"He's tapping into us." Michael responded calmly. "I feel it too."

"What?! How is that possible?" Uriel's rage grew quickly as he pulled the sword from his back ready to fight.

Michael gently placed his hand down on his brother's shoulder. "He is weak. He can't do much. It will be over soon."

"He shouldn't be able to reach us at all! What if he lets something in? Can you see him?"

"He is being chased. They are too strong for him… although…" Michael stopped.

"What?" Uriel asked, impatiently.

"I feel someone is helping them."

"Raphael? Is she giving him power?"

"No, not Raphael, another Archangel. One that is here, with us." Michael smiled, a little impressed that he was fooled so easily.

"What? But who? Who would willingly place themselves in this danger?"

Michael turned to his brother, "The same one that gave Sophie such a beautiful gift." He hinted.

Uriel's eyes widened in disbelief.

The white light grew in front of Alex as tiny feathers brushed past his face ever so gently. Soon, they began to attach themselves to his body. They connected painfully into his shoulder blades, then exploded into giant wings that stretched out magnificently from his back. They radiated a pure white energy towards the evil spirits. They jolted back in fear.

Alex could feel himself beginning to heal. The wings were powerful and protective of him, but the purple haze that filled the sky soon made its way down towards him, it was chasing him. It began to taint the tips of his wings and his speed began to slow with every step, but so did the spirits. His wings flicked the drips of purple from their tips as Alex continued to push forward.

"Alex!" A voice screamed from a far off distance.
Straining to see ahead, Alex tried to make sense of the image
that lingered in the distance. Were his eyes playing tricks?
"Alex, stay strong! Let it out! You have it within your grasp,
let it out!" The voice encouraged.
Alex stumbled again, his knees giving way.
"One magic, one power. One spirit, one might… shatter the
darkness and bring only the light!"
The words quickly poured from his mouth once again and the
white light surrounding him exploded with energy just as the
spirits knocked him to the ground.

Uriel dropped to the ground hard, drained of energy. Michael
took a knee beside him feeling the same.
"It's happening again!" Uriel growled. "How Michael? How is
this possible?"
Michael bowed his head and took a deep breath before
attempting to rise. "He is remarkable,"
"Remarkable?!" Uriel repeated, unimpressed. "This spirit
guide should have been destroyed long ago. For Gabriel to
have such a loose cannon on his hands is irresponsible and
despicable to our kind! No matter if he was a gift or not, this
is not how a spirit guide should act. I truly hope for our own
sake that he doesn't make it out of this alive."
"Do not worry brother, this will be his greatest battle and his
last." Michael assured him.
He then took his brother's hand and helped him back to his
feet.

When I woke the next morning, it felt as if everything was
a dream, until I looked around the room. There was no one
in sight. The apartment was completely silent and nothing
had changed. Everything was in its place. Slowly, I got up
from the couch and stretched my body out. My neck was a
little sore from the way I had slept. I hadn't thought of going

into Alex and Charlotte's room to get a pillow. In fact, I really didn't want to go in there at all. After Alex and the rest disappeared from the apartment last night, it only took me a few minutes to fall asleep. I was mentally exhausted from all of the drama I was experiencing again.

I walked my way over to the kitchen and opened the fridge. I had used a good amount of food in the apartment for Alex's dinner the night before. I'd have to go out and get something eventually, but I didn't want to leave in case Alex summoned. I had to be ready at any second—for anything. So I grabbed a bottle of water from the fridge and swung it shut. I then snagged the bag of bread on the counter to make myself a quick peanut butter and jam sandwich.

Sitting at the kitchen table alone, I thought of all the scenarios that could happen, and what I would say to Nathan if I saw him again. The last thing I said, was that I never wanted to see him again. I told him I hated him, that I wished I'd never met him. I remembered it now, all of it. All the horrible things I said to him. I meant some it, but not all. I think. He had hurt me badly and broken our promises. The Nathan I knew and loved would have never done that to me. He had changed. I had changed and it seemed like we were growing apart too quickly. I needed him to fight for me, to be there, to prove me wrong about my thoughts of Serena. But he left. He chose to leave. He chose her. My chest began to ache again. My feelings were all over the place on this subject. I didn't want anything to happen to him in purgatory. I didn't want him to die there, but I was also scared of his return. I guess it's selfish of me to think this way. Nathan had done so much for me. We had so much history. It seemed crazy that things turned out this way. What happened to our destiny that Gabriel spoke of? I couldn't see any of that now, and what would become of us now that everything had changed? More importantly, what would become of Nathan? Just then, a knock came from the front door.

I looked at my watch, it was close to ten thirty in the morning. Who was Alex expecting? I peeked through the small hole in

the door and saw no one in the hallway.
"Who's there?"
Two more knocks came, making me jump back nervously.
"Who's there?!" I repeated, waiting impatiently for a response now.
"It's me Soph, let me in." The voice said, happily.
"Ben?" I replied, surprised. "What are you doing here?"
"Just open the door silly, I have something for you."
How did Ben find me?
Feeling a little unsettled from his arrival, I walked back towards the door and peeked through the hole again. This time, I saw him on the other side. He was holding some bags.
"I have food!" He joked, holding up the grocery bags.
I smiled, then decided to unlock the door.
"It's about time! These bags were getting heavy." He complained, handing one over to me and walking in the apartment like he'd been there before.
"Um… How did you know where I was?" I asked, following him into the kitchen.
"Oh… a little birdie told me." He laughed, looking around for some pans. Once he found them he turned on the stove top.
"Are ya hungry? You must be." He smiled, taking the bag of food back from me. One by one he pulled the items from the bag. I was still hungry, even after my sandwich.
"Hope you like pancakes, I actually make the best in town." He teased.
I immediately thought of Nathan. How he'd never let me help. My job was the syrup—and nothing else. My stomach started to turn at the thought.
I quickly sat down in the chair trying to contain my emotions.
"What?" He asked. "You do like pancakes. Don't you, Sophie?" Ben asked again, in a different tone.
I didn't know why he was so persistent on making pancakes for me. He must know from last time that I didn't want them. I still don't want them. Not from him at least, but I couldn't talk about it. He continued to stare at me as I battled the thoughts in my head. Then I thought of Ben's words from the

day before. How I had to face the things in life that hurt me the most—possibly meaning thoughts of Nathan. No matter how painful it was. But he couldn't possibly know about this intimate moment Nathan and I shared regularly, could he?

Ben placed his items down and made his way over to sit down next to me at the table. He touched my hand gently. The warmth of his skin was calming.

"You do like pancakes, don't you Soph." He asked once again, but this time it was more of a statement.

I finally nodded, as if I was in a trance.

He touched the side on my cheek, looking deep into my eyes.

"I'm going to make you some delicious breakfast and you're going to love it, trust me." He smiled. "Then, when we are done, I'm going to do another session of Reiki on you. Sound good?"

I continued to stare at him, agreeing without hesitation. As Ben stood up, he leaned over and kissed me on the forehead. He then made his way back over to the stove.

I sat quietly—calmly. I didn't have a thought in my head.

"I know you miss him," Ben spoke, as he mixed the batter up. "I can see it in your eyes."

I didn't respond, but something began to build inside of me.

"Hold it in, Sophie," he quickly said, without looking at me. "Learn to control your emotions."

I felt like I could cry. How did he know what I was feeling? I took a deep breath and sucked it back down as he said.

"You will face him again soon and it's going to be hard, but you must do it." He then poured the mixture into the frying pan.

When he was done cooking, he brought a beautiful breakfast over to the table. Not only were there pancakes, but also some fresh fruit, toast and bacon too. It was definitely something Nathan would prepare. He then pulled two small bottles of orange juice from his bag and placed one of them in front of me on the table.

"Eat up," He smiled, sitting down beside me.

"Why are you doing all of this?" I finally said.

"Well, it seems like you could really use a friend. You seem
sad... and depressed."
"I seem sad and depressed?" I repeated.
"To be honest, yes. You're also more... excuse my words,
bitchy." He smirked, finding the response on my face quite
entertaining.
"I'm sorry." I said, feeling guilty. "It's just... I can't. I mean,
I'm not sure how to deal with anything anymore."
"You don't have to deal with everything at once, just moment
by moment. Day by day. That's all you can do in life. Well,
that and remember to breathe." He joked. "Don't worry about
it, I get the loner stuff. But we loners should stick together."
I smiled. "Ben, how do you always get me to listen to you?"
"It's probably my charm... and of course good looks." He
laughed.
I shook my head, then began to eat the wonderfully prepared
breakfast in front of me.
"Thank you." I said, not looking up at him.
"You're very welcome." He replied, twisting the cap off of the
orange juice in front of me. "Drink up, you're going to need
your vitamins today.

After breakfast, Ben gave me a few minutes to digest my
food. Sitting in front of the window in the living room, I
could feel him studying me from behind as he cleaned up the
kitchen. He was doing that a lot now—studying me. I thought
about Charlotte for a moment, I hoped she was still okay. Then
I thought about everyone else that was still in that horrible
place. Stuck there, like I was. How were they dealing with
it? Were they still alive? Had Alex found them yet? And what
was Fate doing right now? My hand reached up to the pink
stone around my neck. I closed my eyes and tried to remember
my life before I came to Vancouver. When my Grandmother
had helped me apply to acting school. She believed in me
and wanted so much for me. But what I was right now, was
nothing either of us could have expected. Everything from my
past seemed pointless now. All the horrible boyfriends, the

friends I lost, even my parent's divorce—none of that drama
compared to what I was going through right now. It seemed
silly almost—the small things we sweat about in life. There
were so many bigger things happening out there. Things we
humans didn't even know about. All of this was really making
me look at life a different way. It made me think about other
people too. Who else was going through something just as
traumatic? Or worse? Supernatural or not, I began to think
about everyone's fate in life. Where there worse things?
Things I didn't know about? My mind switched again.
What did I want now? What did Fate have in store for me?
And could I actually survive it? Just then, Ben touched my
shoulder.
"Are you ready?" He asked, startling me a bit.
My hand took his, "It still hurts,"
"I know," he smiled. "And it will hurt for quite some time.
But anything can change if you have faith in yourself. Believe
you can change, believe you are strong Sophie. You can have
whatever you want in life if you are willing to fight for it. You
must never give up, especially if something means the world
to you." He then pulled me to my feet.
I leaned in and hugged him tightly. He wrapped his arms
around me, gently stroking the back of my head with his hand.
"Are we doing the same thing as last time?" I asked nervously,
ready to breakdown in his arms.
The more I reflected on myself, the more I was opening up
to the things I missed. The things I think I wanted in my life,
they just seemed a little more impossible now-a-days. I was
having so many mixed emotions and thoughts on everything.
I had regrets—about things I had said and things I didn't do.
All of it was painful to admit and even worse to feel.
"Yes, it should be even more effective this time now that
you're more familiar with the treatment and open to it."
He pulled back to look down at me, then placed his hand
against my stone.
"This will work wonders for you, if you let it."
"What is it about this stone, Ben?" I asked, nervously.

"Alex looked surprised to see it on me."

"It's a stone for the true of heart. Many are given it, but few can ignite it." He answered. "Alex should know about it very well."

I looked down. The stone had generated a warm energy before with the Archangels present. Was that the power he was talking about?

"That's all I can tell you," He then said. "It will work exactly how you need it to—how your heart welds it." He winked, then pulled me towards the center of the room.

By now, I was sure I heard everything and anything there was about the supernatural world and the things that came along with it. I didn't want to admit it out loud, but Ben was beginning to feel very comfortable to me. Like Nathan once was. Although, I still had many questions about him and he still made me nervous at times. But I trusted him—completely. As he pulled me down to the ground, he quickly placed a pillow from the couch under my head.

"Ben?" I asked, looking up at him. "You sure you don't want to tell me who you really are?"

He looked at me oddly, "I'm Ben,"

"Uh huh," I replied with a smile, then closed my eyes.

Like before, Ben went through the chakras, charging each one slowly. Making every emotion in my body spark, just like last time. Only this time, memories flooded my mind immediately. Memories of promises and conversations I once had. Then suddenly, my Grandmother appeared.

I could clearly see her standing across the way from me. We were in a white, round room. Surrounding the room, were twelve white doors with sliver knobs.

"Gram?" I said, my eyes watering at the sight of her.

"Hi Honey." She answered, with a pleasant smile.

I didn't waste a second more, I hurried across the room and dove into my Grandmother's arms. I could feel her as she wrapped her arms around me. She was there, really there. I could even smell her perfume—white vanilla musk. It was wonderful.

"You seem so healthy Gram. Are you okay? Where are we? How am I seeing you?" My mind raced.

"One question at a time, my dear." Gram laughed. "We're in your mind. I'm a memory from your heart. I assume this is where you wanted us to meet? Odd place for a reunion don't you think?" She teased.

I looked up at her, "I made this?"

She nodded.

Whatever Ben was doing, I didn't want it to end. I didn't know Reiki could connect me to Gram.

"I miss you so much." I said. "So much has changed with me. I'm losing myself, I've lost Nathan and—"

"I know everything, my dear," She interrupted. "I've been watching over you. You're not lost Sophie, you're just derailed a bit." She smiled. "I'm not sure what all of these doors mean, but I'm assuming you have a path to choose and you need to pick one."

I glanced around the room.

"Remember what I used to tell you? When one door closes, another will open?"

"But I don't even know where to start," I responded. "Tell me what do you and I'll do it!" I begged. "I don't know what I'm doing with my life anymore, Gram. What should I do? Tell me, please!"

"Sophie, there are many different paths in life. Paths that will teach you many life lessons. Some good and some bad. But there is no correct way to go, my dear."

It wasn't the answer I wanted.

"I've been such a jerk, Gram. I'm afraid my friends won't forgive me. Not this time. I don't deserve it."

"Sophie, your true friends know who you really are. That's why they fight for you, they will be there when you're ready to return to them."

"I'm not too sure of that… and Nathan," I choked up.

"Nathan is a wonderful person with an amazing heart."

"Wait, Gram... Have you met Nathan?"

I had forgot for a moment that I had never mentioned Nathan to Gram—not once. Probably because when she was alive, he was still my guardian angel.

"Oh, I've met him. Long ago, just before he returned to you as a human." She smiled, "He paid me a visit,"

The thought of Nathan visiting my Grandmother on the other side warmed my heart. It also made me jealous that he got to see her. Why didn't he tell me?

"He loves you more than anyone in the entire world. Don't give up on him just yet. I think he may surprise you if you let him." She then stepped back from me.

"Wait, where are you going?" I said, quickly reaching for her. "I need you...."

"No, you don't. You need to follow your heart. Let it guide you. Let them be there for you. Trust in yourself and don't forget your promise to me,"

"Wait, please!" I yelled, releasing the tears I was desperately holding in. "I'm not sure I can do it!"

"You will. I know you will. You are 'My World' Sophie. I love you very much and I'm so proud of what you are and what you are about to become. You're going to love it. Trust me..." Her voice faded as she disappeared before my eyes.

"Gram!" I shouted again, but she was already gone.

Standing alone in the circular white room, I wiped my eyes trying to think of Ben's words to hold myself together, but it was so hard. I hadn't seen Gram in so long. Her passing had ruined me. Emotions were racing throughout my body as I stared around the lonely room.

"Ben?" I said, quietly—hoping he could hear me. "Ben, I need your help... please. Are you still there?" I asked, touching the pink stone again. My eyes jumped from door to door. Was I really supposed to pick one? What would happen if I picked the wrong one? Why were there so many? Anxiety kicked in. I quickly took a deep breath and tried to relax. I couldn't afford to lose it in here. I needed to concentrate and take action like my Gram said. I closed my eyes and tried hard to listen to my heart. I felt myself begin to move around the room until eventually, I bumped into a door. My eyes shot open. Slowly, I lifted my hand for the silver doorknob. My fingers slid around the knob. I quickly turned it to the right. The wind blew softly against my face as the door opened. I lifted my hand to shelter my eyes. There were small particles flying towards me. They burned like tiny sparks of a flame the moment they graced my skin.

"Sophie..." A familiar voice howled.

I froze in fear. *That voice.*

"Sophie..." She whispered again. Then again and again, taunting me like she did before in purgatory. I had let her in. Serena's voice echoed throughout the room as I covered my ears in fear. I wasn't ready for this—not for her.

"Stop it." I cried. But I could already feel her. The ghostly presence, just like before, surrounded me.

"Help!" I shouted, trying to wake myself up.

The cold air picked up around me, making it hard to keep my balance as I backed away from the doorway.

"Sophie, get hold of yourself!" A voice shouted.

My eyes raced around the room, "Ben!" I yelled. "Ben I need you to stop this. I can't do it. Let me out! She's going to take me! Don't let her take me!" I continued to scream frantically. I hurried around the room, tugging at the other doors, but not one of them opened. I felt the room beginning to shrink around me as the haunting continued. Why was this happening again? And why was Ben allowing it to happen?

"I told you I wouldn't let you take him. Now you'll pay for it all..." Serena's voice shrieked.

"Sophie listen to me! You can stop this! You have the power!" Ben's voice shouted again. "Channel your chakras and use them for defense. You know what to do. Look into your heart, Soph! Do it now!"

My eyes raced around the room in fear of seeing Serena's face. I then reached for my stone necklace that whipped in the wind around my neck. I held it tightly in front of my chest and closed my eyes.

"Protect me… Protect me from this—from her. This isn't real…" I said aloud.

I wasn't even sure if what I was doing was right. I was just trying my best to concentrate on what I wanted like Ben suggested.

"That's it Soph, she only has power over you if you give it to her." Ben's voice warned.

"Sophie…" Serena taunted, again.

Her voice seeped into my ears. She was close.

I felt a presence behind me. Before I could turn, a cloudy shape made its way around me and stopped directly in front. With my hand still clenched to the stone in fear, I swallowed hard as the image became clearer. I quickly closed my eyes.

"You're not welcome here!" I shouted, loudly.

Just then, a gust of wind smashed against me and my eyes opened to Serena. I screamed, backing away from her as she reached for me. Then, just as her fingers were about to latch onto my neck, she exploded into bright pink smoke.

Trembling, I dropped to the ground. My eyes found nothing as I searched the room for her. I gripped onto the cement floor below me, trying to stabilize myself. I couldn't catch my breath.

"You did great, Soph. I'm proud of you."

My eyes shot open again to the very familiar voice that wasn't Ben's. Listening carefully, my eyes searched the circular room. It was him, I was sure of it. Tears filled my eyes as I attempted to stand. I continued to search the room for him— for the person I wasn't ready to see. I turned one last time and rubbed my eyes. It couldn't possibly be him. He was still in purgatory—with the others. When I slid my hands back down, there in front of me, was Nathan.

"I've missed you, crazy girl…" He said, kindly. Slowly, he began to walk towards me.

His face was pale and worn looking. His body was thin—very thin—but it was definitely Nathan. My heart sank at the sight of him. I gripped on to the stone again for strength. I couldn't speak. The mere sight of him was disabling me. He stepped

closer, waking me from my trance. I quickly stumbled back
from him then stopped abruptly when I felt a tug at my heart.
It felt like something was pulling me back towards him.
"I…. I can't," I began to cry.
His face softened. "I'm so sorry," He whispered.
I watched as he took one last step towards me. His hand then
lifted and hovered near my cheek. He seemed nervous to make
contact. I definitely was. Tears rolled down my cheeks as I
looked into his beautiful, dark brown eyes. My heart raced as
his fingertips were about to touch my skin. I closed my eyes.
I wasn't ready—not for this. Suddenly, a white light filled the
room around us, devouring everything. Including my vision of
Nathan

●●●

When the blinding light faded, my eyes opened and I shot up
from the floor. Ben quickly grabbed me by the shoulders,
"Soph, are you okay? Can you hear me?"
I was sweating profoundly. My hands shook as I gripped onto
his arms, attempting to stand up.
"Wait. Stay seated for a sec. Calm yourself, what happened in
there?" Ben asked, worried. "You were doing so well. What
changed?"
I didn't answer. I couldn't get the words out. I mumbled,
trying to form a sentence.
"It's okay, just lay back. Don't push yourself." He insisted,
helping me back down. My hands remained attached to his
arms.
"Calm down, you're safe." He repeated, slowly pulling
himself from my grip.
I breathed deeply, staring up at the ceiling. My entire body
was electrified from this unexpected encounter.

●●●

 Nathan awoke rapidly from his resting state against the dead
 tree. Out of breath and completely disorientated, adrenaline

pumped throughout his body from the dream. His eyes searched the area frantically.

"What's wrong?" Gabriel asked.

"I can feel her!" He responded, quickly.

"What do you mean? Feel who?"

Nathan stumbled to his feet, full of energy.

"Sophie! She was right there—in front of me!" He shouted.

Gabriel snagged him by the arm, "Calm yourself, where did you see her?"

"I don't know, one moment I was sleeping, then... I felt this warm sensation from within, like I was being pulled towards something. It was her, I know it. I could feel her—smell her. I almost touched her but..." He paused, then a smile grew on Nathan's face. "Gabriel, she's looking for me—for us."

The Archangel stood in silence, uncertain of how this was happening or if Nathan was possibly losing his mind.

"Are you sure? Are you sure it was Sophie? Could it have been Serena or Fate, or—"

"No Gabriel, it was her. I could feel the hurt inside her heart. She was so mad at me, but so..." He took a breath again, "In love with me still..." Nathan ran his fingers through his hair in relief and began to pace.

"Okay, I believe you. Come here and sit down, you'll cause us another fight if you draw any more attention to us. Be calm, let's talk about this." Gabriel responded, guiding Nathan back over to the tree.

"Where am I?" A weak voice said from behind them.

"Alex!" Nathan raced to his side. "Alex! You'll never believe it, Sophie—she contacted me!" Nathan shouted, "She can reach us! It was definitely her, I swear it!" Nathan's words raced from his mouth.

"Nathan calm down, let Alex collect himself. He's been out quite a while." He then knelt down beside him. "How are you feeling?"

Confused and a little sore, Alex slowly attempted to sit up. Gabriel reached out to help him adjust up against the tree. His body still bleeding badly.

"Gabriel?" Alex couldn't believe his eyes as they came into focus. He then looked to Nathan, who stood directly over him now. "Nate?" He said, smiling a bit.

"You have no idea how happy we are to see you," Nathan replied.

"That is an understatement, it's a miracle we are seeing you right now." Gabriel added. "How did you get in here, Alex?" Alex rubbed his head, exhausted.

"Michael…He sent us through the portal doors. Sent me, and Raphael in after you."

"Michael opened the portal doors?" Gabriel asked, concerned. He couldn't believe what he was hearing. The doors were only opened to banish spirits into purgatory and he freely opened them for an angel and a spirit guide? What was he thinking? There was only one reason he would open the doors for them, and it wasn't good. They gave Alex a few more minutes to collect himself before the conversation continued.

"Where is Raphael?" Alex asked, weakly.

"We didn't see her, only you." Nathan replied.

"What? She was right there…" Alex's voice trailed off. "She's changed," he spoke again. "I fear she may not be on our side anymore."

Gabriel stared quietly back at him.

"Raphael? That can't be, she would never…" Nathan quickly glanced to Gabriel.

"What makes you think this?" The Archangel asked.

Alex took a deep breath and moments later, Gabriel and Nathan were filled in on what had been happening back in the real world since they left. Alex told them everything, including his studies into the dark arts and the voice he heard talking to Raphael in the living room. He filled them in on Sophie, the plan, and the news about Fate taking Charlotte.

"We have to be on our toes," Gabriel said, sternly.

"And we need to get out of here, fast." Nathan added.

Alex nodded, then glanced at Nathan again.

"Did you find Serena?" He asked, timidly.

"I did," He answered. "But no matter how much I tried to

explain things, she just won't change her thoughts. She's stuck in the past. I feel I might be at a loss, especially after my last encounter." He sighed, "I never should have left Sophie."

"But you also couldn't have lived with yourself if you hadn't at least tried." Alex replied. "I know how badly you wanted to save her Nathan, I'm sorry."

Nathan nodded, a faint smile on his face. He then slid himself down next to Alex on the ground.

"Alex," Gabriel interrupted. "Given all that you told us… do you think that Sophie can do it? Do you think she can pull us out of here, alive?"

"I do." He answered, honestly. "She's damaged for sure, but I have a feeling we have an angel on our side in here."

Nathan looked to Gabriel confused, then back to Alex.

"What angel? It can't be Michael, or Uriel…"

"Neither…" Alex replied.

"And it's not Raphael ether," Gabriel added.

"Nathan, what are you going to do about Serena? I mean, if we get back to the real world?" Alex asked, quickly changing the subject again. "And what about you, Gabriel? Anna is fueling Serena, it's just a vicious cycle for all of us."

"I too, like Nathan have to let go. Both Serena and Anna died with rage in their heart. Neither could handle the cards Fate handed them in life and unfortunately there is nothing we can do for them now if we can't reason with them. It pains me to think it, as I'm sure it's crossed your mind too Nathan, but there may come a time soon when we will have to destroy them and it will not be an easy task—for either of us."

Nathan's head lowered at the thought.

"But for now, let's worry about getting out of here."

"I agree," Alex said, attempting to get up.

Nathan quickly laced his arm around Alex's waist, helping him to his feet.

"I've prepared Sophie as I told you both. She knows what to do. Now it's up to you, Nathan. I need you to be open for her. She will not be stable, so you must coach her into trusting you again. You cannot lose her for a second or the connection will break." He warned.

"Of course, I'll do whatever it takes." Nathan replied.

"Alex, are you sure you can handle this spell? You're not at full strength yet." Gabriel then asked.

Alex nodded, "We don't have much time. The fact that Sophie already made contact, means we need to make our move now while the energy is still lingering."

Gabriel lifted Alex's arm over his shoulder, removing his weight from Nathan. "Then let's do it."

Alex reached into his pocket with this free hand in search of something.

"But what about Raphael?" Nathan asked, still worried for his friend.

"What about me?" Raphael replied weakly, from behind.

Their eyes shot around to the fallen angel standing before them. Her hand clenched to a nearby tree for balance.

"You left me, Alex. Why?"

10
Redemption

When I sat up again, I was greeted with a glass of water that Ben forced down my very sore throat.

"Thank you." I managed to get out.

"You're welcome. How are you feeling now?" He asked, a little concerned.

"Better… What was that?"

"I charged you again, but this time you took it to a whole new level." He looked a little nervous, which made me nervous. "Your heart took over as it should, I just didn't expect it to this quickly. It was showing you the way Soph, whatever you faced or saw in there… it's what you need to deal with. It's what your heart truly desires. Do you agree?" He asked, politely.

I sat in silence. I wasn't sure. The sight of Nathan frightened me, but I guess it made sense.

"Soph?" He asked again, touching my hand.

I nodded, unable to admit it out loud yet.

"Okay then." Ben smiled. "Let's get you it." He then stood up and pulled me to my feet.

"Are you sure you want damaged goods back?"

We spun around quickly to Fate.

Ben quickly stepped in front of me. It was odd how quickly he reacted and even odder how he responded.

"How did you get in here?" He asked.

He seemed to recognize her immediately. I stood in fear behind him.

"Sophie, it's so good to see you again." She said, sitting down on the couch and stretching out her legs. Her tall black boots reached up to just below the knee. Her black leggings were skin tight and the corset she had on, hugged her thin waistline just right. Connected together with a thick red and black leather belt, Fate looked as if she had walked right out of a superhero comic with a touch of Hollywood fashion. She was tough—warrior like, especially with the fitted dark leather jacket she wore. At first glance you wouldn't find her too intimidating. She was almost beautiful in the darkest kind of way. Her eyes, the color of coal with a hint of red to them— something hard to take your eyes off.

I glared at her as she tossed her long black hair over her shoulder and leaned back against a pillow. Two streaks of electric red hair rested gently on each side of face. Making her pale flawless skin almost glow in the light.

"I was just thinking that you might want to reconsider your heart's desire," She continued. "I mean, if Nathan does make it back here alive, you're going to have a whole new person on your hands. He'll be damaged goods. Think about it, all of that torment from Serena and the other spirits in there. You'll be dealing with a very different person. It's going to be so hard." She smiled at me. "You know how it is, right? Coming back from purgatory? It makes you a little—crazy, doesn't it?" She taunted, getting up from the couch.

"Remember how you attacked Charlotte? Exciting, wasn't it?" I pushed Ben's arm down. She was pissing me off. I felt a new emotion building inside, one I hadn't experienced with Fate before.

"Where are you keeping her?" I spoke in a cold tone.

"Your little friend? Oh she's… hanging around." Fate snickered.

"Let her go. She has nothing to do with any of this!" I
demanded.
"Absolutely not," She quickly responded. "And you're wrong,
Charlotte does play a very big part in this game. She was
helping her little boyfriend play with the dark arts. She's very
much invested."
I gave her a disgusted look.
"Alex will come for her, so you better—"
"Better what?" Fate interrupted, appearing directly in front of
me. "Go ahead, I dare you. Threaten me just a little and I will
end Blondie's life."
I felt the tears beginning to form in the corner of my eyes. I
quickly turned my head so Fate wouldn't see me wipe them
away.
She began to circle us. I held tight to Ben's arm again. He
continued to stand firmly beside me, watching Fate like a
hawk.
"I think it's best if you go," He said.
Fate's eyes didn't move from mine. She wanted a bigger
reaction out of me. I could feel it.
"You've already lost him, Sophie. Nothing you do now can
bring him back to you. At least not the Nathan you remember."
She then reached out to touch my hair ever so slightly. I
flinched in fear as she made contact. Her long thin fingers slid
through the dry strands, and as they did, one long strand on
the left side of my face turned bright red just as she reached
the tip. Ben and I stood very still as she released my hair, then
leaned in close.
"Now you're one of us." She whispered.
"That's enough!" Ben said, pulling me away.
Fate quickly shoved him hard to the ground. "Stay!" She said,
holding her hand out in front of him. He couldn't move. His
legs, arms, fingers, all of it locked in place.
"Ben!" I attempted to reach for him, but Fate intervened.
Her hand gripped my chin and jerked my face back to hers.
"Listen to me very carefully," she spoke in a low tone. "You
almost had it, you stupid girl. There was no drama anywhere

in your life. Why would you give that all up? Why?!" She
shouted.
My tears began to stain my cheeks, I tried my best to hold
them in but she was making me so angry.
"Because I don't feel whole!" I shouted back. My reaction
surprised me. "I need my friends back. My life isn't the same
without them and I'm going to do whatever I need to get them
back."
"It could cost you your life, Missy." Fate smirked.
I could tell she was annoyed with me. I continued to stare
back, a glimmer of red sparked the corner of her pupils. I
grabbed the stone around my neck.
"I don't care. I'd rather die trying then give up on them."
The pink stone began to light beneath my fingers. It slowly
leaked out and around me.
Fate smiled, then carefully stepped back from me.
"Driven by your emotions…Be very careful with that." She
warned. Her eyes then locked on Ben's. "He's lying to you…"
Ben's eyes shifted to mine.
"Good choice in becoming an actor, it fits you perfectly. She
may not know, but I see right through you." Fate laughed,
fading out of site. "I'll see you soon." Her voice lingered.
I quickly reached for Ben to help him up from the ground.
"Are you okay?"
"Yes, thank you." He replied, straightening his shirt a bit.
"Are you?"
I nodded, then headed straight into the kitchen for water. Ben
followed close behind.
"Listen, about what she said…." He paused.
I was thirsty. So thirsty. I quickly chugged down a glass of
water, then began to fill it again. I took a deep breath, then
chugged the second one down. When I was done, I placed the
glass in the sink and turned to him.
"I don't care if you're lying," I said. "And I don't care who
you really are. I don't want to know. The fact that the sight of
Fate didn't horrify you means you've seen supernatural beings
before. So you're either one of them, or you're a poor soul

like me. But I don't wanna know, okay?" I said, grabbing the empty glass again. I needed one more. I filled it once again and chugged it down.

Ben leaned down on the counter next to me.

"I'm not lying, Sophie. I'm here to help you as I said. I do know about the Supernatural world, maybe more than I let on. That's why I believed you when you told me your story, I believed you because I believe in all of this stuff." He smiled. "I've studied it since I was little and when I got into Reiki, they spoke more about guardian angels, spirit guides and even purgatory. Many Reiki masters come in contact with spirits at some point, so it's very important that we charge our chakras and learn how to control our energy. The same as it is for you... Especially if you want to keep those bad spirits out. Know what I mean? It keeps our body, mind and soul strong."

"Makes sense. I guess." I answered, putting the glass down for the last time. "I'll admit, it's nice to have someone around that I can talk to. You know, and not have to hide this crap." I smiled, then stepped towards him. My hand gently touched his chest as the other took hold of the pink stone around my neck. "Thank you Ben, for everything. I don't know what I would do without you. I mean, if you hadn't come into my life—"

"It's no problem, I'm glad you're in mine too." He replied, then leaned in and hugged me tight.

"I want to make sure you're safe—always. I want to protect you." He whispered.

Suddenly, my stone lit up again. The pink energy emerged from my chest warming both of our bodies. My arms grew tighter around Ben's strong frame. That familiar scent was in the air again—Lavender. I breathed in deeply, feeling comfortable in his arms.

Eventually, the energy faded and Ben pulled back. Whatever this was that was happening to me, I really liked it. It felt safe and beautiful. Especially with him.

"Come on, I want to keep going with you. I feel your time to help will be coming soon. You need to be ready."

I nodded, feeling a little braver from surviving Fate this time.

"Okay, let's do it."
I then walked past him back into the living room. I wasted no time getting comfortable on the floor and quickly prepared my mind for the next treatment. This Reiki stuff was more powerful than I thought and I wanted to learn more as quickly as possible.
I felt Ben's hand cover my eyes just as I closed them. Then I felt his other hand place directly over my heart stone and once again, we began the journey to charge and connect my chakras as one.

●●●

The candles lit up one by one around the room again. Charlotte's eyes slowly flickered open to the fire burning bright.
"Wake up sleepy head," Fate said appearing in front of her. She gripped the chains linked to the cuffs around Charlotte's ankles and yanked her across the floor. She then pulled her up to her feet by the back of her head.
"Get up,"
The strength of Fate, forced Charlotte to her feet. "What do you know about Ben?"
"What?" She said, weakly. "Ben who?"
"You know who I'm talking about. That little creep is teaching Sophie how to channel her Chakras. Do you know who he is?" Fate asked again, quickly annoyed.
"Ben? He's part of her cast… He's just a human, another actor. What does he have to do with any of this?"
Fate glared at her.
"You honestly don't know who he is? And Sophie doesn't either?" She asked, again.
"He's… an actor, she met him on set." Charlotte repeated in pain this time.
"Oh please!" Fate huffed, tossing Charlotte back to the ground. Her head cracked hard against the cement. Blood began to pour from her skull and a numbness soon tingled

throughout her body.

"Just finish me..." Charlotte begged, in pain.

Fate stood silently over her beaten and drained body.

"I'm annoyed—with all of you!" She said, dusting off the sleeve of her jacket. "You're all so stupid. You don't even see what's right in front of you." She began to pace around the room, impatiently. "No matter, your stupidity will kill you in the end."

Charlotte moaned in pain as Fate stopped in front of her, tracing her lips with her index finger in deep thought.

"But I can't be too confident, I better mix it up—just in case." She then reached down and snagged Charlotte by the arm. "Okay Blondie, let's go."

The chains suddenly dissolved from around her ankles, leaving her skin was red and raw. Fate gripped Charlotte's lifeless body tight before they disappeared from sight.

Alex stepped forward slowly, still in pain to speak with Raphael privately. She stared him down as he approached without a single blink. She was worn and beaten. Whatever had happened moments before took a lot out of her.

"I'm sorry, I panicked." He said. "I didn't know what you were doing. You were letting them get to you—the spirits. Please understand, I can't afford to fail this Raphael, not even for you."

She stared quietly, then rotated her left shoulder back into its socket. Gabriel walked to her side and gently touched her.

"How are you feeling?" He asked, worried.

"Gabriel, I'm sorry. I was weak," She responded. "But I'm better now. I want to help. You know I want Nathan back as much as all of you," She said, sadly.

"Of course," Nathan piped up from behind. "What happened, Raphael?"

Gabriel's hand dropped as Nathan joined their side.

"What Alex said is true, they were in my mind from the

moment I arrived. I wasn't as strong as I thought I would be. I was fighting so hard to keep them out, but they kept ripping through my walls."

"That glow, the purple energy that was radiating from your body—what was that?" Alex asked, nervously.

"Purple energy?" Gabriel repeated, "Why were you using that, Raphael? The purple haze is for…" He paused, continuing to stare at her.

Raphael seemed a bit ashamed.

"What's the purple haze?" Nathan repeated.

Neither of them answered.

Raphael ran her fingers through her hair and straightened herself up before she spoke again.

"I was going to sacrifice myself. Doing so, would clear out a large portion of spirits for miles. Giving Alex the chance to find you. It was my plan all along." She admitted.

Gabriel shook his head in disappointment.

"There's no reason for you to do this." He said, keeping his eyes to the ground.

"Brother," She replied, touching his chest with her right hand. "This is my chance to redeem myself. I've been waiting to do something great, something that would affect us all. If I can save Alex and give him the chance to save you and Nathan— which I think he can, then it would be the greatest miracle of all."

"There are other ways," Gabriel replied, still upset.

"I agree." Nathan added, a little shocked from what he was hearing. "Raphael, no one wants to see you go out like that. It's very noble what you're trying to do, but we couldn't live with ourselves if we lost you in here again."

"Nathan, I'm worn… and weak. I only wanted the chance to show the Archangels that I've changed, that my loyalty is to them first and foremost. I want to do this."

Gabriel turned from her.

"Nathan is the most important thing to us right now. I believe in all that Gabriel speaks of and I want to see you all succeed. The end of me will bring such power to you all—especially you, Nathan. Tell them, Gabriel." She asked, kindly.

Nathan looked at the Archangel, confused.

"What's she talking about?"

Alex looked just as nervous.

"When an Archangel dies, all of the power they have within them is sent to the remaining angels. Giving us tremendous strength, leveling us up, including our spirit guides that serve us. But for you Nathan, because you are so special, there's no telling what it would do for you. It could give you strength, knowledge and possibly more power than then all of the Archangels. She's offering it to you as a gift."

Nathan looked at Raphael sadly.

"As you have faith in me Nathan, I do as well—in you." She smiled. "I'm certain you will save us all."

Nathan shook his head—confused and upset now.

"This will give you such an advantage, don't you see that?" She spoke again, stepping towards him.

"Something we really need right now, considering what we face." Gabriel sadly spoke again. "It takes centuries to make our power grow, but with the passing of a single Archangel, especially for noble reasons, the power is enhanced and will spread throughout us immediately." Gabriel paused, "But I can't let you do it. You deserve to live, Raphael."

"There is nothing left of me. I've tried. Please, Gabriel. Let me go out with some pride. Help me achieve what I desire." Raphael begged.

"Whoever brought you out of purgatory, brought you out for a reason and until I—"

"This is my reason!" She snapped. "I'm meant to help you. Only I understand what power you need in here to survive and only I can give it to you."

Everyone was silent.

"I'm sorry, I'm going to do it, whether you like it or not."

"Raphael…" Alex spoke, quietly.

The conversation was over, but Alex still had one last question lingering in his mind.

"Raphael, who were you speaking with in our apartment

earlier? I heard a voice with you. I mean, I heard you say something about wiping memories or something. I truly thought ….”
She stared at him sadly.
“I thought that you had turned on us. That you were working with someone else.”
“Alex, I would never turn on you,” she said, very calmly. “And I’m sorry I worried you.”
Alex sighed in relief. Then she went on.
“Partial of what you think is true. I have been working with someone else lately. He has been helping me calm my inner thoughts, coaching me back to a normal life. I owe a lot of my healing to you all, but mainly to him. He was the one who saved me from purgatory.” She said, rubbing her shoulder again.
“Who Raphael? Who was it? Who saved you?” Nathan asked again. But just as he did, the sky grew dark and the wind picked up immensely.
“They’re here!” Raphael said, spinning around. “Alex, are you ready with your spell?” She shouted, over the howling winds. Gabriel stepped in front of them.
“You’re not going down like this. I won’t let you.”
Raphael’s face softened as she stared back at her brother.
“Tell me, was it him? Did he save you?” Gabriel shouted again. She knew who he meant. A kind smile grew on her face, giving the Archangel his answer.
“I knew it, he’s on our side. He believes too, doesn’t he?”
“More than anything.” She assured him.
A thunderous growl ripped through the dark sky. Gabriel glanced back at Alex who was quickly preparing his spell. He pulled Sophie’s winged necklace from the pocket of Nathan’s torn up jacket.
“We’re going to need this.” He said, attaching it quickly around Nathan’s neck.
“You can do this, I know it.” Nathan said, staring into Alex’s nervous eyes. He nodded, then reached into his own pocket and pulled out some stones. Placing them in his left hand he

quickly grabbed a small bag of salt from his other pocket and opened it carefully, so the wind wouldn't catch it. The screams of angry spirits surrounded them now. Gabriel and Raphael kept their eyes open for the first to attack.

"Take us home, Alex." Nathan shouted.

Alex closed his eyes and with the same black tourmaline stone he used earlier, he began his spell to first surround them with protection.

"The darkness you have created here is bound to you. We do not own your darkness, so you may not share this darkness with us. As long as our hearts beat, your energy shall hold no evil or power over us." And like before, an energy exploded from the stone, lighting it up. The screams around them began to grow. Nathan grabbed the winged necklace around this neck and thought if Sophie.

"I call on the powers from the West, bring us your speed. Powers from the North, bring us your energy, as the powers from the South, bring us your strength to fight."

Gabriel shot around them suddenly as a spirit leapt from the darkness towards Alex, taking it down immediately. He then blocked another from the side. Alex continued,

"I finally call to the East, bring us the fire! Fire to protect, fire to bind us from these spirits!" The fire ball blazed up around Nathan and himself, immediately protecting them from what lingered in the darkness—leaving Gabriel and Raphael on their own.

Raphael turned hearing something behind her, she was suddenly attacked from both sides by raging spirits. They tore at her as she desperately tried to fight them off.

"Come on, Soph… Let me in." Nathan whispered to himself. Alex quickly grabbed Nathan's wrist, he then placed his left hand onto Sophie's necklace hanging low. He closed his eyes and concentrated. He could feel Nathan's heart racing in anticipation.

"Think of her! Call to her, Nate!" Alex instructed, sharply.

"Sophie?" Nathan said aloud, but nothing happened. "Sophie!" He yelled another time. He then closed his eyes as Alex

recited another spell, the specific one he had taught Sophie to
use.
"Repeat after me, Nathan." He ordered. "Perfect love and
perfect peace." He began. Nathan repeated his words carefully
as asked. "Will make conditions right, and from that place
that's not a place, the form will come to light."
Again, Nathan repeated the words as Alex went on.
"I lift my heart to touch you, there is magic to be done and all
I need is knowing, that you and I are one."
Nathan repeated the final words of the spell perfectly and just
as he did a red energy ignited from within.
A spirit knocked Gabriel hard to the ground, but Raphael
was quick to his side to help. As Nathan's light began to
grow, Gabriel could feel a little of his own energy building
as well. It seemed to effect the Archangel each time. Gabriel
concentrated on that energy and forced what he could from
within. A pure white energy rippled down his arm and blasted
from his hand out into the sky—blowing the spirits far from
them. He then turned to Nathan.
"Remember what I taught you!" He shouted. "You have the
power within. Take hold, now is your time!"
The wind that was unbearable now, making it hard for Nathan
to hold his stance.

● ● ●

   My eyes wondered as I walked through the cherry blossoms
in Stanley Park. This familiar feeling warmed my heart. I
remembered walking here with Nathan. The sweet scent of the
blossoms filled the Vancouver air.
"Let him walk with you, Sophie." A familiar voice said in
my mind. This time I knew it was Ben, guiding me. He had
gotten me to a calm place this time. I found a park bench and
sat down quietly. Taking a deep breath in, I tried my best to
remain calm. I was only there for a moment or two before I
heard him speak.
"Hey you," Nathan's voice said, from behind.
I turned on the bench to see him walking towards me.

He was dressed in a white V-neck t-shirt and dark jeans, just as he did long ago as my guardian. My heart sank at the sight of him, emotions flooding my body. I wiped my eyes, trying my best to hold in any tears that were fighting to get out. When he reached me, we looked at each other silently, waiting for the other to speak first.

"Can I sit with you?" He finally asked.

I nodded nervously, after taking a moment to register his simple question. Every hair on my body was standing up. I was a wreck inside—barely holding it together. Mixed emotions of wanting to scream at Nathan, questioning what he was thinking, or leap into his arms and cry my eyes out, swelled up my body. I wasn't sure what I wanted to do.

"Sophie, I—" He began to say.

"Hurry Nathan, please! I can't hold it much longer!"

I jumped, startled by his voice.

"Was that Alex?" I said, sharply. My thoughts immediately went to him. "Alex!" I shouted, "Where are you?!"

"I'm here!" His voice echo in the wind "It's time, Soph!"

But another voice interrupted our conversation from behind. "How could you, Nathan?"

The two of us turned to see Serena standing under a nearby Cherry tree.

Gabriel quickly appeared by Serena's side back in purgatory and grabbed her by the neck. She fought fiercely against him with a blank stare on her face. Her mind was lost within Nathan's dreamstate while her lifeless body fought blindly against Gabriel with rage.

"Look what he's doing with her, Serena! That was supposed to be you, not Sophie!" Anna chimed in from the other side of Alex's fireball. She was guiding Serena's sight, coaching her on.

"Anna! What are you doing?" Gabriel shouted, holding Serena in place. "Stop this, please!"

Raphael quickly appeared by her side.

"If you're going back to the real world, so are we!" Anna shouted, just as Raphael took her down.

Back in the dream state, Nathan moved quickly in front of me as we both rose from the bench.
"Serena, what are you doing here?" He asked, nervously. The sight of her made my body react immediately. I felt the darkness inside trying to climb its way back up, but I held tight to Ben's words and forced it down as I did in the last dream.
"This was supposed to be our thing, you promised me the cherry blossoms!" She shouted, "What were you going to do, leave me to rot in purgatory?! How could you, Nathan!"
"Serena, I'm sorry." He explained. "I tried but—"
"But what?!" She shouted back.
The sky above thundered around us.
"You won't reason with me, look what you've become!" Nathan shouted.
"So you're choosing her?" She asked, "You can't, I won't let you! You're making a mistake, they're all tricking you!"
Suddenly, the sky went black. I glanced up nervously, grabbing my stone against my chest.
"I'm still here..." Ben's voice, chimed in my head.

The spirits surrounding them continued to feed on Serena's jealous energy which also fueled Anna. Giving her a little more strength to fight against Raphael.
"He can't hold it much longer, Gabriel!" Raphael shouted, noticing Alex's weakened state.
"You can't win! You will never get rid of us!" Anna shouted beneath her grip. "You all have that guilt, the guilt of leaving us to die. It's inside your heart—forever. You messed up, Gabriel! We will always be here! Because of you!" Anna growled, pleasantly pleased with how things were going so far. Just then, Fate appeared in front of the fire barrier.

Hanging on her side was Charlotte. Alex's eyes shot to hers.
"Hey boys and girls, I thought I'd bring you a little present."
She said, dropping Charlotte's lifeless body to the ground.
"Charlotte!" Alex screamed, horrified.
His heart started to race in fear.
"Alex! It's a trick! Don't lose your concentration! She's doing
this on purpose to distract you. Concentrate!" Gabriel pleaded.
Alex's barrier sparked a bit, the spirits lingered closer waiting
for it to fall. With Gabriel holding Serena back, and Raphael
holding Anna down, Alex and Nathan would be an open target
to attack.
"I think I might be bored of her…" Fate teased, jabbing
Charlotte's side with her boot. A faint groan came from the
lifeless body as she rolled over.
"Stop it!" Alex's rage grew tremendously.
The sparks flickered again. Raphael looked at Gabriel
nervously.
"Touch her again and I will end you!" Alex warned.
"End me? Hilarious!" Fate laughed, grabbing Charlotte by the
hair and pulling her head up. Charlotte's eyes opened slightly,
her vision blurred in and out until Alex face came in focus.
"Alex?" She cried, weakly.
"Charlotte!" He shouted back in tears.
"Save him…" She said, before passing out again.
Fate then tossed her across the ground—towards him. Alex
flinched at the thought of racing to catch her.
"Concentrate on Nathan!" Gabriel begged again, but Alex's
mind was wandering fast.
He looked back at Nathan who was holding tight to his
necklace. He closed his eyes again, trying to concentrate on
his spell—looking desperately for Nathan and Sophie once
again. It was so hard with Charlotte right there within his
reach. But Gabriel was right, he had to concentrate. It was
surely a trap. He had to think clearly—and fast.
He only hoped Charlotte could hang in there just a little while
more.

● ● ●

Serena charged at us, pushed Nathan aside and toppled me hard to the ground. Fear shot through me as her long fingers gripped my neck as they once did before. Memories of purgatory electrified me immediately and disabled my confidence I had moments earlier.

"I didn't get to finish you before. I won't make that mistake again!" She warned, holding me down by the hair.

I screamed in fear as Nathan jumped to his feet. Just as he reached us his hand flew out to grab Serena by the arm, but disappeared right through her.

"What the?" He said, looking down at his hand. "Alex's power..." He watched as his hand continued to flicker in and out of sight. He couldn't touch us. My eyes widened at the sight, I needed him. She was too strong. She was going to take me—this time for good.

"Alex! I need you, please!" Nathan begged, calling out to him again.

"This is silly! We can't lose him!" Raphael shouted, throwing Anna to the ground. She closed her eyes and concentrated like she did before. A sudden strong energy began to grow from within, and eventually turned into the purple haze.

"Raphael no!" Gabriel pleaded as Anna appeared by his side to pull him from Serena.

Alex's eyes shot back to Charlotte on the ground. She wasn't moving.

"Charlotte!" He screamed. "Charlotte, wake up!" He shouted again as his energy flicked around them.

"Guess you're going to have to choose..." Fate said, watching her game unravel around them. "This was a brilliant move by me, if I don't say so myself."

Alex kept his eyes on Charlotte until he heard Nathan's call. "Alex!"

He looked back at Nathan, then back to Charlotte. Her thumb moved ever so slightly in the dirt as she became more conscious. Slowly, her head turned to him.

"Charlotte, hang in there… please!" He begged.

She smiled at him, then closed her eyes again.

"Stay with me!" He shouted.

The purple haze had filled the area around them now. Alex's barrier slowly began to break down. In between the bursts of flames that surrounded them, a spirit cut through and latched onto Alex's back, tearing into his flesh. He screamed in pain as Gabriel tried to reach him, but Anna held onto him tight—allowing Serena and Nathan to stand frozen in their dream world.

"Alex!" Gabriel shouted, but was suddenly distracted by Raphael who was now lit up completely. The purple haze was everywhere, filling the air with a warm energy just as Alex's energy died completely. The spirits tackled him down to the ground.

"No!" Gabriel shouted, horrified.

Nathan's red energy had grown enough around him to keep him safe in the dream world until his eyes shot open. He began to panic, thinking that he had left Sophie back there with Serena—alone. He looked down at Alex on the ground.

"Alex! Get up! I have to get back to her." He shouted, then noticed Charlotte a few feet away. His energy began to grow in rage as his eyes shot up to Fate who was now in the trees watching over them. Behind him, Raphael was in her final stages of her sacrifice.

"I think that's good enough for now," Fate spoke pleasantly. "I don't want to waste all of my leverage so early in the game." She then landed again by Charlotte's side.

Gabriel fought ferociously to break free at the sight of her, then took all of his energy from within and exploded a white orb from his body—throwing Anna far from him and giving him enough time to race to Alex's side. He eliminated each spirit attacking Alex with the white energy orb, then quickly pulled him to his feet.

Still weak and disorientated, Alex pulled from Gabriel's grip and hurried towards Charlotte. Her eyes opened once more just as he was about to reach for her.

"I don't think so," Fate teased, then snagged her up from the ground and disappeared from sight.
Alex skidded to a stop.
Reappearing in the trees above, Fate held Charlotte's lifeless body in her arms. "You can't have her—not yet." She said.
"Charlotte!" Alex screamed, dropping to the ground again.
"Alex, please!" Nathan called out again. "Help us get out of here. I promise you, we will save her, but right now, we need you!" He begged from within his red energy field.
Gabriel was fighting his way through the spirits towards Raphael to stop her.
"Alex, I demand you to help Nathan!" Gabriel shouted. "You are my spirit guide, you must obey!"
The raging spirits took every shot they could at the Archangel as he drew closer. Alex glanced at Raphael, then up at Fate one more time.

●●●

I scrambled on the ground beneath Serena. I fought desperately, but she was too strong. I felt a heavy blow as Serena slammed my head back into the grass. She hovered close as I tried to regain my focus. Looking into my eyes, I could feel Serena's pain and hatred deep within my soul. The negative energy from her was pouring into me. My eyes locked on hers just as a piece of black hair fell across my face. Then I heard Ben's voice,
"Sophie, let your heart guide you. Pull the power from within," He encouraged.
I blinked, a little dazed from the blow to my head.
"It looks like you've been tainted too." Serena snickered, as her fingers laced through my red stand of hair.
"You're connected to us—forever." She smiled.
Her words bothered me, more than ever. All of this was insane. I needed them out of my life. I had to do something. I felt the energy shift inside. It warmed my body.
"I will never be one of you..." I replied, looking deep into her eyes.

"With perfect love and perfect peace, will make conditions right. And from that place that's not a place, the form will come to light." I began to say.

Serena stared at me nervously, her fingers releasing my hair.

"I lift my heart to touch you, there is magic to be done—"

"What are you doing?!" She screamed, slamming me back against the ground again. The fuzziness seeped through my body, I tried my best to concentrate again. Just then, Nathan reappeared beside us.

"Keep going, Soph!" He urged.

I cleared my throat and forced out the last few words.

"And all I need," I stopped, looking at Nathan, "Is knowing, that you and I are one."

A pink energy detonated from my body—blowing Serena far from us. I then watched the red in my hair change. It grew bright and now glittered a magenta pink in colour.

"Do it now!" Anna screamed. "Don't let her go!"

Gabriel ignored her words and hurried towards Raphael, but before he could reach her, the purple haze exploded.

"Raphael!" Gabriel shouted, covering his eyes. "NO!!!!"

The purple haze burned throughout the sky, lighting every evil spirit up around them, their screams were deafening.

Anna quickly grabbed Serena in her dream state, fearing the unexpected power surrounding them now and retreated as fast as she could. Fate jumped a little higher, staying clear of the power below. Alex scrambled to his feet, fighting off a spirit to reach Nathan again. He then carefully reached into the red energy surrounding him and grabbed his wrist.

The purple haze was hard to see through, but Gabriel soon felt his body begin to power up with energy. He could feel Raphael's soul racing through his veins.

"Gabriel, hurry!" Alex shouted, holding out his hand to the Archangel. Nathan's power ignited again, much brighter than before. Fate watched on from a far as Nathan's fire connected with Alex's energy.

Gabriel looked at him, and then back to where Raphael once stood. He sighed, knowing he could do no more, then raced to Alex and Nathan's side.

"I'm sorry…" Alex shouted just as he reached him—looking back to where Raphael once stood.

Gabriel lowered his head in sorrow as Alex continued his spell.

"I gazed upon your faces, in the darkness and in the light. I sought your wisdom in the stars, in the fabric of the night. I looked in the books both old and new, and heard my own heart beating. I call to you from the city of angels, guide me through!" A pure white energy shot out from Alex, blowing Nathan's red blaze higher and making a tunnel straight up into the sky.

Fate's eyes widened as she watched the powers unite.

Gabriel looked at Alex worried, he knew what he was doing now. Alex was tapping into the powers of the Archangels. Linking himself to them directly—in hopes of pulling them all back into the real world. Gabriel's eyes searched for Fate as the energy grew, but she was already gone.

"Sophie!" Nathan screamed back within the dream state that was now peeling away. The ground, the trees, the clouds— even the cherry blossoms were blowing away. I lifted myself to my knees, my fingers digging into the dirt, trying to hold on.

"Hurry Soph!" He yelled, "Take my hand!"

My eyes met his, this couldn't be it. This couldn't be the end of us. I continued to watch as the world around us ripped away into nothing.

"Sophie!" He pleaded.

My eyes reconnected with his, "Nate!" I finally shouted back, "Don't let them take me!" My fingers slid through the dirt as the wind pulled me back from him.

"Never!" He shouted, pushing forward.

Saying his name aloud ignited something within. A beautiful

sadness crippled me from speaking any more. I reached for
him—our fingers were only cementers away from each other.
"Don't give up!" He shouted again. The sky grew louder
above us. A thunderous sound ripple behind me.
I glanced over my shoulder. The ground was shaking,
diminishing before my eyes.
"Look at me, Soph!" Nathan demanded.
Terrified, I turned back to him.
Nathan's eyes grew wide, making me glance back once more
in fear. A black vortex-like hole was growing behind me.
I could feel the wind pulling at me. My eyes shot back to
Nathan's. This was it. I wasn't going to make it. I could see it
in his eyes. He was just as scared as I was.
"Nathan!" I cried, "I forgive you!"
He stared at me sadly for a moment, then shook his head.
"Don't you say your goodbyes—not now!" He shouted back.
"We're going to make it through this, together! You hear me?
I need you, Soph. If I don't have you, I don't have a reason to
live!".
Tears fell from my eyes freely now. His words pained me.
Nathan's eyes didn't move from mine as the world around us
was sucked piece by piece into the void. I felt ground beneath
my legs began to crumble. I reached for him again. My fragile
hand shaking—stretching to meet his. I needed him. I needed
him to save me—one more time. The tips of our fingers
brushed briefly, before the ground gave away completely.

"I call upon my brothers, give me your strength, give me your
guidance and forgive me for what I'm about to do. Take our
friends, our family, our kind, and give them the strength to
make it back safely. Doing now, what others could never do.
Lend us your strength!"
Gabriel's eyes shot open to the familiar voice in the wind..
Just then, Alex felt a burst of light within. It was from
Raphael. He could feel her now, filling his body with energy.
His lungs filled with clean air and strength. Then suddenly, a

familiar hand touched his shoulder gently. Alex turned to see the Archangel Chamuel. His eyes widened in amazement. "How?" He stuttered.

"I've blessed you with a special gift young one," Chamuel smiled.

Alex stared at him confused, just as another burst of energy filled their circular area. They held tightly to each other as another crack of thunder made the ground beneath them move. Then, Uriel and Michael were by their side.

The four Archangels surrounded Alex and Nathan, their very power within being controlled by a mere spirit guide now. Each of them lighting up fiercely with power from Raphael's sacrifice. Large white wings soon exploded from each of their backs as the heavenly power poured into the world of purgatory around them.

Michael looked at Chamuel, then over to Alex, his eyes glistening ice blue with energy. Uriel struggled from their grip that would not loosen. He was outraged at the thought of being held captive within purgatory, but between Alex's spell, Raphael's sacrifice and the help of Chamuel, they were all linked in there together—unable to move until the spell was completed.

"So you figured it out?!" Chamuel shouted over the wind to Alex. "You found the ultimate spell."

Alex smiled again as the white blinding light began to circulate around them all—slowly lifting them from the ground. Gabriel couldn't believe what was happening. He glanced to his right to see Chamuel smiling back.

"I thought you could use some help, brother." He said, looking around to the rest. "We must take care of each other—always." He said, loudly to them.

Gabriel looked back sadly, to where Raphael once stood.

"It was her decision, Gabriel. Do not mourn her—love her." Chamuel spoke, over the wind.

"This is forbidden!" Uriel's voice thundered. "Stop this, immediately!"

Michael watched on silently, still astonished by Alex's

knowledge and new found powers.

Chamuel shot Uriel a stern glance, then looked over to Alex who was barely holding on—but not from weakness, from great power!

"Take us home Alex, you have our strength!" Chamuel shouted once more.

Alex looked around at each of the Archangels, then nodded. He was surrounded by so much energy right now—more than he could ever dream of. He then looked to Nathan once again in his dream state.

"Hang on…" With his last breath, Alex summoned the rest of his energy from within alongside the energy from each Archangel and shot them all straight up into the blazing white light—through the purple sky—and far from any spirits and all that was purgatory.

When Michael opened his eyes, he was surrounded by warmth. Around him, lingered the glowing gold energy that glittered throughout the room.

"Take my hand, brother." Chamuel said, helping him slowly to his feet.

"You—" Michael began, but suddenly Uriel charged, slamming Chamuel back against the wall. Even in their weakened state, Uriel's strength was still immaculate. Immediately, the gold glitter that surrounded them disintegrated away as Uriel pinned his brother still.

"What were you thinking? You could have killed us all!" He shouted. "Taking us into purgatory? Letting that spirit guide tap into us? It was you all along—wasn't it? You've been helping them!"

"Of course. He's also been assisting Raphael. Isn't that right, brother?" Michael added. "Helping her redeem herself?"

Chamuel smiled as Uriel held him tightly against the wall.

"Chamuel, angel of love. I should have known." Michael smiled, slightly. He then looked at Uriel. "Let him speak," He commanded.

Uriel huffed, then released the Archangel. "At least Raphael is out of our hair now."

"She did it." Chamuel said, proudly. "She saved them all."

"True, a noble sacrifice." Michael agreed. "Putting herself on the line to give them all enough energy to survive. Quite remarkable, I'll admit." He paused. "She has earned her forgiveness. It will not go unnoticed."

Chamuel face softened.

"But you… What do we do with you?" Michael pondered, stepping closer. "Just because your power gives you the strength to connect Heaven and Earth within a human heart, does not mean you attach us into the equation. I'll give it to you, it was very smart of you to use Sophie and Alex as one, but still…"

"He gave me his guidance," Chamuel interrupted. "He wouldn't have done so if he didn't approve, correct?"

Uriel looked at Michael oddly, then shook his head in disbelief. "Unbelievable, why would He approve such actions? We were never told of any of this!"

Michael continued to stare into his brother's eyes.

"I will need some time to think about this. What you did was very dangerous—for us all."

Chamuel nodded, understanding completely.

"Even with His approval, I am still in charge here. So, until I decide, rest up brothers." Michael then rubbed his forehead, about to turn away from them. "But I wonder," he then said. "Where was Fate in this?"

"She retreated earlier." Chamuel replied.

"Retreated from battle?" Uriel huffed.

Chamuel nodded. "The moment Nathan ignited his powers."

"Well, perhaps Nathan has proven himself too then." Michael replied. "He did seem stronger, and not because of Raphael."

Both Uriel and Chamuel's eyes lit up, but only one of them in disbelief.

"I believe now," Michael spoke again, staring directly at Chamuel. "He is… the one."

A smile grew on Chamuel's face as Michael motioned to Uriel.

The Archangel snarled at Chamuel one last time before exiting the room after his brother.

Taking a seat on the white stone bench next to him, Chamuel sighed in relief. "Beautifully done young ones."

11
Far From Perfect

My eyes flickered as I awoke from my dream state. My head was pounding and I could feel the weight of someone against me. His scent was familiar, but mixed with the smell of dirt and smoke. I reached up and rubbed my nose. Suddenly, his body jolted—frightening me a bit. Nathan's glance shot straight up at me. Resting against his chest, he felt weaker then I remembered. I was scared, nervous, thankful and frozen all at the same time. I couldn't believe he was actually here. I could feel his chest rising beneath me.

"Soph?" He said, clearing his throat.

I felt his shaky hands slide up my back. I attempted to sit up with his guidance. Looking around the room, I quickly noticed we were alone. I only hoped it was back in the real world. It looked like the real world—*I think*. Alex's apartment was quiet and everything was in its place, but something still felt off. My eyes met his again.

"Sophie," He said.

His heart was racing, I could feel it. So was mine. We were unsure of what to do first. I wanted to hug him—*I think*. I wasn't too sure. His hands continued to shake as they raised to touch my face. He stopped just before my cheek, just as he did in my dream, surely waiting to see if I would pull from him. Then I felt his fingers lace through the magenta pink strand of hair to the side of my cheek. I gasped from the sight. I'd forgotten about it. He then smiled.

"I missed you—crazy girl."

I bit my lip, holding in my emotions as he pulled me in close. His arms held me tight, tighter than ever before. I felt his chin rest down on my head.

"I can't believe it. You did it." He said. "I love you so much. I'm so sorry—for everything. I never should have left you. I'm sorry for all that I've put you through."

There was too much happening and as much as I wanted to hear everything he was saying, I also wasn't ready for it. I couldn't process it—any of it. My mind shot to Ben, where was he? It wasn't like him to suddenly disappear after a treatment. He was always there when I woke up. Where was he? I felt myself push back from Nathan's grip.

"Nate," It took everything in me to hold it together—to not break down. "I'm... glad you're safe." It was all I could say. He smiled again. Then, just before he spoke, a voice startled us from behind.

"Nathan?"

We turned quickly to see Gabriel. He was worn and tired looking.

"You're here!" Nathan said, happily.

But the look in Gabriel's eyes made my stomach turn.

"Alex," I cried. Gabriel didn't respond.

My heart dropped immediately. I quickly pulled from Nathan's arms and jumped to my feet in a sudden burst of energy.

"He's in his room," Gabriel said as I raced by him.

Reaching the doorway, my hands shook in fear of what I might see when I entered the room. Slowly, I turned the knob.

The room was quiet and normal. There was no magic, no supernatural stuff lingering in the air—it was nothing but a plain old bedroom. Then I noticed the lifeless body lying in the bed.

"Alex?" I choked at the sight of him. "Alex? Are you okay?"

He didn't answer.

When I finally reached the bed, I carefully pulled down the gray blanket. There were cuts on his skin with blood seeping from them everywhere. His body was shredded to pieces. It was hardly a body at all. I sat down beside him, horrified by the sight. Carefully, I brushed the hair from his face.

"No," I cried, resting my head down against his. "Alex… You have to be okay."

Nathan stepped into the doorway, weakly. He too, couldn't believe the state Alex was in. Eventually, joining my side, he knelt down.

"He's not responding, Nate…" I said sadly, looking up at him. Nathan didn't speak.

"Didn't you hear me? He's not responding—like nothing, I can't hear him breathing!" I cried. "I can't hear him. He promised me. He said he'd come back. He said he knew what he was doing…"

"I know Soph," Nathan finally spoke.

"Alex!" I screamed, giving him a hard shove. "Alex, wake up!"

"Sophie," I felt Nathan's hand touch my arm. I quickly brushed it off and continued to push at my friend.

"Stop," Nathan begged, then grabbed onto my hands, releasing them from Alex's body.

"No! I promised Charlotte! I promised him! It's all my fault! I should have helped him sooner! I wasn't strong enough for him…"

Nathan quickly wrapped his arms around me and pulled me back towards him. I screamed and cried into his chest as Gabriel appeared beside us.

"It's not your fault," Nathan whispered.

He was wrong. It was totally my fault. I wasn't ready.

"He's right, none of this is your fault Sophie." Gabriel spoke. "We lost Raphael too, but we all knew what we were getting ourselves into. Sacrifices were made to free us all." He said, sadly.

I looked up at him in shock.

"What did you say?" I asked short of breath. "Raphael's gone?"

The Archangel nodded. "She sacrificed herself, to save us all."

The sickness in my stomach began to stir again. It wasn't fair. Like me, Raphael had managed to survive purgatory once and was finally pulling herself back together and now this? How had she ended this way?

"I won't let her sacrifice go in vein." Gabriel then said, stepping closer to Alex's body. "We will complete this. She would want us to." Carefully, he pulled the covers completely off of him as Nathan pulled me aside to give Gabriel room. He knelt down and hovered his hands over the pale, torn skin and what was left of his worn clothes. A white glow began to grow from beneath his palms, radiating across Alex's body. We watched as the blood and dirt from his cuts suddenly cleared away. Gabriel was attempting to heal him from all physical impurities. His light was blinding to Nathan and I, but felt amazing. The Archangel slowly made his way from head to toe, healing all that he could. We knew he couldn't heal his body completely, but it was better than nothing. Minutes later, the open wounds were gone, and the blinding light faded. As Gabriel backed away from the body, I could see the faint war scars still left on his bare skin. Even with the enhancement to the Archangel's power, it wasn't enough to fix the spirit guide. It wasn't enough to wake him.

"He isn't gone yet, do not lose hope." Gabriel said, quietly. "I've healed his body, but what's within… I cannot touch."

I looked up at him, confused.

"He's quite remarkable you know?" He spoke again, "Now it is his turn. We will have to see if he is strong enough to heal his own soul."

I glanced back at Alex as Gabriel exited the room. "He's still alive…"

Nathan released me and I rose to my feet. I couldn't look at him a second longer. I quickly raced out of the room and into the kitchen. I was going to do whatever I could to help Alex recover and I had no time to waste. Nathan soon followed.

"What can I do to help?" He asked.

I scrambled around the kitchen ignoring his words, nervous to speak to him at all. I pulled a pot from under the stove. Fumbling around, I dropped it on the way up to the counter. My hands were still shaky. I was doing my best to push the emotions back down. I had to. Alex needed me.

"Here," Nathan said, picking it up. "Go to Alex, I will make him something to eat."

I stared at him with no expression, then turned and hurried off. I wasn't prepared to be here alone with Nathan—not right now. Everything inside of me was twisting from just his presence alone. I really needed Ben's words of encouragement right now or at least another body here so it wasn't so awkward.

I stopped at the bathroom to grab some vitamin lotion and a few other things from under the bathroom sink. I then hurried back into the room for Alex. Gabriel had cleaned up his wounds, but there were still scars left on his body. Carefully, I took the small bottle of vitamin lotion and rubbed it on every single scar, hoping it would help him heal. He didn't flinch, not one bit at the touch of my fingers. He couldn't feel me at all. I then quickly cleaned his bedroom up and placed a clean blanket over him. Searching through his stuff, I had hoped to find something—anything that could help us more—to help him more. There were many objects and gadgets, but nothing I could really use. Alex handled powerful stuff, nothing I could ever understand or even handle. Then I came across a small candle of Charlotte's in the closet. We had bought it long ago down on Granville Island. The smell of Nag Champa soon filled the room as I lit it up and placed it on the night stand next to Alex's bed. The lady in the store said this scent was good for cleansing a room and clearing the mind. I only hoped the scent would do just that for him. I needed something to trigger his mind, to awaken his spirit again.

Twenty minutes later, I was still sitting on the floor beside his lifeless body. My knee bumped something under the bed, I reached under to find a small book and opened it.

The pages were filled notes. The stuff he was studying was outrageous and seemed very dangerous. Every spell, every piece of magic written in here seemed to come with a price. My mind shot to the Archangels and what they would do to him if he ever came to. What would his punishment be? He had truly broken every law in the angel world. He was doomed for sure. I wish I knew more about what happened in purgatory. How had he gotten enough energy to pull them all out? Was it truly from my connection to Nathan alone? It seemed too simple and what about Raphael? I wanted to know more. There had to be more to this. I continued to flip through a few more pages of Alex's messy notes. He seemed to use a lot of energy stones. The stones represented the angel studies and natural life on earth, while the spells were more of the dark arts. Together, they were most powerful and unknown as to how much magic they could actually generate. There were locater spells, healing spells and of course protection spells that were always needed. For a moment, I pondered to myself. Maybe I could learn some of this? Maybe some of this could be of help in our situation right now? If I connected with the pink stone that hung around my neck, maybe my energy would be much stronger. Maybe it could help us. The Archangels did say that I had some hidden power still to learn about. Maybe I just had to find other ways to tap into it. But would Ben approve of this? Would the Archangels punish me if they found out? I dropped the book, frustrated. Resting my chin down on the mattress, I stared at Alex.

"We need you." I whispered. "You have to make it through this. Tell me what to do Alex, please."

Just then, Nathan appeared.

"How's he doing?" He asked, carrying a tray with a bottle of water and bowl of soup. He placed it down on the nightstand beside the bed. I didn't answer. I didn't even look at him.

"Here, let's feed him something." He said, twisting the cap off of a bottle of water.

"I'll do it." I said, holding my hand out for the bottle.

Nathan looked at me, then smiled sadly, handing it over.

I quickly adverted my eyes to Alex again. I could feel his gaze
still on me. It felt horrible, but I couldn't deal with him right
now. I carefully turned him over in the bed, adjusting his head
on the pillow.
"I'll let you know if we need anything else," I said.
Nathan quickly got the hint. He then headed over to Alex's
closet and snagged a few clean clothes.
"Okay, I'll leave you two be. I'm going to shower up."
Opening Alex's mouth just a bit, I poured a little water down
his throat. Not too much, just enough to keep him hydrated.
When the soup cooled, I attempted to feed it to him. But it was
too hard for him to get down. His body was rejecting it. I had
to think of another way to get some substance into his system.
I really needed Ben right now. He always had an answer for
everything.

When Nathan was done showering, he threw on a pair of
jeans and a gray shirt that had three quarter sleeves. He
was thankful that Alex and he were the same size. He then
looked through the bathroom cupboards until he found
some mouthwash. He quickly took a swag of it and swished
it around his mouth. It felt amazing to shower again and
thankfully the smell and taste of purgatory was almost gone.
He still felt weak and his nerves were a little on ends, but
other than that, he was in one piece—a lot better than he
thought he would be. He couldn't believe he was back in
the real world. He thought for a moment as the mouthwash
continued to swirl around his mouth. He really didn't have
a plan to get back in the first place. What was he thinking
acting on his emotions like that? What if he had ended up
getting stuck there—permanently? Could he really handle it—
forever? Never seeing Sophie, ever again. It was stupid of him
to have gone in there. He understood that now. But sadly, it
was too late. Many others had already paid for his actions.
After spitting the mouth wash into the sink, Nathan glanced up
into the mirror. His hand traced his chin where stubble began
to grow. His skin felt rough and nothing like it used to feel as

a guardian. Mixed emotions raced through him as he continued
to stare. He felt horrible for not being able to help Serena. He
felt horrible for putting Sophie through all of this and most of
all, he felt horrible for being so selfish. He had to let go of his
past—of Serena, and truly move on. He needed to concentrate
on the moment and making things right. He wanted Sophie,
and to keep her, would mean that she would need one hundred
percent of his attention here in the real world. He only hoped
that she would forgive him. They hadn't had a chance to talk
about everything yet. It was awkward between them right now.
But he was willing to wait. His fingers laced through his hair,
tossing it off to the side.
"You're back with her now, don't mess it up." He said to
himself, then flicked off the light before exiting the room.

In the kitchen, Nathan sat on his own, eating a small snack
he had prepared. He hadn't eaten a full meal in what felt like
forever, so snacking was all his stomach could handle right
now. He also drank a few tall glasses of clean water, trying
to hydrate his body back to a normal state. His condition was
much better then Sophie's was after returning from purgatory.
He wondered if it had anything to do with the changes he was
experiencing. Was this new power helping him? Helping his
body grow stronger and if so, how much would it change? Was
he still going to be human?
"Nathan," Gabriel said, appearing behind him.
Startled for only a second, Nathan turned to the Archangel.
"How are you?"
"I'm fine." He responded.
"We need to talk," Gabriel then glanced down the hallway.
"But not here."
Nathan looked at him nervously, "But what if she—"
"She will be fine. It won't take long." Gabriel urged.
Nathan nodded, then followed the Archangel out the door.

As they walked through the nearby park, Nathan was flooded
with memories. The cool Vancouver air blew strongly around

them. When they reached a bench, Gabriel motioned for Nathan to join him.

"Alex is very damaged Nathan and I'm unsure if he will return to us." He said first. Nathan didn't respond. "We've lost Raphael and Charlotte is still missing. We were too careless in our choices." He said. "I need you to understand how important it is for you to inhabit the powers within. Your subconsciousness is holding you back."

"What are you talking about?" Nathan snapped from his silent state. "You saw me in there! I had the energy strong. I used it to connect with Alex and get to Sophie. I was even protecting myself when Alex went down. Did you miss that? What am I not doing?"

"Do not let your feelings for Sophie get you worked up right now, we need to discuss this calmly."

"I'm not! What do you want from me, Gabriel? I just got back and she won't even look at me. I'm back to how she was when she first came back from purgatory." He yelled, getting up from the bench.

"Calm down Nathan, you knew it was going to be tough. I told you that when we left. You knew what you might come back to,"

"I know! I just thought that… in our dream, she said that she—"

"That she had forgiven you?" Gabriel interrupted. Nathan stared back at him.

"What are you saying? She didn't mean it?"

"I'm saying, now that she is safe, she needs time to process. Do not push her. I warn you, whatever made her agree to helping Alex—to helping us, is a miracle on its own." Gabriel said, rising to his feet. "But know this, she did agree. I truly believe she still loves you, Nathan. But you must take this slow."

Nathan's face softened, "What if we don't have enough time for slow, Gabriel? Who knows what will happen tomorrow. We could be killed."

"It could happen, yes. But nothing you do or say will change

what is between you two right now. You have to let it fix
itself. Just be there for her—protect her. Become what you are
meant to be." Gabriel reached his hand out to touch Nathan's
shoulder, but he quickly stepped back.
"That's what this is all about, isn't it? You just need me to
become what you want. You don't even care about what I'm
feeling or what Sophie needs, do you? Don't you remember
what we agreed to in purgatory?"
"Of course, but what you don't understand is how your power
can help you."
"Help me? How could this help me?!" Nathan harped.
"We need to get rid of Serena and Anna for good. This will
make things better for us all. But none of us can do it without
your help, Nathan. Think about it. Even Fate ran at the site of
your energy—she fears it!" Gabriel explained.
Nathan began to pace in frustration, "I need to be alone.
Please, give me some time to think." He said, leaving the
Archangel behind.

The knock at the door startled me. I got up from the bed
and slowly made my way to the front door. Just as I peeked
through the hole, I heard him speak.
"Soph, it's me, Ben. Let me in!" He sounded desperate.
I quickly opened the door.
"Hey, how are you doing?" He asked, stepping in and hugging
me immediately. I wrapped my arms around him, thankful for
his embrace.
"Where did you go, Ben? What happened to you?" I said,
holding him tight.
"I'm sorry, I just ran out to get some stuff while you rested. I
knew you weren't alone." He replied, looking down at me.
His hands traced my face. "How are you feeling? The
treatment seemed to knock you right out this time."
I looked up at him, confused. Why would he leave me? I
needed him, he had to know that. My eyes began to water. I
couldn't hold it in anymore.

"Ben, it's Alex… He's back and he's not…" I broke down and cried into his chest.

"It's okay, I'm here." He said, holding me tight. "Please, take me to him." He insisted.

I nodded, then sadly lead him down the hallway.

When Ben stepped inside the room, a cold sensation trickled down his spine. "There's something in here…"

"What?" I asked nervously, grabbing onto his arm.

"I can feel it. He brought something back with him. He must have used a lot of magic—and dark magic at that."

Ben then backed out of the room quickly for a moment, pulling me along with him.

"What are you doing?" I asked, worried about leaving Alex in there.

Ben quietly reached into his bag and pulled out a small pouch of what looked like dried leaves tied together with twine. He then reached in for another item—a lighter.

"We have to protect ourselves first. This is white sage. It will force the negative energy away from us while we are in there." He then lit the leaves on fire, letting it burn for a moment, and then blew it out. The remaining smoke lingered around us. He then guided me in front of him. He began to circulate my entire body with the smoke from head to toe. Then did the same to himself.

"What's in the room Ben?" I asked, again.

"I can feel it. It's very heavy." He repeated, tracing the doorway with the sage before stepping back into the room again.

I followed close behind, holding tight to the back of his shirt. Ben made his way over to Alex on the bed.

He knelt down in front to grab his wrist and check for a pulse.

"He's barely alive," He said, worried. "Although, it looks as if his body is healing quite nicely." He pondered some more, looking him over. "Somebody has healed his wounds…."

"Exterior only," I added.

He then placed his bag down beside the bed and began to

search through it. He pulled out a small little stone, green in colour.

"What's that?" I asked as he stood up and held out his hand to me.

"Come here, I need your help." He said, kindly.

Slowly, I took his hand and joined his side. He held the green stone out in front of me. "This is a Green Kyanite stone. Before we can attempt to heal him, we need to clear the energy. This stone is the only one we can use. Do you know why?"

I shook my head no.

"Because this stone will not accumulate any negative energy— ever. It never needs cleansing, no matter where you take it. And, it can never be tainted. It is that pure and true." He spoke, placing my hand over it.

I flinched a bit at the touch. "It's cold," I said, smiling back at him.

"It is always cold, like the wind. It keeps evil away."

"Amazing," I replied, hovering my hand over it more.

"Not only will Kyanite clear the chakras... It will also bridge any energy gaps that may have been created by accidents or trauma in the past—ones that have still not been healed. For Alex, it's recent, but should work just the same."

"Are you using it for his heart chakra, like mine? To help him heal?"

"Sort of, but what Alex needs is much more intense. You see, spirit guides don't have a heart."

I looked at him oddly. Alex didn't have a heart?

"But their soul is just as strong—if not stronger than a real heart. Unfortunately, his soul took a horrible beating in battle—his body as well. But what happened to his body and soul are two separate things. They aren't connected anymore, Soph."

"What do you mean?"

"His soul is so broken that it won't connect back to the body. And the body took such a hit from the dark arts, it too has given up on him. If the soul is not connected to the body, it cannot encourage it to heal which gives him no chance. If they don't connect soon, we risk losing him forever." He said, sadly.

Lose Alex—forever? I began to doubt if Alex could really make it through this. That was a lot for him to take on in such a weakened state.

"We need to connect his thymus chakra, back to the rest."

"Thymus chakra?" I repeated, choking back my tears.

"The thymus chakra is the seat of the soul, it's also the bridge between your emotions and your intellect. Working closely with the heart, it creates a connection between your soul body and physical body. This chakra is associated with the thymus gland, one of the earliest glands that develop in the fetus while in the womb. It's also related to the immune system and has within it, the pattern for your DNA and your karmic design for this lifetime. This chakras location aids communication too— the spoken word resonates from here, creating a powerful healing effect. Do you follow?"

"Sort of, that's a lot of information." I replied. "So, even though Alex doesn't have a heart, you still think this will work?"

"I'm hoping, it's worth a shot—right? Miracles happen all the time. I mean, you came back." He smiled.

I couldn't help but smile at Ben's moving words, but my smile soon faded. "Ben," I hesitated with my next question.

"Yes?"

"What did Alex see? Or, what did he do… that broke his soul this badly? Was it because I told him that Fate took Charlotte?" I asked, feeling a little guilty.

"No, and calm yourself Sophie." He quickly, replied. "I need your energy contained to do this. I'm sure it worried Alex, but he must have seen something far worse than he could of handled at that time to have this effect. We'll never know, we just need to help him. Okay?" Ben then placed his hand on my shoulder. The heat from his palm slowed my breath and calmed me instantly.

"What can I do?" I asked.

"I just need your heart." He smiled.

I looked at him oddly as he placed the green stone down on Alex's chest. He then pulled me closer to them. With his right hand over the green stone, his left hand reached out for the pink stone that hung from my neck.

"Remain still. Think positive thoughts of Alex. We need to cleanse his body."

I did as he asked without question. Closing my eyes, I began to think of my friend. I thought of the first time I met him. When he was on set with Matt in one of Charlotte's photo shoots. I remember speaking with him for the first time. I remember us talking about hating to hike. Mostly, I remember him jumping into purgatory and dragging me from the spirits within. He was the only person I wanted to see right now— more than anything. I wanted him to be okay. Alex had done nothing but care for me since I met him. Even when I was a total jerk to him and Charlotte, he was still there for me.

My eyes began to water as I felt the pink energy radiate faintly from my chest. I opened my eyes to his lifeless body on the bed. The green stone was glowing brightly on top of him now. The energy moved like water from his chest up to the top of his head, then melted over him all the way down to the tips of his toes—cleansing his body of all negative energy from purgatory. The green glow was very warm and cool at the same time.

"There is a lot of dark energy in there, can you feel it?" Ben asked quietly, looking up at me.

I nodded.

"The warmer it gets, the more it's fighting the negativity."

I was starting to feel a little light headed. I wiped my head from the sweat that began to dip down my face.

"Hang in there, it's almost done." Ben insisted, moving his grip from my stone, to hold my hand.

"It's pretty hot Ben, it's getting hard to breathe." I said, starting to sway a bit.

"Almost done,"

Just then, we heard the front door open.

"Soph?" Nathan called out.

I glanced to the doorway, only to see him step into it for a split second before I collapsed.

   It felt like I was out for quite a while when I heard him call out to me.

"Sophie!" He shouted. "Open your eyes!"

I had heard those words before, long ago, but I couldn't remember when. My vision blurred in and out as I desperately tried to clear my confused mind.

"Come on, Soph. Wake up. Please!"

I blinked a few more times before a shape came into focus.

"She will be fine. She just needs to rest."

I recognized that voice immediately. When my vision finally came into focus, I was in Nathan's arms.

"Sophie? Thank god." He cried, pulling me in close.

I began to sweat in his embrace. I needed air. I felt warm—too warm. "Ben?" I said, weakly.

Nathan glanced up at the young man as he approached.

"Who the hell are you anyways?" Nathan snapped, pulling me back as Ben reached for my hand. I immediately reached back for his. Ben paused.

"It's nice to finally meet you, Nathan. I've heard a lot about you."

"From who? Answer me quick, before I—"

"Nathan, calm down. I will explain everything."

Suddenly, the heat from Nathan's body began to burn against me. "You'll tell me everything or I'll—"

"Let me go," I cried in pain.

Ben quickly reached for my hand, "She's burning up. You must let her go. Your body is—"

Nathan immediately released me.

"Sophie, I—"

●●●

Adjusting himself in the kitchen chair, Ben finally spoke. "As I said, it's nice to finally meet you. Sophie has mentioned you many times." He said, politely.

"Who are you? I won't ask again," Nathan repeated, impatiently.

"Nathan, there's no need to get defensive. I'm a friend of Sophie's, so I'm a friend of yours."

Nathan sat silent—studying him.

"Alright, have it your way. I'm Ben."

"Where did you meet her?" Nathan questioned.

"On set, we've been on set together for the past little bit."

"You're an actor? Who do you play?"

"Actually, I'm her on-screen boyfriend."

"On-screen boyfriend, huh?" Nathan repeated, not impressed.

"Why are you here? This is pretty personal stuff happening. Nothing you need to involve yourself in."

His jealous tone was more than obvious, but Ben didn't seem to mind.

"She needed me, and no one else was here for her. I thought I could be of some help."

"She has friends… and me."

"True, but where were they, or you recently when she's been crying her eyes out?"

Nathan didn't answer.

"She's in a very fragile state, you know?"

Nathan huffed at him.

"But there is a beauty inside of her, something that has never been harnessed. I want to show her the way. She needs to believe in herself. She needs someone by her side to encourage her and keep her moving forward."

"Well thank you for worrying, but you can go. Like I said, I'm here now. I'm her real-life boyfriend and—"

"Boyfriend? Funny… she never spoke of you that way. What I heard is that you abandoned her—left her—broke her heart,"

"You don't know anything about me!" Nathan snapped, getting up from the table. "So don't go assuming things until you know the entire story! I love her more than anything in this

entire world and as far as I'm concerned, we are still together.
I had to do what I did and Sophie just doesn't understand
that yet. She didn't think I would come back to her, but I'm
here—standing right here and I'll wait as long as I need to
get her back. So why don't you back off and mind your own
business!"
Ben smiled slightly. "Good. That's what I wanted to hear." He
then stood up from the chair.
Nathan paused, a little thrown by his words.
"But I'm not going anywhere, she needs me too." He then
said. "I promised her I wouldn't leave, so I'm not going to.
If you want her, then you'll have to fight for her and trust
me, it won't be easy." Ben then held out his hand for Nathan.
Lingering in the air for a second, his hand waited for Nathan's
exchange, hoping for a friendly shake.
Slowly, Nathan took a step closer. He was about an inch taller
than Ben, but unfortunately much thinner due to purgatory. He
grabbed Ben's hand tight and shook it.
"You have no idea what I've been through for her or what
we've been through together. Nothing will scare me off." He
said, confidently.
Ben smiled again, then pulled his hand away. Heading to the
front door, he stopped once to look back at Nathan.
"Talk with her, there is lots to be said still."

12
A New Strategy

Pacing around the room annoyed, Fate stopped in front of Charlotte's lifeless body.

"Your boyfriend got lucky back there." With a swift kick to the gut Fate spoke again. "You listening, girl?"

Charlotte didn't move. Fate knelt down and flicked a strand of hair from her pale face.

"Looks like I might have been a little too rough on you. Hey, wake up!" She shouted a little louder this time.

A subtle moan and a slight twitch of the hand gave Fate the sign that the human was still alive. Pacing around the room again, Fate continued to talk to herself. Another painful moan came from the floor behind her.

"Alex…" The blood from Charlotte's mouth dripped down onto her dirty hands as she attempted to open her eyes.

"I wouldn't even bother, Blondie," Fate responded. "He's not going to save you anytime soon."

Staring down at her, Fate crossed her arms sadly.

"Listen, I gotta be honest with you, the toll your BF took from purgatory will most likely be the end of him. Totally sucks, I know…"

Charlotte's eyes began to water. She swallowed hard, trying to

form words as her eyes followed Fate's wandering feet.
"That Nathan… What to do with him?" She pondered aloud,
bringing her attention back to her own thoughts. "I need a
new strategy. He and the Archangels are playing my game too
well. But on the other hand, now that Alex is out of the way…
perhaps—no. He still has Gabriel. Ooh that Gabriel makes me
mad," She huffed. "What I need is something to distract them
from advancing any further."
"No," Charlotte finally managed to get out.
Fate paused and looked over her shoulder.
"Don't worry, you'll have a part in this. Nathan still cares for
you, even if your boyfriend gone." She taunted.
Charlotte's head dropped into her hands, unsure if what Fate
was saying was actually true. Quietly, she began to cry.
Fate slowly walked over and knelt down again. Gripping her
thin fingers into Charlotte's long hair, she pulled her head up
from her hands.
"Stop crying, it's annoying." She demanded. "Don't worry,
the end is coming soon." She then released her and stood up.
"Stay here, I'll be back for you."

.

"You had your chance! I lined it up perfectly for you. I
practically gave you an opening to kill her!" Anna screamed,
pacing around the cave.
Stressed, Serena snapped back quickly, "I know! But it's
Sophie! I'm so confused, when did she gain powers? I don't
know what happened—"
"Who cares where she got them from," Anna hollered, ripping
Serena to her feet. "You should have been stronger. You can't
let your feelings take over. They only create an opening for
you to be attacked. Do you want Nathan back or not?!"
"Of course!" Serena shouted, trying to pull her arm free, but
Anna was much too strong.
"Then pull yourself together!" She hollered, pushing Serena
back down to the ground.
"Girls, girls, there's no need to fight." A sudden voice said

from behind.

Anna quickly spun around.

"Relax." Fate said, "I'm not here for that. Believe it or not, I'm actually here to lend a hand."

"Why?" Anna asked, suspiciously.

"Because I'm feeling generous today." Fate smiled. "You know, I could've had you killed a long time ago if I wanted."

"Then why didn't you?" Anna spoke again.

"Because you... I like." Fate smiled. "You make things interesting. You're still annoying, but—entertaining to say the least." Fate then turned and held out her hand to Serena

"So, you're trying to get Nathan back are you? You realize he's alive and you're, well—dead. Right?"

Serena nodded slowly, unsure of Fate's change of heart and intentions. She stared for a moment, then finally took hold of the pale thin hand.

"So how do you expect to achieve this goal of yours?" Fate asked, pulling Serena to her feet. Before she could answer, Fate spoke again."I have an idea, I could help you bring him to your side." The girls stood silently, caught off guard by the offer. "But on one condition," Fate paused again.

Serena looked at Anna, worried.

"Well... don't you want to know what that is?" Fate asked, getting impatient with them. "Speak!" She demanded.

"What are you getting at?" Anna finally said.

"I will help Serena get Nathan back to the side he should have stayed on only if... you swear to pass on with him. Then the two of you will be together forever—and out of my hair."

"Where will we pass on to?" Serena questioned, nervously. "I don't want to be stuck here anymore, I want to be—"

"Yes, yes, I know. I will make sure that you and your precious Nathan go up to heaven together, forever."

"You can do that?"

"Of course I can. The angels don't control me. If I tell them so, it will happen. So, do we have a deal?"

Serena looked at Anna. It seemed like a pretty solid deal, but there was no way that it could be that easy—not with Fate.

"And don't worry Anna, I haven't forgotten about you either."
Anna's eyes tightened. "My plan is to release you both—fully,
back into the real world. Right now." Fate waited for their
reaction. "You will have full power to do as you please to get
your boys back—or in your case Anna— kill Gabriel—if you
wish. But, if you kill him, you die with him. It's only fair."
Anna stared at Fate. "Deal." She agreed, without hesitation.
Shocked by Anna's harsh words, Serena stepped towards them.
"But I thought you—"
"Mind your own business. Just worry about your precious
Nathan. My plans for Gabriel are my own. We accept your
offer, Fate." Anna said, confidently.
"But you love him, don't you?" Serena asked, still confused.
"Be quiet." Anna snapped.
"Alright, then it's settled." Fate smiled. "Oh, and I almost
forgot, one last thing…"
Anna's eyes widened, waiting for that last bit of malicious
detail Fate would have to offer.
"Alex may have been the hero pulling everyone out of
purgatory, but he also messed up,"
Everyone was silent.
"He made a tear in your world here," Fate explained. "There's
an opening. I'm surprised you haven't noticed."
Fate then turned from them.
"I'll point you towards it before I go, and feel free to take any
'thing' with you. If you know what I mean. It may help you on
your quest."
Anna's eyes widened with excitement from Fate's words.
"I knew that would please you." Fate stepped to the edge of
the cave. "I want to give you one last gift…" She smiled,
before turning back to them. "The gift of prayer."
The girls stared at her, confused.
"Not that kind of prayer," She chuckled, staring at their faces.
"The gift of listening in on one's prayers. Trust me, it's a lot
of fun."
"And why would we want to listen to anyone's prayers?" Anna
questioned.

"Because people are at their weakest when they pray. They open themselves up and become vulnerable to the outside world. Human energy in desperate times is quite powerful. It would be a shame if the wrong things were to listen in," She snickered. "Just a thought. Use it how you may."
With a snap of her perfectly painted finger nails, Fate jolted the girls with a burst of energy. They gasped for air, then began to breathe much different than before.
"And Serena… Sophie just about gave up back there. You almost had her. Why don't you bring her a few souvenirs from her pleasant time over here? You know, to really make her feel at home."
A smile grew on Serena's face as Fate turned from them again. "The opening is at the end of the dirt road below. Call to them, you will need as many as you can get." Fate looked over her shoulder once more. "Don't say I never gave you anything," She winked, then vanished from sight.
Anna raced to the edge of the cave, Serena quickly by her side. Below a dirt road began to manifest leading straight into the forest of dead trees.
"Can we really trust her?" Serena asked.
"Who cares, this is exactly what we need to make our move. Let's go."

A few days passed with no word from Gabriel. Nathan continued to tend to Alex's lifeless body and now Sophie's as well. She hadn't woken from Ben's last treatment on Alex. He quickly became annoyed with Ben showing up every day trying to care for her—and whatever it was he was doing to Alex in his room, clearly wasn't working. Nothing was working. They were wasting time. They had to come up with another plan before someone else did. Nathan also worried for Charlotte and only hoped that she was still alive. He needed Alex to wake up, he needed his help. Another thought leaking into Nathan's mind was Fate. She hadn't shown herself since purgatory and it was making him nervous as to what she might be up to. Even more, what were the Archangels up to? Everything was too quiet—too still. It was affecting his sleep at night.

Nathan sat on the couch quietly with Sophie's head rested in his lap flicking through the channels on the television. It felt too real—too normal. Something he wished for, something he longed for—a normal life with her. The life they almost had, but so much had happened between them recently and a lot had changed. He needed to get things back to normal as fast as possible in fear of losing her. He glanced down at her again, she seemed peaceful for the moment. At least she was here with him. He didn't care what kind of person she was now or how all of this might have changed her. He still wanted her—all of her. No matter what.

As she continued to sleep, he brushed his fingers through her course hair that used to be silky straight. She was definitely different. A drastic change had happened since he left. Not only in her looks, but her personality too. The energy he once felt from her as a guardian was completely gone now and in its place, something new—something dark. This change was much different than her last, when she came out of purgatory. He thought that was bad, but this was different. He could still feel the darkness lingering, but something new was stirring in her now. Something he didn't recognize. When he left her months ago, she was damaged and angry. Something Gabriel warned him about but now, she was indescribable and a little frightening. Not to look at but to be around. Only because she was too quiet, too introverted for Nathan's liking. She used to confide in him all the time, now she ignored him and barely made eye contact. He couldn't read her, not even if he tried. This scared him the most. That one power he still had from being a guardian was something he held special in his heart. He liked that he had the power to check-in on her if needed. He liked that he could read anyone if needed. It was a gift that was helping him settle easier into this new life, but it was gone now. At least for Sophie. Why was it gone? Had purgatory disconnected them somehow? As he continued to flick through the channels, he eventually stopped at the sound of a worried news broadcaster. The woman spoke about power outages happening throughout the city and not only around the city of Vancouver—across the world. As he continued to listen, the broadcaster spoke of adults passing in their sleep and children going on about constant nightmares. About horrible dreams they had about their parents right before they died. Nathan turned up the sound a bit, then looked down at Sophie once again. It didn't seem to bother her. He listened carefully as the news report continued. The stories only got worse. It was something out of a horror story. The videos on screen showed children attempting to explain these horrifying nightmares and their lack of sleep. It reminded him of Sophie years ago—when she too suffered from nightmares— nightmares that turned out to be Serena. The horrified look in Sophie's eyes after returning from purgatory was the exact look these children shared now. But why were people passing in their sleep? And even more unbelievable was the numbers. There were hundreds passing, randomly, in no sort of order or pattern! None of it made sense. There was no spread of disease or threat by terrorist happening right now, so what could it be? He wondered what the Archangels thought of this. Did they know, where they watching as well? Nathan's thoughts stopped abruptly. Then carefully, he slid out from under Sophie, careful not to wake her, then began to pace around the room in thought. We wondered if... They were back. He didn't want to believe it, but... Just then, Ben entered the apartment. "You!" Nathan said, turning to him immediately. "What have you been up to?"

Ben walked casually into the living room, a little surprised by Nathan's reaction to him today.

"I'm sorry, I'm not sure what you're talking about?" He responded, politely. "I'm here for their daily treatments, you know that." He then headed straight for Sophie.

Nathan quickly placed himself between them.

"Don't touch her." He warned. "I want to know exactly what you're doing in there with Alex!" He demanded. "Are you practicing some sort of dark magic?"

"Dark magic?" Ben laughed. "I don't do that stuff, I'm not a wizard, you know?"

"Don't mock me, you know what I'm talking about. I don't trust you one bit…" Nathan shoved him back, then pointed to the television. "What do you know about this? There's too much crazy shit happening around here and I feel like you might know exactly what's going on, now talk!" He hollered. Ben listened for a moment to the broadcast then sighed.

"It's horrible isn't it?"

"You think this is funny?" Nathan spoke again, raising his voice.

"Definitely not, it's quite alarming actually." Ben answered with his hands in the air. "That's why I'm trying to heal Alex as quickly as possible. We might need him."

"What are you talking about? What's happening out there?"

"Whatever it is that's killing all of those innocent people, isn't human. I believe they come in the night—"

"Spit it out already! What are you saying? That it's some sort of Boogeyman we're dealing with?" Nathan pushed, playing a little dumb. He needed to know how much Ben knew.

"Actually, I think you know exactly what this could be. I don't know why you're waiting for me to confirm. You're a smart guy Nathan." Ben replied with a straight face.

Nathan ran his hands through his hair, worried why Gabriel and the rest of the Archangels didn't catch this? How did this guy know more than the Archangels? What were they doing up there and more importantly, why was this Ben guy so familiar with supernatural stuff? Is it possible that he could know about Serena, or Anna for that matter? But how?! Nathan knew very well that there were only three possibilities of who would be causing these deaths, but he couldn't say it yet. He hoped for some miracle that she might not be involved.

"How do you know all of this? I mean, since you don't practice magic, right? How did you—"

"Nathan, everything you are thinking, is wrong." Ben began, cutting him off.

"You have no idea what I'm thinking." Nathan snapped again. Ben shook his head then stepped around him towards Sophie. "When will you just accept that I'm here to help? Stop asking so many questions when you know the answers already. I hold no threat to you or your friends. You must learn to have faith in people. Now please, calm yourself and let me check on her."

Quietly, Nathan took a step back, studying him again. Ben's tone was changing. It didn't sound so human anymore. Ben carefully knelt down by the couch and touched Sophie's forehead gently. Her skin was still warm. His left hand then slowly hovered over her pink stone lying directly in the middle of her chest.

"Watch your hands, buddy." Nathan warned.

Ben smiled to himself, then continued to concentrate.

"Sophie," he whispered. "Wakeup, it's time. We need you back here," Suddenly, warm air filled the room and a pink haze began to radiate from Sophie's chest.

"What are you doing?" Nathan asked, nervously.

Ben didn't answer.

"Sophie, come back to me. You are healed." He then leaned in and kissed her on the forehead. Nathan quickly reached for the back of Ben's shirt and pulled him to his feet.

"What do you think you're doing?!"

Before Ben could reply, they heard my voice.

"Ben?" My throat was dry.

Nathan quickly released him, shoved him aside and stepped towards me. I felt like I over slept. My head was heavy and dizzy feeling as I tried to sit up.

"It's so warm in here," I complained, blinking a few times, trying to regain focus.

Ben stepped past Nathan and placed his hand against my forehead. "You're burning up from the treatment, don't worry it will pass soon." He then pulled my long sleeved shirt up from my waist. Carefully, he lifted it over my head and tossed it to the floor. "This should help a bit," He said, rubbing my back.

I was sweating. The tank top I had on underneath the long sleeved shirt was drenched. I glanced up at Nathan. His eyes were tight. He didn't like this—any of this. I watched his hand clench into a fist below. He took a deep breath, then released it.

"Soph?' He finally spoke, "How you feeling?"

Nathan motioned for Ben to move aside. As Ben got up I quickly grabbed his arm.

"Don't leave…" I said, nervously. I couldn't look at Nathan. I didn't mean to ignore him, I was just more worried about Ben. I needed him here.

"I'm not going anywhere," he replied quickly. "I'm just going to get you a drink. You need to hydrate yourself and I need to check on Alex." He said, with a smile. "I'll be right back." He then headed into the kitchen to grab a glass of water.

Nathan stood silent for a moment, still waiting for a response from me. Then slowly, he sat down next to me on the couch. Ben returned moments later and placed a cold glass of water on the side table, then headed off to check on Alex.

"Are you alright? You scared me," Nathan spoke quietly. His hand touched mine. "Sophie, please. Talk to me. It's killing—"

"I'm fine." I replied, sharply. "How is Alex?"

Nathan paused, hurt again. "No change,"

I still didn't look at him. I could barely stand that he was touching my hand. It hurt, everything hurt. His touch, his smell, his presence. He hurt me by just being here.

"Are we ever going to talk about us?" He finally said.

No. I didn't want to talk about us at all, because I didn't know what I thought yet. I didn't know what was happening around us or to the rest of my friends. I needed to save them still. I needed more time to figure out what I felt about him and what I wanted in life now. It was too much for me to think about right now and I didn't want anyone bugging me about it either. The pressure was too much. I felt the emotions rushing inside of me. They were getting out of control again. My eyes began to fill with tears. I hadn't even noticed until one slipped down my face. I quickly wiped it away. I didn't want his pity.

I could feel him pitying me without even looking at him.

"I'm so sorry, Soph—for everything. But I'm here now like I promised, and I still love—"

"I don't." I interrupted.

I didn't mean to say it. Not like that—at least *I don't think.* It just came out. He quickly got up from the couch. My heart started to race as my eyes finally met his. I watched his chest rise and fall as his breathing picked up.

"Sophie..." He said, looking down at me. "You don't mean that, do you? I know you're hurt and, I know I broke your trust but... what do I have to do to get you to trust me again?" He asked, clearly upset. "I'll do anything Soph, we've been through too much. I'll do whatever you want..."

I still didn't answer. His eyes remained on mine, waiting for me to say something.

Space. I hear myself say in my mind.

He swallowed hard, still waiting, still thinking of what he should say next. I didn't want to talk about this, about us. Not right now.

"Are you really saying that you don't... love me, anymore?"

I sat silent again, my eyes shifted to the ground in shame. I was really hurting him—on purpose again. I could feel it.

"You can't be serious!" He then said. His tone changed quickly. "Think of everything we've been through!"

I kept my eyes to the ground as his anger began to build.

"We deserve our happiness. We deserve to be together Soph, just as Gabriel said! You can't honestly say that suddenly all of your feelings are now gone for me? I can't believe that. I won't! What we have is so huge, so powerful, so rare!"

I still didn't look at him. *Please stop.*

"Sophie look at me! I deserve that!" He shouted.

Slowly, I raised my head. Trying my best to hold back the tears and emotions swelling within.

"Tell me to my face that you don't love me..."

I could see the tears building in the corner of his eyes. It broke my heart. Nathan never cried.

"You can't, can you?!" He went on.

I swallowed hard again, the pressure was eating me up inside.
He then knelt down in front of me and gripped my shoulders,
forcing me to face him completely.
"Go on Sophie, tell me you don't love me!" He said, giving
me a shake. My body was numb in his hands. I felt the tears
staining my cheeks as his grip tightened. I didn't even care
that his grip on me was beginning to hurt. I welcomed it. I
welcomed anything other than this conversation we were
having.
"Say it!" He pushed again.
"Nathan, that's enough!" Gabriel spoke from behind.
Ben quickly entered the room again and hurried to my side.
Nathan released me, turned and shoved him back.
"This is the last time I'm going to warn you!" He hollered.
Ben stood still as Nathan then turned back to me.
The look in his eyes scared me now. I didn't know why I said
it, but he had no idea what I was going through right now. So
much had changed since he left. He didn't know me anymore.
I didn't know me. I didn't even know what I was doing right
now. I began to feel sick again.
"She can't say it!" He shouted again. "Can you, Soph? You
can't say it because you know it's not true. Your lying! You
love me and you know it—say it already!" He pleaded. His
voice then softened. "Say what's in your heart, I know you
feel it. Please..."
He grabbed onto me again as I attempted to turn from him.
"Nathan, I'm warning you, let her go!" Gabriel demanded,
then appeared by our side. He motioned Ben to step back
again. "Please. Let her go, Nathan." He then said very calmly.
"Sophie..." Nathan whispered, trying desperately to hold back
his tears. I glanced up at him one last time. "I need you. I need
you, please..." He begged. "I'm nothing without you."
Gabriel looked at him sadly, then placed his hand down on
Nathan's arm. "Release her," He repeated.
I quickly wiped my face and looked to Gabriel. I only hoped
he could hear what was scrambling around in my mind right
now. It was too much for me. I wasn't trying to be mean, I just

wasn't sure what to do in this moment. I was still damaged. I wasn't enough yet—for me—for anyone. I wanted to be stronger and I just wasn't. Looking back at Nathan, his head dropped and I watched as tears slid down his face.

"Nathan," I finally spoke, doing my best to hold it together. He lifted his head with hope in his eyes.

My body was trembling. I had to be honest with how I was feeling. I was sure this was right. *I think.*

"I'm sorry," I began. I didn't know if the words would come out. They were too hard to think about and ever harder to say out loud. "I don't love you anymore. Please stop this,"

Everyone was silent, surely in as much shock as I was.

It seemed as though Nathan had stopped breathing. He was silent for a moment in a dead stare. I continued to look into his sad brown eyes, every part of him was tightening up.

I knew I was sucking the life from him with my horrible words, but I wasn't ready. For any of this.

I watched as he attempted to step back from me. Gabriel grabbed his arm noticing his legs trembling beneath him. Finally, Nathan breathed, his back against the wall now across from me. Gabriel's hand rested gently against his chest trying desperately to help him calm down. His eyes were glued on me. I immediately felt fear. What had I done? I watched as he swallowed hard and blinked a few times.

"Then there is nothing left for me here." He said, pulling himself sharply from the Archangel. He began to stumble. My heart shattered on the floor. The future we had both dreamed of, the one that was pretty much impossible for anyone to achieve, the one we had fought for and beat the odds was gone now. Instantly.

"Nathan, calm yourself." Gabriel warned, stepping towards him again.

Nathan's eyes quickly shot to Ben, "You changed her!" He growled. Gabriel held him still as Nathan began to push back against him, trying to get at Ben once again.

"Nathan, it's not what you think." Ben began.

Nathan pushed at the Archangels a few more times, then

pulled back from his grip and headed towards the door.
Gabriel appeared before him.
"I warned you not to push her," He said.
"Move aside, Gabriel!"
But he didn't.
"We still have work to do, you can't let everything go because
of some meaningless words. What about Alex, and Charlotte is
still—"
"Don't you get it?" Nathan shouted. "It's Sophie I care about!
There is nothing left for me if I don't have her. I don't care
about anyone else and I don't care about your stupid issues
with Fate, Anna, or even Serena now! How many times do I
have to tell you all? Sophie is my life and nothing else. Stop
trying to control me. You just want me to serve you. That's all
you ever wanted!" Nathan hollered. He began to sweat as his
body suddenly lit up with energy.
Gabriel slowly removed himself from the doorway and backed
towards the living room. The energy continued to build.
Then suddenly, exploded, throwing Gabriel back onto the
floor. Nathan's breathing stopped for a moment in shock. His
entire body vibrating from the charge. He looked at Gabriel
nervously as the Archangel attempted to get up.
Nathan's eyes met mine again. I couldn't believe what was
happening. My body began to tremble again. I watched as he
swallowed hard, about to say something, then hurried out of
the apartment.
Gabriel dropped his head for a moment to rest—a little shaken
by the sudden attack. He then turned to Ben, who looked at me
now. My eyes were wide and full of fear. Gabriel rose to his
feet and came towards me. Kneeling down in front of me he
asked me very calmly, "Are you alright?"
I didn't answer. I looked to Ben again, then back at the
Archangel. I felt horrible, just horrible.
Before Gabriel could ask again, I threw myself into his arms.
"I didn't mean to..."
Gabriel glanced up at Ben, then wrapped his arms around me
tight. Never had he let his guard down this much with me.

He held me tight as I continued to cry into his neck. I felt
his arms tighten. His scent and embrace of his body was
calming. I felt safe in his arms, the same way I felt in Ben's.
I didn't care if this was wrong, I didn't care if Archangels
didn't do this. I needed to be held. I wiped my eyes and tried
desperately to calm myself. I waited for my breathing to slow
before pulling back from his chest. My hands still gripped to
his shirt.
"Breathe, you can handle this." Ben spoke from behind.
I felt his warm touch against my back.
My eyes met Gabriel's finally. I suddenly felt a little awkward
and embarrassed. I felt like a child for crying like a baby
into his arms, but he only smiled back at me. Assuring me
everything was fine. I turned to Ben, suddenly realizing the
power and situation he had just witnessed.
"Ben, this is…" I paused. Pondering over how to introduce the
Archangel. I was confused as to why Gabriel showed himself
to a human once again. Wasn't Charlotte too much already?
"Gabriel, yes. I already know."
I froze. Confused again. Gabriel took my hands then helped
me to my feet.
"But how…" I said.
Ben reached for my hand and guided me over to the chair.
"You better tell her." Gabriel insisted.
"Tell me what?" I asked. Suddenly my thoughts and feelings
for Nathan were put on hold. Ben sat down beside me on the
arm of the chair and held my hands tight.
"Sophie dear…" His tone quickly changed. Like it had before
in my apartment. I pulled my hands from his worried.
"I'm not one hundred percent, Ben…" He began.
My eyes shot to Gabriel. He smiled again.
"He's only living in Ben's vessel," Gabriel added.
"What are you talking about?" I asked, not liking where this
conversation was going.
"My name is Chamuel. I too, am an Archangel."
My felt my jaw drop. "But Ben… he and I are—"
"Don't worry, Ben will return to his normal life when my time

is done with him. I'm actually helping him too. He's special
like you and has seen magnificent things in life."
I didn't know what to say. The only person that felt normal to
me right now was Ben. I needed him to be normal, but now, he
was different. "Why?" I asked, sadly.
"Because you needed a friend," He replied.
"Sophie, Chamuel is the angel of love." Gabriel spoke clearly.
"He specializes in helping people heal their hearts. He
connects your soul and heart as one. For you, he also helped
you connect with the pure heart within."
I dropped my head into my hands.
"I don't believe this… I knew there was something off
about—" I then lifted my head again, thinking of all that I had
said and done with Ben. "Oh god, I kissed…"
"You kissed Ben," Chamuel smiled, a little amused.
"This is so embarrassing," I dropped my head again.
"There's nothing to be embarrassed about. Ben was the perfect
vessel for me to get close with you. He was alone and had
doubts in his own life, just as you did. The little bits he told
you about his life are true. He's still the same person. He's
still an actor, trying to make it in Vancouver, just as you
are. But when he began his research into Reiki, I knew there
was something more to him. He wanted more in life and he
wanted to heal as I know you do as well. He truly saw you.
He connected with you, Sophie. His heart is just as strong as
yours and he's fully aware of the journey ahead. He knows
how much he can help you grow, and how much he can
himself in return while assisting me. He is another pure heart
Sophie, just like you. He wants to help you."
"Can he hear us now?" I asked, timidly.
"Both of us hear and see everything, but we take turns coming
forth. His body is protected by me while I inhabit him and
when I am gone, he will return to his normal life at the same
point I entered. He will be healed, more informed and very
healthy—mind and body. Giving him a much better chance at
life. But he will also be unaware of anything that happened
while I was here. His mind will be erased when I am done

which will help him move forward with a better perspective. It's kind of a gift." Chamuel smiled again.
I had to stop and think for a moment. I wasn't sure how I felt about this. I mean, I was happy that Ben wanted to help me, but also upset with myself that I didn't see this earlier. I felt for him, knowing he was hiding pain like me. It reminded me of my old roommate Julie. I missed her still. This information, as surprising as it was sadly made me feel a little more connected to him now. We had a lot more in common than I thought. But unlike me, he was clearly trying harder to change and better himself. He noticed his slump in life and wouldn't accept it. He was stronger than me. He was just another person helping me when I couldn't help myself. Maybe I hadn't made as many changes as I thought I did recently. I was still weak. I sighed, feeling like every conversation nowadays brought more for me to worry about.
"I apologize for the deceit, but you understand why I couldn't tell you, right? You would have never trusted me."
I nodded.
When Ben entered my life it was like a breath of fresh air. Exactly what I needed. I couldn't be mad. Not at him.
"No wonder you believed everything I told you," I then said in a lighter tone. "No human in their right mind would ever believe anything I said. I just don't know why I couldn't see past you." I laughed a little. "I guess I thought you were one of those guys that was deeply into spiritual healing or something. Or maybe, I just didn't want you to be anything other than Ben. I don't know," I paused, looking up at him. "So now what? I don't know how to act around you anymore." I said, rubbing my arms nervously.
"I'm still the same person Sophie, and I'm still going to help you heal. Nothing has changed." He said, touching my back again. A slight smile grew on my face as another thought entered my mind. It was a little embarrassing to ask.
"I don't mean to make things more awkward than they already are," I began. "But how come you angels are suddenly so touchy?"

A slight smile grew on Chamuel's face.

Before he could speak, I quickly cut the Archangel off with another thought.

"Wait… what about Nathan? Does he know about any of this? He must think…" I paused again, remembering what just happened. "Oh god…Nathan," I said, sadly.

Standing up from the chair I suddenly felt very guilty.

"He thinks you… I mean, does he know who you really are?"

"No. He was very hard to talk to. I didn't get a chance to explain."

"Leave Nathan to me," Gabriel interrupted, stepping towards me. "Sophie, everything has changed and we need you more than ever now. A lot has happened in the time you've been asleep."

I looked at him worried.

"You must work with Chamuel and train your heart to be strong. I feel there is a battle coming very soon."

"A battle?" I repeated.

"There is a darkness taking over, and not just here in your city, but throughout the world. We're going to need all the help we can get, especially since Raphael is gone and Alex is—"

"Alex!" I shouted, cutting him off. "Is he healed?"

"There's still no change," Chamuel replied, sadly. "But let's not lose hope. I'm going to continue to work on him and I will need your help—if you are up for it?"

I nodded slowly. Why hadn't Alex come back yet? The mere thought turned my stomach again.

"But Nathan… What if he? I didn't mean to hurt him so much, I just…" I wasn't sure how to explain my horrible words.

"Concentrate on Alex," Gabriel replied. "Plus, we still have to find Charlotte. She won't have much time left—wherever she is."

There was so much happening. How could we possibly save everyone? I couldn't help but begin to doubt us all. Then Gabriel spoke again.

"We know why you said what you said,"

I stared at him. "I didn't—"

"Let's get you something to eat." Chamuel suggested. "Then we will tend to Alex. Let's do this for now. One thing at a time. Shall we?"
I choked back the lump rising in my throat. "Ben… I mean, Chamuel. I mean,"
"Call me Ben, it's much easier." He said, taking my hand and guiding me towards the kitchen.
I looked back at Gabriel as we walked.
"I will worry about Nathan. We'll talk more soon."
Then he was gone.

13
Future

Gabriel pushed at the large white doors that stood tall in front of him. Although they were heavy, they didn't make a sound as they slowly slid open, revealing a long white hallway. The floor glimmered with white crystals below him as he walked down it. On the walls of the great hallway were large carvings of angels. The angel realm was sometimes referred to as Heaven, mainly because most humans are misinformed of their secret world. His creations actually knew very little of how things really worked up here. It was not the place that you went to when you died. That was a completely different world. The angel realm was for those who became guardians, archangels and sometimes spirit guides—and it was even more beautiful than Heaven. But like Heaven, it was a quiet, calm, and serene place. Here in this realm, angels could watch peacefully over life below, control the world of darkness, and look to guidance from Him whenever they needed it. No light was needed in this great hallway— ever. The walls shined bright and were complimented by the glimmering floor below. They reached high above Gabriel's height to a ceiling that soared as blue as the sky above. It was pure bliss to anyone that walked this realm. On top of this, the scent in the air was relaxing, almost intoxicating and although it was very silent, silence was enough. For your thoughts were never so clear than they were in this hallway. Helping all that walked it find their peace and answers they were looking for. As the Archangel reached the end of the hallway, in front of him stood a round pool of water. In the center, a fountain that glimmered in a diamond-like shape pouring crystal blue water from within to the pool below. Gabriel stepped up to the edge, then knelt down. Bowing his head to the water, he listened to the sound as it rippled around him.

"I am sorry, Raphael." He spoke, quietly. "I'm sorry, for failing you." His right hand shook ever so slightly as he ran the tip of his fingers across the water below. It was cool to the touch. The crystal fountain in front of him reflected brightly off the water as his voice echoed faintly in the great hallway. "What should I do?" He humbly asked.

Suddenly, the water came to a halt from the crystal above. It seemed to completely freeze—as still as a painting.

"You did not let her down, my son." A voice whispered though the air.

Gabriel raised his head to the sound of His voice.

"When will you learn to forgive yourself, Gabriel?" The voice spoke, lovingly. "Raphael was cast away as a result of her own actions. Her fate was chosen by Michael, not you—you believed in her. You may not have persuaded your brothers to forgive her, but Chamuel—he listened to every single word you said. Nathan too. That one, is a beautiful soul because of you. You do great work Gabriel, know that you did not let anyone down. Raphael got her second chance and saved everyone as she wanted. A very noble action, don't you think?" His voice echoed.

Gabriel dropped his head, "She deserved better. She didn't have enough time," He replied. "I should have saved her much sooner..."

"She had the correct amount of time she needed, Gabriel. It is a much better thing that you encouraged someone to care for her, even after her chosen actions with that human long ago— enough to want to save her." The voice then paused. "It was him, you know. Chamuel. He was the one that pulled Raphael bravely from purgatory,"

Gabriel looked up and nodded.

"You encouraged his heart to defy the rules and do what he thought was right. Something very dangerous—but honorable in my books. He entered purgatory to save her, then worked with her one on one every day—helping her find herself. She only wanted to have an impact on you all, as you did on her." His voice assured.

"That journey into purgatory took a toll on Chamuel and still does to this day, even if he does not show it. His heart is strong like yours Gabriel. He believed so much, but he knew your brothers would not approve. Which is why he kept this secret from you all. Do not be angry with him."

"Why didn't he ask for my help? I would've been there if he had only said the word—"

"He didn't want to make things worse between you and Michael." The voice interrupted. "You know, Archangels have a will as well Gabriel. Your choices are your own, and I still love you all no matter what you do—including Raphael."

"Then why did you let her go?" Gabriel asked, sadly. "Why let her go through all of this? And why not punish me as you punished her? She only repeated my actions…"

"Because Michael made a choice, and I trust his judgment. She was heading down a dangerous road. She was getting careless and we feared for her as we once did for you." The voice paused. "But you returned to us. Raphael chose differently. She chose William. Which caused Michael to make a hard choice. Gabriel, you know what becomes of those who decide to part from their duty. What they become is something I cannot protect anymore. Fate, she is cruel and would have surely made Raphael's life worse. She, like you, would not have seen the bliss you were hoping for. Even if I had allowed it, Fate would not. She requires us all to be in our places and there is no changing her design. That is why I am so thankful that you returned. I don't want to lose you and believe me, it pains me to have lost Raphael. Twice."

Gabriel sighed in pain.

"They still have faith in you…" His voice spoke again. "Even if you have stepped down. They still know the power you hold inside."

Gabriel shook his head in disbelief.

"Do you not believe the words I speak?"

"Of course, I would never doubt you," Gabriel replied, rising to his feet.

"It is a tough thing dealing with Fate. She is reckless and cares not for any of us or those below. But we must continue to persevere because we deserve to live and that is why I have you Archangels. I'm certain with all of your help, we will change things for the better one day. Do you not agree?"

Gabriel stood in silence, a million thoughts racing through his mind.

"You are unsure of the future now. That is understandable my son, but do not lose faith in yourself—or your brothers."

Gabriel raised his head, "Nathan… there's no doubt in my mind that he is the one." He spoke, confidently. "He will save us all. I am certain, but… his heart is so broken now. I feel his pain within me very deeply."

"I'm sure you do, and no one will ever understand better than you. Not only because you have been through it and pulled yourself back on track, but because you are Gabriel, the Angel of Mercy. You feel remorse, pain, and love more than any other Archangel—even Chamuel."

"It is my weakness…" Gabriel spoke again.

"No." He answered, "It is what gives you great strength. You were once the leader of angels, up until the day you felt you didn't deserve to be followed. It was you that denied yourself a future, Gabriel. Your outstanding service and loyalty to myself, including the rest of the angels, is impeccable. But I still feel as if you are cutting yourself short. I hear you speak to Nathan about my greatness, but what of yours? What of the great Gabriel's force?"

"I broke the rules. I do not deserve to lead. Michael is a better fit." Gabriel responded, quietly.

"Indeed, Michael serves us well, but he does not have the heart like yours and he knows it. Strength and wit are one thing, but a strong heart to guide us is much greater. But you must decide that for yourself. I cannot force you. But I warn you my son, be careful what you preach if you cannot act on your own words."

Gabriel nodded. "Thank you for your wisdom. Nathan is my focus now. I must continue to help him but I am unsure of what to do next. Do you believe he can do it?"

"He is very lost and very broken, but... I believe what you believe. For someone can only get another chance if others believe and encourage them. You have your work cut out for you, Gabriel. It will not be easy and Fate is worse than ever. Her motives are not what they used to be. It is a bigger game for her now. We will need great power and great numbers to win this battle. Something all of our hearts are not ready for. But to be absolutely clear—yes, I believe."

Gabriel sighed, deep in thought again. "I fear we do not have enough time for him to fully transition."

"Agreed. Our world is in a critical state. There is a tear. Purgatory is now free to enter the real world which means the minds of all humans are in danger..."

Concerned more than ever, Gabriel crossed his arms in thought. He had felt something was off, but was too concerned with Alex, Sophie and Nathan to check in on it. He should have seen this sooner. Another mistake.

"Alex was too strong with all of us attached... We messed up." He then said. "How did Uriel's portal not protect us from that spell?" He questioned. "I should have seen how powerful Alex had become. I should have known that this would cause a tear. It's my fault."

"Do not punish yourself. It was a choice, and a good one at that. It was the only way to get you all out of there and yes, there are some repercussions, but if your senses are correct and Nathan is the one... Then it will all be worth it in the end, my son."

Gabriel turned back towards the fountain.

"Every step you took on this journey from the day you left Anna, to when you found Nathan, even down to protecting

Sophie on a human level were all necessary to get you to this point. If you believe this is your path—then it is the correct path."

"I'm certain he is the one." Gabriel repeated.

"Then I am certain you are right," His voice replied. "You must work together with your brothers. Now that you are all magnified with power there is a much better chance at success. Believe in yourself. Believe in Nathan, and believe in those who care for you."

Gabriel nodded, then turned from the fountain. There was much work to be done and no time to waste.

"Gabriel…" The voice said loudly, stopping him in his tracks once more. The archangel glanced back over his shoulder.

"Do not be afraid of your greatness."

Gabriel smiled slightly, then nodded before talking the long walk back down the beautifully sculpted hallway.

The doors silently closed behind him as he exited the room. Gabriel rubbed his temples, a little exhausted from his recent conversation. His eyes adjusted to the right to another set of large white doors. The portal room. The room solely protected by his brother, Uriel.

"How are you doing, brother?"

Gabriel turned to see Chamuel.

"I'm fine." He responded with a smile.

Chamuel slowly walked up and placed his hand on Gabriel's shoulder. "I too tried to talk her out of the idea, but she was set on it. I have to admit, it was a good plan and luckily enough it worked. I am sorry again for my actions—for deceiving you. I'm sorry I made you all doubt her."

"Why didn't you just tell me?" Gabriel asked, a little upset.

"Because you would've never allowed it. Your heart cares too deeply for us all. You would never allow any of us to sacrifice ourselves. Not even Uriel…" He joked.

Gabriel smiled. "Perhaps you're right," He answered. "But why risk yourself going into purgatory alone to save her? You could've been killed Chamuel and that would have really upset me."

"I know," He replied. "But your heart was broken so badly after Anna, and then the loss of Raphael… I wanted you to get back to the old Gabriel. I hated seeing you step down and belittle yourself like you did. You deserve more. I wanted to bring you some hope."

Gabriel looked at him sadly, then stepped closer to hug his brother. "Thank you—for everything. But you care too deeply, yourself." He replied. "I'm not sure how you survived, but I'm glad you made it back to us."

"You'd be surprised how much the heart can protect you…" Gabriel looked at him suspiciously as he stepped back. Chamuel then confessed once more.

"I'm sorry for Sophie as well, I should have told you I was going to work with her. I just didn't want any chance of her finding out. It was the only way I could get close to her. I hope you understand."

Gabriel looked at him with a smirk on his face. "An actor huh?" He teased.

"It has been a secret wish of mine…" He replied. Then Chamuel's face then went serious. "I would never defy you, Gabriel. You know I will always follow you loyally—until the very end."

"I know brother, thank you. But Michael is our leader now. It's best if you do not cross him."

"Of course, I will be more careful." Chamuel smiled as they stood for a moment in silence. "What now? What is your next step?" He then asked. "There is a horrible force taking over down there."

"I know." Gabriel sighed. "We need to act soon. But first, we must both do something very difficult."

Chamuel looked at him, uncertain of his words.

"I need you to find Nathan and make him understand about you and Sophie. Make him understand what he needs to become without revealing too much. It still needs to be his choice."

"Of course, as you wish." Chamuel nodded.

"But be cautious." Gabriel warned. "Nathan is a loose cannon driven by uncontrollable emotions. You must expect the unexpected."

"And what of you?" Chamuel asked, watching his brother head towards the portal room.

"We are going to need more than just Nathan. I must make amends with our brothers and ask for their help."

"Then I wish us both luck," Chamuel spoke positively, before vanishing from sight.

A week later, things were worse than ever on earth. Young people across the world were waking in the middle of the night only to find out their nightmares were real. Adults were passing in their sleep. Institutes were being filled with children telling stories of evil spirits and a young girl haunting them. The stories got bigger and more unbelievable by the day. Humans were not advanced enough yet to understand this type of presence in the world. To them, it looked like ghost stories, cults and more. But no one could deny the deaths that were happening on a regular basis, no matter what they believed, and officials had no leads and no idea of how to help anyone. People became paranoid with the lack of explanation from their leaders, and soon began to sought out help from religious leaders. Even those not so religious looked for some type of guidance out of fear. They were even looking to the unconventional that practiced spiritual and natural healing. They were reaching for something—anything to believe in. None of it made any sense and the media only made things worse as expected. The most recent, topped them all.

It happened in the city of Boston. A young boy, eleven years of age woke from a nightmare in his bedroom that was ignited in fire. The bedsheets burned brightly with raging flames, yet he did not burn himself. His horrifying screams were heard by neighbors who charged heroically into the house in search of the boy and his family. They pushed their way into the flaming room with a fire extinguisher. They quickly pulled the pin and began to fight the fire as another person jumped courageously through the smoke to reach the screaming boy on his bed. They thought they extinguished all the flames at one point, but then suddenly, new flames ignited—this time from the palms of the boy's hands. A woman tried frantically to cover them in blankets, hoping to put them out, but they would only ignite again within seconds. Scared out of their minds from what they were witnessing they evacuated the house, leaving the boy behind to call 911. The boy screamed hysterically racing after them, out of his bedroom and into the hallway. He stumbled in fear towards his parent's bedroom, tripped and fell to the floor, then began to crawl desperately towards their door. His hands lit the ground on fire until he reached for the doorknob. Choking on smoke, the boy pushed his way into the room. From the doorway, he called out to his parents, but they did not answer and they did not move. As he dragged himself towards their bed, he noticed the covers pulled up high over their heads. Shaking, standing over the bed, he pondered how to pull the covers off without lighting them on fire. He called out to them another two times. They still didn't answer. The boy cried harder hoping they would wake and when they didn't, he decided to reach for the covers. The touch of his hands erupted the blankets into flames. He quickly ripped them off and tossed them to the floor.

Falling back in fear, the horrified boy caught glimpse of his parents. Their bodies—were burnt to a crisp. There was nothing left except bones. His father's jaw hung low from his face, then eventually disconnected and fell to the bed. Firefighters broke into the room at that exact moment and were just as horrified. They quickly wrapped the boy up in a fire retardant blanket and raced him from the house. As they reached the front porch and pulled the blanket from over the child's head, his hands no longer burned with flames. He was perfectly fine. There was no trace of anything.

After checking him over completely, the boy told officials of his nightmare. He then told them that the voices had stopped the moment they pulled him from the house.

He said everything was quiet now. He said he felt fine. They
didn't believe him, so they checked his vitals once again while
the firemen put out the last of the flames in the house. It was
true, he was fine. Perfectly healthy, like nothing happened.
Afterward, the Police made their way back inside. They
walked through the house and up the stairs, everything seemed
normal. When they reached the bedroom of the parents,
they cautiously stepped in. The sight of the room shocked
them. There were no signs of a fire anywhere now. No burnt
walls, no lingering smoke, nothing. Making their way over
to the foot of the bed, something else had changed. They
leaned over to the bodies in the bed, then froze—completely
confused by the sight. The bodies were no longer burnt. In
fact, their bodies were in perfect condition and looked as if
they were sleeping. All traces of fire in the parent's room
and the boy's were gone. Like it never happened. A medic
stepped up and checked the pulse of each body. Although
they looked to be sleeping, they were in fact, dead. Just like
all the others who died peacefully in their sleep. The boy was
then taken in for more questioning and eventually put into an
institute to examine further. He could no longer function in a
normal society. He only spoke of evil spirits now. He warned
everyone he could of a young girl that was coming for them
all, a girl that could speak to the dead.
Stories like this one were spreading across the world like
an infectious disease. Faster by the day, and the Archangels
were quickly running out of time. They tried everything from
making rounds during the night to desperately speaking with
the children in their dreams while they slept, but their minds
were always too scrambled to understand. The darkness
had a strong hold on all of them. They couldn't predict the
next attack and there were not enough of them to make it to
everyone in time.
    Eventually, Gabriel came across a young girl named Rachel.
She was sixteen. She reminded him a lot of Sophie. The way
she spoke about her dreams was exactly how Sophie did after
purgatory. She was the only who gave who gave them enough

information to work with. That innocent girl, even in her dreams, only had a piece of her mind left after surviving her recent attack. Her parents, like the boy's, were found dead in their bed. He could feel how terrified the young girl was as he tried desperately to keep her attention in the dreamstate. She asked if he was God. She asked if he was here to take her away. Unfortunately, the more Gabriel tried to speak with her, the more confused her mind became. She begged for him to end her life. She told him she didn't see what happen to her parents because the spirits kept her locked away in her room for two days. She said the spirits warned her that if she left her bedroom for even a split second, they would finish her parents off. For two days they taunted her with visions of her worst fears and visions of family and friends dying. Just as they did with Sophie. She even feared herself at times, losing all capability to figure out what was real and what was not. And like Sophie, the young girl had many thoughts of killing herself, just to escape the madness. It was everything Alex had told him about which only meant one thing. It was becoming clear now, there was only one answer for all of this. They were here, and they brought more than just themselves.

Serena and Anna had to be leading this crusade. They had found the tear in the portal and were now here in the real world, reaping all the fear they could into every human mind. They were here for revenge.

Gabriel needed Nathan now more than ever. They needed to complete their training but unfortunately, Nathan had refused to speak with Chamuel when he approached last and was now ignoring Gabriel too. They had tried numerous times to get through to him, but Nathan's temper was growing worse by the day. They couldn't keep him still long enough to explain things. They were running out of time. The evil was spreading. They needed to create a plan now, and amongst this all, remember to get Charlotte back.

It was becoming too much. He needed more help. Even Gabriel failed with his attempts to talk with his brothers. Uriel was skeptical about working alongside him—especially if they continued to try and heal Alex. He didn't want anything to do with that spirit guide anymore. He knew Uriel wouldn't budge on the subject. What he needed was to persuade Michael to lead this journey so the others would follow. Gabriel needed a break. He was desperate now. He needed something, anything to show a bit of hope to them all. How was he going to get through to Michael? Without Michael, he wouldn't have enough strength on his side.

●●●

The sky in Vancouver was darker than usual and the sun didn't rise over the mountains like it used to anymore. It was overcast and gray in the day—every day, and in the evening, it was more silent and black then ever before. There was no one in the streets, and no sounds from animals in the woods. There was nothing. This once vibrant city was now dead silent in fear. Everyone was on edge, especially when officials placed a five o'clock curfew on the entire city. Unfortunately, that did not stop everyone. Crime took over. For those who did not fear the darkness saw this as an opening to take what they wanted while others were too weak to defend themselves or their belongings. Officials were too caught up trying to solve murders to stop any criminals doing petty crimes.
As for the ones who feared the darkness—they did not sleep anymore. Most gathered with loved ones in a single home— scared to be alone. Hoping to keep each other awake, but exhaustion soon took over humanity. Businesses closed. No one wanted to go outside with all the crime. People were becoming very weak and sickness soon spread. Infecting everyone, everywhere, like wildfire. Everyone was affected, everyone but one person... Nathan.
He walked the streets alone as if nothing had changed. He feared no one and cared less about his health or human body. Stepping off of the SkyTrain at the Burrard Station, he calmly made his way towards the escalator that once carried he and Sophie up into a vision of pink snow at ground level. But now,

it was nothing more than a cold damp stairway. The escalator didn't move and all the trees were dead at ground level. When he reached the top, he turned to walk down the pathway of fallen cherry trees. Suddenly, in front of him, a young girl appeared. Her back was towards him. She had long blonde, beautiful hair. She reminded him of Sophie and for the first time ever, he hoped it wasn't. Slowly, she turned as he stepped closer.

"Hello Nathan," her soft voice spoke. It was Sophie, or at least a version of her. He didn't answer. Her hand slowly tucked a strand of hair back behind her right ear. The vision blurred in and out.

"Fate." He growled, giving his head a shake. He quickly took a step back.

"Cool trick, huh?" She smirked, morphing back into her own body. Her hair remained blonde though. "Thought I was your little girlfriend, didn't you?" She teased. "Oh wait, she's not your girlfriend anymore, is she? Ouch, that had to hurt."

He looked away—annoyed. "I don't care."

 "You don't care?" She repeated.

"She has Ben now, I messed up. I don't care what she does with her life now. I don't even want to be here anymore, so do what you wish to me." He replied, looking her dead in the eyes.

Fate stared back at Nathan's cold look.

"You don't want to be here anymore? Well, I'd hate to waste your wishes…" She said, stepping closer. As she walked forward her hair stripped from blonde to jet black with the front two pieces switching back to their original shade of electric red. A flame sparked within her pupils just as reach reached Nathan. She extended her arm sharply and touched his chest, running her long thin fingers down his body. Nathan didn't react.

"You sure you're ready to die?"

"Yes." He answered.

Fate smirked as the wind picked up around them—her long black and red hair lifted and swirled in the air. There was no scent to the ghostly body that stood in front on him.

"Then I shall grant you your wish." She whispered as her eyes lit up.

Nathan sighed in relief. He wasn't scared to die. He was serious about the words he said back in Alex's apartment. He didn't want anything if he couldn't have Sophie.

Her left hand lifted to the side of his face, then from her fingertip a red ribbon slid out in a snake like manner, she grabbed it quickly before it escaped her grasp. Her right hand taking the other end of the ribbon ever so carefully. Slowly, she raised her hands over his head to the back of his neck where the ribbon now rested gently against his skin. His body tensed up immensely waiting for her next move. Fate's ribbon was thin as a strand of hair, but as deadly as the slice from the sharpest blade. She leaned in once again, breathing deeply with excitement as she spoke into his right ear.

"Goodbye, Nathan…"

With one quick slice, the ribbon of death slid forward through his skin like water—decapitating him. His body fell heavily to the ground. She then released it and watched as the ribbon floated down and eventually landed on his chest.

"No!!!!!!" I screamed from behind.

My heart raced as I ran down the pathway towards them. I didn't know what I was going to do when I reached them, but the rage inside pushed me forward. Tears ripped down my cheeks as I reached deep into my pocket. Fate stood patiently ahead of me. I held out my hand in her direction that now carried a black stone. I then lifted it high into the air and ignited it with an electric red energy. The heat from the stone burned at my skin.

"Nice try, little girl!" Fate growled, suddenly appearing directly in front of me. Her hand laced around my neck tight, cutting off all airways. I desperately struggled to break free. "You will never beat me!" She snarled. Then suddenly, a sharp pain stabbed me in the gut. I looked down weakly. Fate had impaled my stomach with a long silver blade. Her eyes glistened as she watched my body slide down.

The pain was excruciating. The tearing sensation as the metal slid from within—tugging at my insides until I was fully released. I hit the ground hard. I felt my heart begin to slow. I glanced over to Nathan's lifeless body, before releasing my very last breath.

$$14$$

Nightmares

I felt the cold Vancouver rain drip from the trees above onto my forehead that now pounded in pain. My eyes flickered a few times from the dampness before I eventually opened them to a pink blurry sight above. I blinked a few more times trying to clear the rain from my eyes before the scenery became clear to me. Above me, hung the branches of a beautiful pink cherry blossom tree. I could smell their sweet scent in the air around me. A sadness filled my heart quickly and a tear fell from my eye.

"You're safe," A voice said.

I felt a hand on the side of my cheek. I turned my head.

"Nate..." my voice broke.

"No Soph, it's me—Ben." He said, running his hand down the side of my face. Then I remembered the awful site I had just witnessed. "Nathan!" I flew up from the ground, my throat choking up, gasping for air. "Oh my god... Nathan! He's— he's dead, Ben! She killed him! It's all my fault!" I cried looking around for his body that was no longer in sight. "I couldn't get to him in time—"

"Sophie, stay calm. You're still inside your mind, this is just a dream. You let her beat you again. None of it was real." He assured me.

"No Ben, I saw her... she stabbed me with..." I quickly

looked down to my stomach. There was no blood on my shirt, or a hole. I lifted the material up—nothing. I dropped my shirt in relief and began to breathe again. "It felt so real…"
"I know." He said, wrapping his arms around me. "It's time to wake up, sweetie."

● ● ●

When I opened my eyes, I was back in Alex's apartment. "You were doing so well," Ben began, hovering over me. "But I think your recent interaction with Nathan took you back a few steps." He said, helping me up to my feet. "No matter, we'll continue to push forward."
"Ben, how long do I have to do this?" I asked, sadly.
"Until you can beat them all." He smiled. "I need you to believe that you can win—no matter the situation.
"But what if I can't…" I sighed. "And Nathan… I just don't think I can—"
"You can." He insisted. "Be patient with yourself. You'll figure it out. I promise."
"How come I didn't wake up after I died? Isn't it a bad thing to die in your sleep?" I spoke again.
"You didn't die, I was right there with you. Your body and mind only went to sleep when she killed you. That's why I had to step in and wake you. It was a defense tactic by your chakras. You never have to worry, alright?" He assured me. "Nothing will ever happen to you as long as I'm here. You trust me, don't you?"
I nodded immediately.
"Good. Now come, let's check on Alex."
As we began to walk toward Alex's room, I grabbed Ben's wrist and stopped him.
"Thank you," I said. "I mean, for sticking with me and not letting me get lost. I know I'm a pain to deal with." I said, looking down from him.
"You are nothing but a joy, Sophie." He said, kindly back.
Liar.

209

I was definitely not easy to handle—for anyone.

"I know your part angel or whatever, but you're still Ben to me. So seriously, thank you." I repeated.

He smiled, then suddenly pulled his arm from me and closed his eyes.

"What?" I asked, nervously.

"Hmm… It seems I have some other business to attend to first."

I looked at him oddly.

"I'll be back shortly." He then pointed up. "Brotherly conflict," He smirked. Then he was gone.

Gabriel entered the portal room determined to make Uriel listen. Confidently, he made his way into the middle of the arctic white circular room—towards the large portal doors in front of him. Uriel quickly appeared behind him.

"You have some nerve, Gabriel." He said, sternly.

Gabriel took a breath before turning to face his brother.

"Yes, because I need you to listen to me,"

"We've had this conversation before. We will not work with those who dabble in the dark arts." He hissed.

"You do not understand. Alex had to, and I will not punish him for it. If it were not for him and his dark arts… Nathan—nor I, would have survived purgatory."

"That we were prepared for," Uriel admitted.

Gabriel looked at him sadly. "Why do you say such a thing?"

"We knew very well the possible outcomes when we heard that you had entered yourself freely into that damned place. Such a foolish move by an Archangel. You are an embarrassment to us brother."

Gabriel's fist clenched tightly, "I could not let Nathan go alone, and I too had unfinished business."

"Exactly. You still haven't learned, have you? This is why you do not lead us. You are weak. You care too much. Isn't that right, Michael?"

Gabriel turned to the Archangel behind him.

"It is true, Gabriel. You care too much for the humans. Can you not love them for what they are from above?" He asked, approaching them both. "We care very much as well, but we also understand where to draw the line. You sadly determined your fate the second you kissed that girl long ago." He spoke, placing his hand on Gabriel's shoulder. "And your precious Nathan followed closely in your footsteps, didn't he?"

"There's no way that Nathan could be the one, he's too foolish!" Uriel's voice raised in frustration.

Michael shot him a quick glance, then looked back at Gabriel. "I admit, I did not believe you when you first said that Nathan was the one. Although, I saw and heard some things that did not make sense. It still wasn't enough proof for me. Then, when I heard you had entered purgatory of free will, it hurt me brother."

Gabriel stared back at him.

"But it also sparked something, because if you were willing to enter that world to save him, there had to be something more. And I knew, if you were correct, Nathan would return to us. I only hoped it wouldn't be at your own cost." Michael smiled.

"Then why let Alex and Raphael in if you believed we might return?" Gabriel questioned.

"Because it was the quickest way to get rid of sinners." Uriel interrupted.

Gabriel shot him a nasty look, then glanced back at Michael. "Brother, tell me honestly, did you send them on a path to their death?"

"Alex broke every rule we aligned for spirit guides. It's true. I knew he wouldn't survive the journey but, I did believe that he may give you some sort of an advantage being in there. The darkness had already taken him. My actions were for the good of you—not him. It was a sacrifice I was willing to make."

"And Raphael?" Gabriel asked, again.

"Raphael needed to be tested and this would be the ultimate of tests. Not only did she need to protect Alex, Nathan and yourself—she needed to keep her head on straight and make good choices."

Gabriel stood silent.

"I am sorry that I have upset you but like Uriel said, this is why I lead. Your feelings get the best of you and you always end up making the wrong choice." Michael then slowly walked past Gabriel towards the white bench to the right of him and sat down. With his arms rested on the top of the bench, he calmly crossed his legs—as if to be relaxing on a beautiful summer's day. He took another deep breath before speaking again.

"What I did not expect was for Raphael to sacrifice herself." Gabriel looked at him, surprised.

"I had no idea that Chamuel was working so closely with her—only he could have taught her that. The ultimate sacrifice of love." He smiled.

"It was him, you know…" Gabriel spoke sharply. "Chamuel was the one who entered purgatory to save Raphael in the first place. He did it all on his own."

"I suspected that once we connected with you all in purgatory. Seeing his power connected with Alex and Raphael…" Michael paused. "You know, the only way that could have worked as well as it did was if Raphael truly loved us. Her feelings had to be true. It really was a noble act of devotion to Him—and to us. I fear I was wrong about her." He sighed, "But it is too late now, we can't go back. Also, your attitude towards humans seems to be rubbing off on our brother." He then hinted as Chamuel entered the circular room.

"Indeed," He smiled, walking towards them. "It's true. I find Gabriel's vision of humans to be quite enlightening. It makes me wonder if there is more to them that we don't understand. Do you not think?" He asked, sitting down next to Michael.

"This conversation is getting out of sorts. Do you hear yourselves?" Uriel interrupted. "How deeply do you expect us to care for these humans? Are we to sacrifice ourselves for them? They are creations of Him, they are below us. Our job is to protect them as best we can. That is all, but there is a limit. That spirit guide could have pulled us all into purgatory for eternity if he were not so lucky! The only thing good that came from all of this was the extreme power that we inhabited from Raphael's sacrifice. Gabriel has taken too many chances for these humans. If it were my choice, I would let those humans choose their own path in whatever hand Fate deals them. Their life is their own responsibility. We should only worry about those who are on the right path—we cannot protect them all."

"My brother, I would watch your words." Chamuel warned, standing up.

Uriel huffed turning his back in disgust.

"Uriel, no matter your thoughts on them, they are His creations. It is true that they are below us, but we must also act as we are—which is a higher community." Chamuel spoke more calmly.

"We were created to protect them—all of them, so that we can build a world of order and hope against Fate's will. That is His desire." Michael reminded them. "His vision was for the humans and us to have a peaceful world, this must never be tainted or questioned. It is disrespectful to think otherwise."

"I would never—" Uriel harped, but Michael's hand silenced him.

"I am not doubting you, Uriel. Be calm."

They watched as Michael thought long and hard on the subject at hand and what to do next.

"My brothers, we all feel the pressure of Fate and we all worry for the day she will come for us as the prophecy once spoke. A time when she feels we are not needed anymore in her game. It is true, our jobs would be much easier if we did not have to deal with her—we can all agree to that. But we must face our reality that she is getting stronger by the day." Michael stopped, thinking to himself again. "We need to be prepared for what she might be planning. I feel this attack on earth is only the beginning of her fun, so we must take it very seriously."

"Yes. This is why I have come to you, Michael. Now is not the time for us to fight. We must look past our differences and

come together to fight for all that He has created." Gabriel said, passionately. "We do not know how much time we have left. She could come for us at any moment. We must act now!"
Uriel appeared by Michael's side with his arms crossed.
"For centuries, nothing has broken through this doorway and I'm not about to let that change…" He growled.
"You fool. It's already happening. She is stronger than us, don't you see? She's just holding back and now that she has released spirits from purgatory into the real world with Anna and Serena, she's got everything below us covered." Gabriel shouted back.
"That's because your foolish spirit guide tampered with the dark arts!" Uriel snapped, then turned to Chamuel on the bench, "Something you assisted in! You two ruined it for us all! I don't know why He hasn't punished you both by now!"
Tension in the room began to grow. Gabriel turned from him, clenching his fists down low.
"But Nathan, he is our answer." Chamuel said lightly.
"Did you see how he blew those spirits away? He is truly remarkable. Fate was fearful of his powers. I believe Gabriel's suspicions about him are correct. I have no doubt in my mind now." He encouraged.
He then stood up and walked over to Gabriel, placing his hand on his shoulder. "Be calm…" He whispered.
Slowly, Gabriel relaxed his fists.
"It is true, whatever it is that lies within Nathan… there is no doubt that Fate fears it." Michael pondered, "I too, believe now but we still have no idea as to how Nathan will defeat her. Where are we to begin with him?"
Gabriel's face softened.
"First, we need to find out what kind of power Nathan truly has." Chamuel spoke again. "We need him to accept it, to control it, but I fear his mind is not in the right state at the moment."
"What do you mean?" Michael asked.
"Sophie…" He spoke again, "He needs her. His heart is controlled by her."

"Who cares what his heart wants…" Uriel snapped, again. "He needs to make a decision. If he is who you say he is, then he has a responsibility!"

"Not Nathan," Chamuel interrupted. "He is a very different being. Driven by love and emotions. He has great power, but will not tap into it unless driven by a strong emotion—responsibility or not."

"It's true." Gabriel agreed. "Sophie is the pure heart that will train his to exceed all that we dream of. I'm sure of it."

"Then what is the problem my brother?" Michael asked, confused.

"I've tried to reach out to him, but he will not listen. He believes that Sophie does not love him anymore." Chamuel explained.

Uriel rolls his eyes, annoyed with their conversation.

"Humans and their emotions, don't you see how this is hurting us all?" He complained. "We must force him then."

"You cannot force him, Uriel." Gabriel harped.

"And why not?"

"Because Nathan would rather die than live without her—that I am sure of." He responded. "He will end his own life before we get the chance to force him."

"Some prophecy! The fact that he would sin because of some girl, disgusts me!"

"Enough!" Michael shouted, annoyed with the quarrels. "Please, my brothers listen to Gabriel. If I ask only one thing of you ever again, it would be this. Think about it. Truly think about it, "He" let Gabriel do all of this without punishment, and not once has He stepped in to ask you to stop him—or end his life." Chamuel explained. "We must be on the right path. He wouldn't allow it if this wasn't true and Nathan, we can change him if we work together. We just need to approach him very carefully and from the heart."

Michael took another moment deep in thought. He then looked at each of his brothers. "The rules for our guidance are set in stone. There is no need for him to intervene. He trusts my choices…"

"Agreed, but maybe he is testing us all... " Chamuel added.
"Testing us, for what?" Uriel asked, a little insulted.
"Testing us to see if we can look past our differences, and make the right choice, no matter our opinions... You must know that he wants us to work together. He is testing us—always. Humans were his greatest creations. He assigned us to protect them and guide them from danger. But if we do not work as one.... Even you, Gabriel... even after," He paused, looking over at the Archangel. "Even after you stepped down as our leader because you felt undeserving. It was you that decided your own Fate, not us. Michael stepped up because you let him." Chamuel's eyes shot to Michael. "I am sorry brother, but I speak the truth." He said, kindly.
Michael didn't respond.
"Michael is our true leader, Gabriel is weak. He cannot lead us or His intentions. He isn't strong enough." Uriel accused.
"That is true, he is not. But only because he will not allow himself to be." Chamuel replied, touching Gabriel's arm again. "If you had demanded our following—even after Anna—demanded our understanding and forgiveness, if you had spoken true from your heart of your intentions we would have followed you. It was you brother that damned yourself as a follower."
Gabriel stood silently.
"This is what He is trying to teach us—all of us. I am certain. We only deserve in life what we allow ourselves to have. We can give it, or take it away. Don't you see that this is how Fate wins? When we decide that we are not worthy of something? We are lowering ourselves to a level she can control. Do not let her win, Gabriel. How do you know that she is not testing us—right now? Maybe she is waiting for us to break from each other. You must believe in yourself as much as you believe in Nathan. Only then, can we believe in you as our leader."
"What are you saying? That we are to follow Gabriel now?" Uriel growled, his temper rising as he looked to Michael who stood quietly.

"I understand what you say my brother, I do. But we will follow Michael." Gabriel finally spoke. "All I ask… is that we work as a team. Which includes Nathan and Sophie. I need us to look past our beliefs and think outside the box." He then turned to Uriel. "We need to try for the impossible. To see if our prophecy will come true. I need you all to try, and if not now, then when? After another one of us is sacrificed?" He said, sadly.

"I agree."

Uriel's eyes shot to Michael, surprised.

"I will lead us. Gabriel is not strong enough. That I know."

"Thank you." Gabriel replied, with a bow.

"But we must seek His guidance first. There is too much happening now and our first steps must be the correct ones." Michael then took a step towards Gabriel.

"Brother, find Nathan and bring him here. Let us speak with him. Tell him it is an order. We need to see if he is willing to join us. The rest of you come with me into the great hall. We will wait for his return there."

"What about Sophie?" Gabriel asked.

"Chamuel can continue to work with her if it makes you feel better."

"I understand." Gabriel bowed again. "But there is also another girl," he spoke. "She is held captive, by Fate."

"One thing at a time, Gabriel. Please, no more questions." Michael said, walking towards the doorway. He then paused, feeling Uriel's racing emotions.

"Uriel, come—now." He demanded.

The archangel sighed, then raised his head high before following close behind. As he reached the doorway, he turned. Pulling the large sword from his back. The Archangel ignited the room with a gold blaze in one swing. An angel protection spell, to watch over the area for the time he was gone. This would ensure the portal to the other side would remain shut. Once they were gone, Gabriel turned to Chamuel.

"Thank you."

"You are most welcome." He replied. "Let us hope this

works," He then vanished from the room, leaving Gabriel to his duty

●●●

I sat quietly on the floor next to Alex's bed. He hadn't changed, not a single bit. It was really beginning to bother me. The sight of him made me want to burst into tears. I needed him to make it through this. I tucked a few strands of hair behind my ear, then resting my chin down on the mattress—staring at his resting face.

"It feels like we're worlds apart, Alex." I spoke, quietly. "All of us are so far apart." I reached up an brushed the side of his face. "I'm beginning to forget what life was like before all of this happened. I can't even remember the last time I spoke to my family," I joked. The silence was killing me.

"You need to wake up, Alex." I whispered. "We need to find Charlotte, she's counting on us." I began to cry. "I just want things to go back to normal."

"Then do not give up on him, Sophie." Ben surprised me from behind. "You need to fight—for all of them. You have the power within. You just need to believe in yourself."

"I don't know about that," I replied. "Before… when I had Nathan, I felt different. I mean, when we were in…" I paused at the thought.

"In love," He said.

I nodded. "But I think I've changed too much. I'm not the same person I used to be. My heart isn't the same. I'm not sure if I will ever love him again. And even if I wanted to, I'm not sure my heart will ever get past what has happened between us. I feel we will never get the future we once hoped for—none of us."

He walked over to me and sat down next to Alex on the bed. "Your future isn't determined yet. It changes by the day with each decision you make. But you do not need to decide this right now. Your friends—"

"I know." I cut in. "They need me, and I will do my best to not let them down. I just feel like there might be nothing left for me when this is over. I mean, if we make it through this alive.”

“I understand what you speak of, but like I said, let’s see what happens, alright? Try to concentrate on one thing at a time. Alex needs you, so concentrate that beautiful heart on your dear friend. We need him to find Charlotte.”

“Alex knows where Charlotte is?” I asked, confused.

“Of course, they are linked. As I believe you and Nathan are. There is always a link when love is in the equation. I also believe there is no world he cannot enter now. We just need to help him find her.”

“Do you think he will wake up soon?”

“Wake up… no. But if we can heal enough of him on the inside, he may be able to work with us and subconsciously cast a spell to reach her.”

I didn’t understand how that was going to happen. Alex was clearly out of it. How could he possibly find her?

“That’s where you come in.” He replied, as if to read my mind. “You have to connect with him—in his mind.”

“A spell?” I repeated. “Ben, if he does anymore dark magic the Archangels will surely come for him! We can’t let him do that.”

“Sophie, it’s our only chance, and don’t worry, I feel the Archangels will not be so hard on him now.” He smiled.

“What do you mean? Did you talk with them?”

“Never mind about all that. Let’s get to it, alright? We don’t know how much time we have left.”

I nodded. I still had many other questions, but I was also eager to see how I could possibly connect with Alex. I got to my knees and took Alex’s hand in mine.

“Let’s begin.”

Once again, Ben placed the green Kyanite stone on Alex’s chest.

“Wait…” I said, getting up from the ground.

“What’s wrong?”

“I want to be closer to him,” I replied, stepping over him onto the bed. Carefully, I moved myself down next to him.

My head rested gently against his shoulder, my right hand
holding the pink rose quartz stone hanging against my chest.
"Okay, go ahead."
Ben placed his left hand over my forehead and his right over
the green stone on Alex's chest.
"May these words bring him encouragement and let him
receive my interest in this moment. I invoke the high power
and give it to our son at his time of need. Among the obstacles
he has faced, and will face ahead, awaken the motivation
within his heart. Awaken his soul to help him find his rock.
As visions of good return to his mind, the spark of positivity
is lit. Let the strength rise within him. It is my wish, that you
guide his steps during this difficult time. May this honest
prayer push him forward—push him to fight, and make it
safely back to us with the guidance of his dear friend."
As Ben finished the prayer, the room around us was already lit
up in a pink haze. The sweet smell of lavender filled the air as
I lay quietly against my friend's chest. My eyes became heavy,
then finally closed. Pressure filled my mind as my eyes raced
back and forth in the darkness. Ben watched on as I fell deeper
into the dream that had now begun in Alex's mind

My eyes opened to a very dark hallway. This was a much
different beginning to my treatments then I was used to.
Usually, it began with a beautiful scenery, but this time I
wasn't in my own mind. Ben had connected me to Alex. I
had to remind myself quickly that this was a dream and only
a dream—no matter what happened. I couldn't afford to get
lost in here. Alex was depending on me. I continued my walk
further down the dark hallway. I passed numerous doors with
locks on them. Why were they all locked? Was it a piece of
Alex's mind hidden away, something he couldn't face?
Suddenly, the wind picked up around me. A cold strike of air
ripped up my spine. My arms hugged my body as I shivered
in the wind. This place—it reminded me of the circular room I

saw in my own dream.

"Alex?" I finally said, aloud. "Alex it's me, Soph. I'm here to help." The floor creaked as I took my next few steps. It seemed to get darker the further I walked and the hallway seemed to be never-ending.

"Alex?" I called again.

"Alex…" a haunting voice whispered from behind.

I whipped around in fear. "Alex?"

Just then, the hallway became very silent and the wind came to a halt. I stood still in the darkness. I wanted to speak again—to call out to him, but I was scared. I covered my mouth. I was breathing too loud. I worried for what might hear me. I had no idea what things lingered in Alex's dark mind. Suddenly, it felt as if a strand of hair brushed across my left hand. I jumped quickly, trying to sense what was around me. My hands searched the darkness but found nothing.

"Who's there?" I trembled.

"I've missed you, Sophie." The voice taunted.

I froze. That voice. I know that voice.

"Did you think that you could escape me?" She spoke again. "You may have beaten me before, but now… I have backup." Fire ignited the hallway. Lighting up every rotted torch on the wall. The darkness now burned bright with the flames of purgatory.

Run! Run now!

My senses were on high alert as I took off in the other direction. I ran fast, and as I ran I glanced up at the torches. A shadow ripped by each one alongside me. It was just as fast as I was, maybe faster.

"Run little girl. Run until your legs give way." Serena teased, her voice howled down the hallway.

The screams of the spirits began to mess with my head.

"Do you remember them?" I heard her yell. "I knew you would. They are very upset they didn't get to finish you off." I suddenly tripped and fell hard to the ground.

"No! No! Stay away!" I screamed hysterically as the spirits surrounded me. "Ben!" I called out, desperately.

"Ben, help me!"

"I wouldn't expect your friend to help you in here—he can't."
She teased again.

"Ben!" I shouted again. "Why aren't you answering me?!" I
pleaded, ignoring Serena's words.

"Because he's right here." She then said, appearing before me
with Ben in her arms.

"I'm sorry Sophie, I didn't know they could break through
our treatments." He said, weakly. "I messed up, but you can
still—"

"Shut up!" She shouted, tightening the grip around his neck.
"You see, Fate taught me a little trick. A trick to listen in
on the prayers of others. How do you think we were able to
access so many minds throughout the world?"

"You're sick!" I blurted out.

"It only took one prayer for Anna to get into a family's mind.
One single prayer by a parent who was teaching their child
to dream—to hope. To ask for guidance or protection. Then,
after we made the news, city by city people began to worry.
They began to pray for those who had been hurt, and more
importantly, pray for themselves. Cool, huh?" She said,
tossing Ben to the ground.

"And it was only a matter of time before an angel casted a
strong enough prayer for us to enter here. Of course, it was a
little easier with the help of Alex's messy mind." She smiled.
"Want to know another cool fact?"

"Just stop, Serena. Please! If it's Nathan you want, he's not
with me anymore. I left him! So leave everyone else alone,
please!" I begged.

"It's about time! You don't deserve him. You never have!
Where is he now?" She said, a little thrown off by the sudden
news.

"I don't know. He's gone."

Serena stared at me, unconvinced.

"It's the truth!" I yelled.

"No matter, that will only make things easier for me." She
replied, turning back towards Ben.

"As I was saying," She continued, shoving her foot hard into his side. He groaned in pain. "Your friend thought he could beat us again since he had done it before in purgatory, but he got lucky. Things are different now. They've grown—they're stronger—all of us are, thanks to those silly human minds."
"Leave him alone, please!" I begged. I didn't understand why Ben wasn't fighting back. Did he have no power on this side?
"We really surprised you, didn't we?" She spoke again, looking down at Ben. "You never expected us to show up in Alex's mind and break through your little barrier, huh?" She nudged him again on the ground. When he didn't respond, she continued. "Did you know that when an angel inhabits a human's body, he is connected with them until he releases himself fully? Meaning, he can't leave until he actually helps that human heal and see his true path in life."
"What are you getting at?" I asked, worried.
"If an angel hasn't completed his job and by chance is… oh I don't know—killed during his inhabitation time. Both souls will be forfeited and lost forever."
My eyes widened. Lose Ben—forever? No, I can't—not Ben. Serena smiled at my reaction, then quickly pulled a long dagger from her boot.
"Ben, get up!" I screamed. "Serena, I beg you. Don't do this!" But she didn't stop. She knelt down next to him, placing her knee down hard against his chest. I scrambled to my feet, desperately trying to get to him, but Serena was too quick. With one quick stab, the blade plunged directly into Ben's chest.
"No!!!" I screamed, diving into Serena and knocking her back to the ground. Our bodies rolled across the cement floor. The sounds of spirits screeching, howled throughout the hallway. Serena fought back hard and threw me off. She quickly reached for the blade again. Ripping it from Ben's chest, he moaned with what little life he had left in him. I jumped to my feet once again.
"Go head, come at me!" I screamed in rage. My heart was racing. "You won't take him from me!"

Serena charged once again. So did I.

Just as I reached her, she spun around me. Her long fingers intertwined in the back of my hair, gripping on for dear life. She then lifted the blade again as I struggled within her grip. With one quick slice, it ripped across my hair. I watched as my once long and beautiful hair fell lifelessly now to the ground before me.

As it touched the floor, the dirty blonde color turned to a dark brown—then eventually to black and disintegrated before my eyes. My heart stopped as Serena now held the dagger to my throat. Anger was rising inside of me as I looked down at Ben's helpless body.

"Sophie," He whispered.

His voice ignited the stone against my chest. My voice was trembling as I began my spell—the spell Alex once taught me. "With perfect love and perfect peace, will make conditions right. And from that place, that's not a place, the form will come to light."

Serena snarled at me, surely remembering these words.

"Not this time," She said, pulling my head back.

But I continued, even louder this time.

"I lift my heart to touch you, there is magic to be done. And all I need, is knowing, that you and I are one." I completed the spell as a single tear fell from my eye. I felt her grip tighten. This was it, she was going go finish me off right here. Suddenly, another spell filled the air.

"I call to you from the city of angels. Protect me—guide me through!"

Serena's body jolted from mine. Before I could blink, she was tossed across the hallway, into the wall. She fell hard to the ground. With a breath of relief, I turned quickly to see who had saved me.

Alex.

I could barely speak, I quickly ran to him and wrapped my arms around his body. "Alex!" I cried, into his chest.

"Sophie, help me," He said, collapsing against me.

"He is not strong enough, hang onto him." Ben said, pulling

himself up from the ground. He gripped his chest in pain.
"You fools! You can't win in here! I control you all!" Serena screamed, taking a run at Ben once again.
Quickly, Ben's hand lifted, shooting a bright yellow light from within it—directly at Serena. The yellow blaze flashed before our eyes. I was amazed by his sudden burst of power. Serena was completely blown from sight.
"You'll never get out of here alive!" Her voice echoed. Then everything went silent once again.
I turned to Ben, "I thought you were—"
"You can't get rid of me that easily," He replied, with a smile. Then slowly, he sat down to rest. Taking a deep breath in, a warm energy began to radiate from Ben's body, but it didn't last long. "I'm afraid I'm not strong enough to heal myself completely." He said.
His words worried me.
Carefully, I lowered Alex to the ground. I touched his pale cheek gently. He was so worn, so beaten, so... Sad.
"I figured the spell you taught me might link me to you," I spoke quietly. He didn't answer. "Alex—"
"Soph," He finally responded. "I can't bear it," His voice then broke. "It's all my fault. She died... and Charlotte..." He began to cry. I quickly hugged him.
"Stop it, Alex. None of this is your fault..."
"You didn't see her..." He whispered.
"You saw her? You saw, Charlotte?" I replied, looking down at him.
"She was barely alive, Fate has taken most of her life," He cried. "Her body was beaten to the point of—she tossed her around like a rag doll—I couldn't save her," He stuttered.
"I had Nathan and the rest at my fingertips—and Fate—she pulled her right out from under me,"
"Alex," I pulled him back in. That was it. That was what he saw. That's what ruined his soul. How horrible.
I began to think about all the horrible images I saw when Nathan was killed in front of me over and over again. When my mind was completely lost. It was torturous.

"It's okay, we're going to get her back." I said. "I'm just glad you're here."

Ben slid his way over and touched Alex's shoulder.

"Alex, can you sense anything of Charlotte? Anything at all?" He asked.

Alex swallowed hard, then shook his head no.

"That's alright, rest for a moment." Ben replied, getting up from the ground. He glanced around the darkness, the hallways were endless. He turned back to me.

"Sophie, I apologize. I should have been more careful. With all that's been happening on earth, I should have expected that she could break into my prayers. I let you down."

"Ben, it's fine." I said, "I trust you, and we have Alex now, so it was worth it—right?"

He nodded, then stepped towards me and held out his hand. "Unfortunately, resting time is over. We cannot afford to linger. It's too dangerous."

I took his hand and together, we pulled Alex to his feet. He then rested Alex's arm over his shoulder, taking the weight from my own.

As made our way down the dark hallway, the torches were still burning bright around us. In the distance, the faint sounds of spirits lingered in the air. They had been blasted away with Serena, but it wouldn't be long before they caught up to us again.

"She'll be back," I warned, looking behind us as we continued to walk.

"We have to prepare ourselves..." Alex responded, trying to stand on his own. "I could try a location spell. If Charlotte is being held anywhere in a supernatural realm, we'll be able to locate her. But I fear I'm not strong enough to keep the energy going. If we find her, I'll want to attach her to myself. I need to bring her home with us, but..."

"But what, Alex?" I asked, worried.

"If he attaches himself onto her, he won't survive the journey back this time." Ben said, quietly.

"What? What do you mean?"

"This is his dreamstate. If he links onto her with a spell and pushes us forward—back into the real world, then he must remain behind. He is too weak to pull all of us out. He has to choose. Charlotte, or himself."

"No," I cried. "Alex, there's got to be another way,"

I immediately began to rack my brain for other ideas. I couldn't face the fact that I had to leave my friend behind. I wouldn't do it. It's not what I had planned.

"There's no other way, Soph. My body is already gone in the real world. I'll have to use everything I have left. I'll need to give it to her, so she can make it back safe." He looked at me, then smiled. "She deserves a life—just as you do. I will die happy knowing that you and Charlotte are free. Please, let me do this for her—for you." He then took my hand in his.

"I'm so happy you came for me. You too, Ben—Chamuel." He winked. "You've awakened me. I know I still have something left to give, so let me show you. Besides, the angels are upset with my actions. If I did live, they would surely punish me anyway." He laughed, then moaned in pain again.

"I can't accept that, I'm sorry Alex. You're going to try and you're going to make it out alive." I said, squeezing his hand. "Now tell us what you need,"

He sighed, then shook his head at me, but before he could speak, the walls began to shake all around us and the ground below began to move. We tried desperately to keep our balance. The torches along the wall ignited bright, then went out as one—creating a pitch black atmosphere and a heavy presence around us. Silence took over.

"Listen to me," Alex whispered, "Chamuel, if you can create fire, I can use it to scry,"

"Whatever you need." Chamuel agreed.

Nervously, I listened as Alex went on with his plan. We had no choice but to try it. Time was running out.

15

Dream Within A Dream

Flame scrying was another forbidden art form for the angels. It had the ability to find someone anywhere between the real world, the dream world, and even purgatory. It reached all realms and was very powerful. It also took someone with much knowledge of the dark arts to perform this act—Alex was confident that he could do it. Especially with Chamuel and myself by his side. I knew this was too much for him. It was beginning to leave scars mentally and physically on him. We could all see it. I was scared. I knew how badly he wanted to save Charlotte—so did the rest of us, but I also knew there would be a bigger sacrifice for this if we did succeed. Alex sat down one last time to rest before preparing his spell. Chamuel was able to light a small ball of light before us, so we could see each other.

"Sophie, sit with me." He requested, patting the ground beside him.

I did as Alex asked. Lacing my arm through his, I sat closely to him on the ground. His body felt weak. It was usually so fit and in shape. He wasn't healthy at all now and it was only getting worse. From what Alex had told me, spirit guides didn't have to worry about staying in shape or being healthy because they were created. They always stayed the same. This is why I was concerned. It was not the same for Ben. I mean—

Chamuel. Since he was an Archangel inhabiting a human's body, he was still required to take care of himself—eat well, and stay in shape. But Alex had changed drastically and we all knew why. The darkness was taking over.

"I guess it was time for a new look, huh?" Alex teased.

I sighed, running my fingers through my now very short hair. It barely touched my shoulders.

"I don't think my agent will be too happy with me," I joked. My smile soon faded. How could I ever think of that world the same way. I couldn't even see a normal life or a future for me right now. Acting, going to the movies, all of it seemed like a dream compared to what I was dealing with—what I'd been dealing with for quite some time. It seemed hopeless to wish for that anymore. But I couldn't ever admit that out loud—especially not to Alex—not now anyway. I needed him to make it through this. I needed Ben too. I selfishly wanted them both in my life for as long as I was alive.

"I like the pink though," I then said, trying to lighten the mood. Alex continued to stare at me, then spoke again.

"When we get back to the real world, can you promise me something?" He asked, kindly.

I nodded with a smile.

"Promise me that you will forgive, Nathan." He said, very seriously.

I heard Ben sigh in relief. I knew he wished it too. Everyone wanted this, but I couldn't. I was still so hurt inside.

"Alex… I—"

"Soph, you have no idea what he went through. Remember how you felt after returning from purgatory? Like no one would ever understand you or what you went through in there? Except for me of course." He smiled again.

My eyes started to swell up as I nodded.

"Well, when I was in there with him, he did nothing but speak of his everlasting love for you. It was the only thing that kept him going. Did he tell you that he made Gabriel swear to give him a normal life with you once this was over? And if something was to happen to you, he too would want his life to

be over. He only wanted his second chance if it was with you."
I stared at him.
"You have to believe that he was in there to save Serena, only
as a friend. He doesn't love her like he loves you and after
trying for quite some time, he knew he had a new decision on
his hands. He saw how precious time was. He had to decide
right then and there, if it was more important to continue to
fight for her—or return to you. He had to let one of you go as
painful as it was."
I wiped a tear away, trying to contain myself.
"He chose you, Soph." Alex smiled. "He loves you more than
life itself. Don't make him pay for fighting this hard—for
something he believes in. He was only trying to do the right
thing," He then grabbed my hand. "You need to listen to your
heart. You know him better than any of us. You just have to
listen to yourself and all your questions will be answered."
I rested my chin down on my knees as I pulled them in tight
against me. I felt Alex's arm remove from mine and place
down gently across my back.
"You have to tell him, before it's too late." He said. "Don't
let it end like this. I already regret not telling Charlotte my
feelings earlier. We didn't even have a chance to live a life
together. I can only assume that's how Serena felt. Think
about it, Soph," he sighed, then spoke again. "I won't end up
like her. I'll do what's best for the one I love—something that
will make Charlotte's life better. I want her to live a long and
happy life and I need your help. I'm asking you to help me
Sophie, please. Don't let me die with regrets."
My eyes shot to his. *Die?*
He rested his forehead against mine, he was really scaring me
now. I released another deep breath, then finally replied.
"I won't," I whispered. "But please, don't give up Alex.
Promise me you'll try. She'll be heartbroken if you—"
"She won't." He interrupted. "I won't make her live in pain.
Trust me,"
His words created an uneasy feeling inside. What did he mean
by that?

"Attached with this enchantment is a memory spell. If I am to die, she will forget that she ever knew me. It's the best way— so you must play along."

"No, Alex, I couldn't." I quickly responded. "You want us to just forget about you? That's impossible! I won't be part of that! You deserve better," I cried. "How could you ever ask me to do this? You're my best..."

"You will, Sophie. I'm doing it, whether you like it or not."

He couldn't be serious? How were we to just forget that Alex ever existed? He had done so much for me, and Charlotte. She loved him. It was too much to ask. I refused to let him go out like this.

"You will only hurt her more if you don't let go of me." He then said.

My heart was racing again. How could things end like this? I couldn't accept this outcome. I wouldn't!

"Let's take a break from this conversation and move forward," Ben interrupted. "We will do as Alex wishes, in respect to him and to save your friend. It is a very noble cause. We will make sure you do not end up like Serena. You have our strength, my friend."

I stared at Ben. I knew he could feel my emotions, how I refused to lose my friend but before I could argue, she spoke.

"Will you all stop talking about me as if I can't hear you!" Serena's voice echoed throughout the hallway.

"I've had enough of you all. You know nothing about me and you never will." She shouted.

My body tensed up again as Chamuel's ball of light went out before us.

"Be ready," Ben whispered.

I felt his presence beside me now as the ground began to rumble below us, making us rise to our feet. I quickly reached down to help Alex up. From a distance, the faint sounds of spirits grew closer until their high pitched screams surrounded us completely. Flashes of purgatory raced through my mind as I covered my ears in fear. I remembered the dirty bed I was tied to for what seemed like forever—their nails—the pain.

I hated the darkness. I grabbed onto Alex's arm again.
"Remember what I taught you, Sophie." Ben said, one last time.
"I'm ready," I lied. "
"Then let there be light within this dark realm," he said quickly. Suddenly, one by one each of the torches along the wall ignited with flames again. The sound of spirits grew louder as their shadows danced across the walls. A spark in the middle of the hallway startled us as Serena appeared in a blaze. Ben quickly turned to me feeling a warmth behind him. I was holding onto the pink stone—it was reacting to her presence. A beautiful light pink shield soon surrounded us all as my right hand rested on Alex's shoulder. I was trying hard to concentrate on the outcome I wanted from this horrible situation—who I wanted to save, and how much I cared for my friends. I wanted my love, my strength, and whatever else I had left deep inside to protect us from anything we were about to face. Clearly, it was working from the look on Ben's face. The magenta pink streaks in my hair began to glow bright as Serena stepped towards us, making Ben's attention return to her.

"You know, Fate told me about you Chamuel… How silly of you to bring this young boy into the picture. It's a shame I will have to get rid of his pretty face." She said, then launched through the air towards him—a dagger secured tightly in her right hand. Ben moved quickly to meet her halfway, dogging her strike and tackling her to the ground. He was trying to give us time, but he was also not in my protective barrier anymore. I glanced over at Alex. His eyes were closed tight, concentrating as he began his spell.

"Scorching depths as you dance, give me now the secret glance. To find the one I long for most, I welcome you on my journey as my host," His body began to tremble. "Make me intuitive. Make me clairvoyant. Scorching depths I command you to burn bright and show me hope as I evoke the power of second sight."

As the last few words slipped from his mouth, the torches that lined the hallway blasted up to the ceiling with fire.

Alex's eyes shot open. But they were no longer Alex's eyes. They were cold—pitch black, and wider than the eye should be.

"Alex?" I said, nervously.

His eyes raced back and forth in search of Charlotte. He was lost in the sight of the flames—surely trapped in another dream within a dream.

The spirits surrounded us now, waiting impatiently for my barrier to fall. I glanced over at Ben, who still had his hands full with Serena. I quickly closed my eyes, concentrating hard on my task at hand. I couldn't lose it. Alex needed me.

Before entering this dream state, Ben had warned me how dark Alex's mind would be. He worried if we could even break through and find him. Lucky for us, we could. But he also warned me of something else.

Since Alex's mind was so scatted, if we did find him and were able to talk to him—for him to cast a spell and connect to another would be a miracle. He couldn't control his mind anymore. He had too much racing through it and now we knew that the sight of Charlotte in purgatory had completely messed him up. Between that, and the dark arts that were taking over, it was hard to say what we were dealing with and what power Alex actually had left. Alex didn't care about the rules anymore. He just wanted to do whatever it took to save Charlotte—to save me. He was different now. He was not the gift Gabriel received long ago.

I was told for centuries, the Archangel would not accept a spirit guide by his side. Gabriel's independence had always bothered Chamuel a little which originated the idea of crafting the perfect spirit guide for his brother. He took his time, implementing every one of Gabriel's beliefs and strengths into this being. And after the Archangel's encounter with Anna, Chamuel had even more work to do. This spirit guide would need to follow Gabriel's morals, but also encourage the angel he used to be—for Gabriel had lost hope in himself.

Chamuel wanted Gabriel to grow confident again, to return to

where he belonged—leading the Archangels. So he also added
a few traits of himself into the spirit guide. When Alex was
finally ready, Chamuel presented him to Gabriel—insisting
that his brother take him under his wing. Alex's quick charm
and easy going personality won Gabriel over instantly. The
Archangel was impressed by how open minded, loyal and
intelligent his gift was. But the others did not feel the same.
To them, this spirit guide had too much free will—too much
realness to him. Something that was never put into their
own creations because it was too human-like. Chamuel then
watched as Gabriel taught Alex many things that opened his
mind to the real world and eventually, it made him much more
powerful than the other guides.
Alex had mentioned to me once how different he felt from the
rest. He said that something was growing within him, but he
couldn't explain what it was exactly. I meant to ask Ben about
it, but it slipped my mind until now. I only hoped that it wasn't
the darkness, but I also couldn't deny what was happening
right in front of me now.

  Alex's mind flashed in and out of both dream states in search
of Charlotte. Suddenly, the second dream state locked.
Squeezing his eyes tight to hold onto it, he felt his body
shift. He then opened his eyes to find himself in a cold, dark
hallway. He hurried down it. Water dripped from the cracks
in the cement ceiling above—creating an echo effect as they
splashed against the floor below. He began to pick up speed.
He didn't have time to waste. The dampness of this hallway
soon got worse as the wind picked up around him. He began
to hear the faint growls of spirits around him once again. But
this time, he was not within his own dream state. The fire had
taken him deep into a dark world he had never seen before.
His feet slid across the wet floor as he approached a large
doorway. With a quick glance behind, he reached into his
pocket to grab a stone. When he pulled it out, it wasn't the

stone he thought it would be. In his hand, was green Kyanite.
He wiped it clear of any dirt. The stone radiated with heat
from a familiar energy source. He smiled, then placed it back
into his pocket. Placing both of his hands on the door in front
of him, he pushed with all his might—making the old wooden
door eventually slide open. The sound of the door scrapping
across the floor screeched throughout the hallway. Once he
could fit his body through, he quickly pushed it close from the
other side.
After taking a moment to catch his breath, the growls on the
other side of the door soon silenced. He then turned slowly,
hoping this new area was safer than the last. In front of him
was a very small room. It was cold and smelled of mildew.
His eyes searched the darkness for any signs of life. Suddenly,
he heard the door lock behind him. He quickly turned and
gave it a shake—nothing. It wouldn't budge, he was trapped!
A sudden sound of chains scratching across the cement floor
startled him again. His eyes blurred in and out of focus for a
quick moment. He wasn't sure how much longer he could hold
onto this vision.
"Who's there?!"
A faint murmur came from the ground as his eyes continued to
search the darkness. Just then, he felt something brush against
his leg. Turning quickly—prepared to fight, he noticed a soft
pink glow begin to resonate from the floor below. The smell of
lavender then filled his lungs.
"Sophie," He whispered.

● ● ●

   Serena threw herself at Chamuel and once again he repelled
her back against the wall. I watched as a spark from a flame
above floated down to the ground before me.
"Ben!" I hollered, "It's getting harder to hold on…"
He quickly appeared in front of me when he had the chance.
"Keep going, Alex needs you!" He urged, before Serena
landed on his back and pierced his right shoulder with the
dagger. Chamuel dropped to his knees.

"Ben!" I cried.

"Don't lose concentration!" He pleaded as my hands reached for him.

"Drop your act! Come out here now and face me! Do it, or I'll kill him!" Serena threatened, holding onto the back of Ben's neck.

I glanced down at Alex, and then back at Ben who had very little strength left. When I didn't move, Serena stabbed him again. This time in the side of the neck.

"You're making it very hard for his body to heal, Sophie. Are you prepared to lose another person you love?" She taunted.

"Ben, fight—please!" I begged him.

The spirits surrounding our protective barrier caught glimpse of Ben's weakness in Serena's hands and raced to her side.

"I'm willing to share—be patient." She said as they snarled at her. "You know, they can smell fear—Ben's I mean." She spoke again. "They know he cannot do this alone. I only need to say the word and they will finish him."

Ben stared directly at me, a slight smirk began to grow on his face. "Do not lose faith," he spoke. "Save him, as you promised you would."

I didn't know what to do. I couldn't leave Alex, but I wanted to save Ben as well. I closed my eyes sadly as a tear slid down my cheek. "I'm sorry, Ben…"

A burst of energy illuminated around us again as I continued to concentrate on Alex. The warmth from my stone lit up Alex's body making him twitch in his meditative state.

When I opened my eyes again, spirits covered the spot where Ben once stood. Their howls ripped through the room as they devoured him and I could do nothing but stand there and watch. Serena eventually emerged from the circle with nothing but a smile on her face.

●●●

Alex jolted with a burst of energy once again. He could feel support again from the other dream state. He could feel strength—and love. Carefully, he made his way around the dark room. His hand eventually came across a section of wall that felt as if a small stream of water was pouring down it. The water was very cold. He followed it down to the ground. His fingers traced the small stream across the floor until suddenly, his right hand touched a cold piece of metal. His fingers slid across what felt like a chain, up to a cuff. Then flinched at the touch of what felt like flesh beneath it.

"Damn it," A voice said from behind. "You found my surprise."

Alex turned in fear. One by one, candles lit up the edges of the circular room. His eyes shot around nervously for what might appear. Then suddenly, his eyes froze to the floor below him.

"Charlotte!" He said, dropping to his knees beside her.

He pushed the hair from her face, touching her cold cheek gently. "Oh god, come on... Talk to me." He cried, desperately.

"Sorry she's not in the best of shape," Fate teased from behind. "But beggars can't be choosers—right?"

"What did you do to her.?!" Alex growled.

"Nothing. I swear. Well... I mean, I didn't feed her or give her water but, she has that nice stream running below her face if she wanted to take a sip,"

Alex looked at her furiously.

"I'll admit, it's a bit cold in here. Hope she doesn't get sick," Fate spoke, sarcastically.

Alex continued to feel around for any signs of life from Charlotte. She wasn't responding. She was so cold.

"Okay, I did kick her once or twice," Fate continued to tease. Alex's eyes shot back to her in rage.

"What?" Fate complained, "She's annoying,"

He quickly tucked Charlotte into him as Fate approached.

"I'd be more worried about her mind though. Traveling here to my dimension, then into purgatory and back? I mean, wow. I'm surprised she's survived this long. What excitement she's brought to my game, am I right? You had some big decisions to make back there in purgatory, didn't you?" She stopped in front of him and smiled.

"Why do you insist on ruining everyone's life?" He hissed.

"Ruining? I'm not ruining anyone's life. I'm testing you—to see if you deserve a life at all. By the way, you're all failing miserably. So don't go blaming me for your horrible choices." She defended. "What I do is simple. I design a path with a few minor obstacles and all you have to do is make the right choices and you get to have your so-called beautiful life. But like I always say, humans are ruined by their stupid emotions and you Alex, have become too human as well—haven't you?" She teased.

"As if it wasn't bad enough that you fell in love with a human girl, you also tampered in the dark arts, which only confused your mind even more from your spirit guide lifestyle. I'm very interested in seeing what becomes of you."

Alex's fist tightened. "If I've messed up, then make me pay for it—not her! Take me!" He shouted.

"How noble, but it doesn't work that way." Fate replied, walking towards him again. "Move," She demanded, then lifted her hand towards him. Alex tightened his grip on Charlotte.

"Fine, be difficult." Fate then reached out towards him again and with a flick of her hand shot the two of them across the room where they slammed hard against the cement wall.

Alex trembled, trying to get to his feet as fast as he could as he watched Fate reach down to touch Charlotte's head.

"You weren't the only one who messed up Alex," Fate spoke again. "She too, messed up. I lined her up perfectly with that young man... I think his name was Matt. Unfortunately, Sophie's life got her too caught up in the supernatural and she fell for you. She only has herself to blame for her outcome. I had planned a very simple life for her. A few job obstacles and such, but compared to all of yours... she would have had it the best. Such a shame..."

Just as she gripped her fingers into the back of Charlotte's head, Alex collided with her. He struggled trying to fight her back from Charlotte, trying to do the impossible and take Fate out!

"You won't be touching her anymore," He warned.

She smiled, looking at him, challenging him to try his worst! She shoved him back, slamming him against another wall, making him hit his head again. She then leaped from him into the air. Alex jumped after her, forgetting the weakness that once filled his body. Fate grabbed his wrist just as he reached for her and threw him back to the ground. Alex rolled across the cement, through the cold water on the floor and hit the wall hard again. Appearing over top of his body now, Fate took her opportunity and began hitting Alex in the face. Once, twice, a third time. She lifted him up and slammed him back down. She repeated this another two times before releasing him. She watched as Alex rolled over to his stomach, trying to catch his breath. She was surprised by how persistent he was. The pain was shooting through him now, he could barely function. His legs wobbled as he attempted to stand.

"I'm impressed," Fate smiled. "Look at you, trying to hang in there—especially in your state. I'm also pretty impressed that your friends were able to enter your mind and awaken you. You must feel horrible that their attempt to save you will be at a loss,"

"It won't. I'm still here." He replied, wiping the sweat from his forehead.

"Now, what makes you think that I'm going to let you take that girl from me?" Fate teased, again.

"Because I know that you would enjoy seeing me die much more than some silly girl."

Alex's honest words made a smile grow on Fate's lips again. "True, it would be a much better sight. But on the other hand… It baffles me how much everyone wants to save this stupid girl— including yourself." She stepped slowly now, "But you. Killing you would bring me great joy. A being that was created specifically for the Archangel Gabriel," She paused, "Wouldn't that be something?" She continued to mumble. "And I can already feel Serena, she is close to finishing your other little friend off,"

Alex's eyes widen as he reached into his pocket again, the stone was warm still. Which was a good sign his friends were still alive.

"Don't believe me?" Fate asked, twirling a strand of Charlotte's hair around her finger.

A rush of emotion swirled through Alex's body as the strand of hair in Fate's hand turned into a red ribbon.

"Careful there, you don't want to lose your train of thought." She then disappeared and reappeared in front of him—knocking him hard to the ground again. Alex's head smashed against the cement floor. Straddling him now, Fate held the deadly ribbon right against his neck. He quickly gripped onto her wrists holding them stable with all that was left of his strength. He knew it would only take one slice from her ribbon to finish him off.

"Alex…" a weak voice spoke from behind.

He glanced to the right as Charlotte's eyes open slightly.

"Charlotte!"

Suddenly, Fate's eyes lit up with a red flame and Charlotte's body began to rise from the ground. Smiling down at Alex, Fate watched as he began to panic at the sight. Charlotte's body now hung like a rag doll high above them.

"Let her go! You have me!"

"Okay," Fate replied, happily.

With a single blink, she released Charlotte's body from the ceiling. Alex's heart skipped a beat as an unplanned invocation spell spilled from his lips, "Gabriel… wherever you are! I appeal to you on the wings of words that fly. Whatever the distance—traverse time and space…appear in my presence now. Protect us!"

Out of nowhere a white energy coated the room from the ground up, catching Charlotte's fall with a soft cloud. Her body now floated in the white fluffy air. Fate snarled at the sight.

● ● ●

I struggled now, holding onto what strength I had left. I could feel Alex's energy going back and forth. I didn't even know if he could feel me anymore. My hope was starting to fade until a familiar hand blessed my shoulder.

"I'm here," He said from within my energy field.

I looked up, Gabriel. I almost died right there. I was so happy to see him. His glance shot to Serena who was now frozen in fear of the Archangel.

"Send Alex all of your energy! He needs you—now!" A tear slide down my cheek. I was tired, so tired. "I will handle her." He then said, bursting from my protective energy field—directly at Serena.

She retreated from his path. He landed hard in front of the spirits that hovered the area where Chamuel once stood. His shoulders straightened as he collected everything within and shot his orb out blinding at them all. I watched as spirits exploded—their screams deafening. I covered my ears in fear. Gabriel's strength continued to grow. One by one he cleared the area. He was so powerful! My eyes looked for Serena. She was nowhere in sight now. She escaped... Again. She probably knew she had no chance of beating Gabriel on her own. I wondered where Anna was. Surely she couldn't be far. My mind suddenly regained focus. Ben. I searched the room until I saw the lifeless body in front of me about ten feet from us. He was shredded to pieces, gone. It felt like something stabbed me in the heart. I couldn't peel myself from the vision of him.

"Gabriel!" I heard myself scream horribly.

He glanced back, his eyes followed mine to his brother's body. He disappeared, then reappeared by his side. "Chamuel..." He spoke, softly lifting him into his arms.

Suddenly, a burst of energy electrified me—I could hear Alex's voice.

"Gabriel!" I shouted again, his eyes met mine. "It's Alex! He needs you, he's in trouble!" Just then, Michael appeared next to Gabriel, catching him off guard.

"We linked ourselves to you—in case you needed us," He said, pleasantly.

Gabriel smiled in relief.

"Now go, brother. Help Alex. I've got him."
Michael then lifted Chamuel over his shoulder and looked directly at me. I swallowed in fear.
Gabriel thanked him, then reappeared by my side. Startling me for a split second.
"Let me in to help him." He said, taking my hand from Alex's shoulder and placing his down. I took Gabriel's free hand in mine and concentrated.
Gabriel closed his eyes. "Take me to him," He demanded.
I wasn't sure how I did it, but I quickly launched the Archangel into Alex's second dream state

Fate leapt from Alex's body back against the wall as the Archangel appeared below Charlotte. His hands raised high into the sky as the warm air floated her down into his arms. Alex's heart dropped at the sight.
"You heard me," He said, weakly.
"How?" Fate questioned, moving a little further back from them both. She then collected herself quickly and reappeared behind Alex. Her bony hands gripped onto his shoulders tight as her long nails dug into his skin. He struggled beneath her. She then gripped his neck, taking full advantage of his weakened state and ripped him up to his feet.
"Well done boy…"
"Let him go!" Gabriel warned, but Fate squeezed tighter—making Alex gasp for air.
"Who do you want to lose, Gabriel?" She questioned. "It's your choice,"
"I'm not playing any more of your games, Fate. I warn you, let him go!"
"Life is a game, Gabriel! It's the greatest game of all, so get used to it!" She shouted back. "Now choose!"
Alex looked at him, a slight smile grew on his face.
"Thank you…" He managed to get out.
Then suddenly, Gabriel heard Alex's thoughts loud and clear. As much as it pained him, the Archangel nodded—agreeing to

the spirit guide's terms. He then took a deep breath, glancing at Alex one last time before his white light manifested again from within—creating a thunder-like sound around the room. Fate stumbled, but managed to keep her grip on Alex tight. Holding Charlotte's lifeless body in his arms, Gabriel spoke one last time, "I have faith in you…" Then he was gone.

●●●

I was startled by Gabriel's sudden appearance back in my pink energy field. My heart stopped at the sight of Charlotte in his arms. Then, just as quickly, appearing outside of my energy field was Uriel in full force.

"Take my hand!" He shouted reaching out for me.

I looked at him nervously, then back at Alex's body that was completely still beside me. Why wasn't he waking if Gabriel had returned? I reached out for his hand. It was cold as ice.

"Alex!" I shouted. "Alex, wake up!" I cried, desperately.

"Do not be stupid girl, take my hand!" Uriel demanded, impatiently.

The haunting sounds of spirits began to surround us once again. Uriel looked over his shoulder, then quickly pulled a sword from his back.

"Alex!" I continued to shout. I shook his body hard, but he didn't respond. I felt Gabriel touch my shoulder.

"Let him go, Sophie" He said quietly.

"What? No!" I pushed his hand off me and reached for Alex again. "I need him to wake before we can leave! He needs to wake up!" I tried desperately to pull at his body, he was so heavy, too heavy for me alone. I tumbled over trying to pull his body up into my arms. "Alex, please." I cried.

I thought I heard something mumble from his lips, but the sound of Uriel's golden sword lighting up—startled me. It was electrifying, a blazing light that vibrated with energy. He began to fight off the spirits one by one as they hurled themselves at him from within the shadows. The torches that once burned brightly around us were fading fast now. It would soon be dark again—our window or opportunity was closing.

243

I could feel it.

"We don't have much time, let's go!" Gabriel urged, pulling at me again.

"What are you talking about?!" I yelled, upset with him now. I worried that if we left this dreamstate without Alex being awake, we might severely harm him—if not kill him. My lips rested down on the top of his head. I ran my fingers through his hair, trying desperately to communicate through energy alone. "Alex, please.... Come back to me. I need you." I whispered. "You're my best friend."

"We're going... Now." Gabriel growled.

My eyes shot up to his. He had a horrible look on his face. A look of defeat. Then I got it. He was going to leave Alex here!

"No!" I cried. "Please, Gabriel! We can't! We can help him still!" I begged. Then suddenly, I heard Alex's voice whistle in the wind. Another spell was being formed.

"Gracious God, lamp of light, hear my words—protect my friends until their fiery end. Cover them with your wings and guide them out of this hell! In return, I leave you with my body, my sacrifice, and all that you need to offer them ultimate protection."

"Alex no!" I shouted, but his voice continued.

"And for the one I love, let me leave her thoughts and memories. Let me take the pain she has incurred as if it was never there—so she shall never shed a single tear. Brighten her heart once again with positivity and warmth. Let her leave all that was us behind—until the end of time. So mote it be!" Alex's voice echoed throughout the hallway as we listened tragically. Uriel sliced away the last bit of spirits just as the torches blew out completely.

I felt him slip from my grasp.

"Alex!!!" I cried hysterically.

I tried desperately to find him, but I couldn't see a thing. I was so tired. I had no strength left. I could barely stay upright. It was too dark.

Where was he? Why couldn't I find him?!

Only the golden light from Uriel's sword was visible now.
I heard a loud thump beside me.
"We don't have time for this!"
Uriel.
I ignored his words, desperately searching for my friend
before it was too late. There was a shuffle of movement, then
someone grabbed my arm and yanked me up from the ground.

Find out what happens next in:
You're Not Alone. The epic conclusion
to **The Guardians Of Your Heart Series.**
